MURDER THIS CLOSE

A Gold Coast Mystery
Book 2

Timothy Cole

Pace Press
Fresno, California

Published by Pace Press
An imprint of Linden Publishing
2006 South Mary Street, Fresno, California 93721
(599) 233-6633 / (800) 345-4447
PacePress.com

Pace Press and Colophon are trademarks of
Linden Publishing Inc.

ISBN 978-1-610353-85-4
first printing

Printed in the United States of America
On acid-free paper.

Library of Congress Cataloging-in-Publication Data on file.

For Peter, Leslie, Sasha, Tula, Andrew and Isa.
How lucky am I?

Very few of us are what we seem.

—**Agatha Christie,** *The Man in the Mist*

1

You're Under Arrest

Dasha Petrov held out her hands so Chief Anthony DeFranco of the Westport Police Department could slip the handcuffs over her frail wrists and snap them closed. Sensitive to the emotions of the moment, she beheld the chief's stricken face and tried to buoy the man as he went about his duty.

"Chief, you're just doing your job," she told him soothingly.

"Procedures, Dasha," he said sadly. "I'm sure we'll get it all cleared up, and you'll be back home before you know it. You have the right to remain silent . . . "

Dasha absorbed the Miranda warnings impassively. Of course, she'd been arrested before. The Gestapo had made a sport of picking suspects off the streets in Prague, where she grew up and later operated during the war in the secret cell called Marigold. Back then, her many offenses were deemed crimes against the Reich—stealing secrets, committing sabotage, luring Nazi kingpins to their demise. She had nearly been killed on her way to destroy the Germans' secret rocket assembly plant inside the mountain at Dora-Mittelbau. She'd needed to get inside, and she'd been *trying* to get arrested.

Now Dasha Petrov was being charged with more mundane crimes—your garden-variety double homicide. Chief DeFranco had wanted to do it himself. He couldn't have assigned an underling to bring his friend in for questioning or, as appeared likely, to issue formal charges at an arraignment. He knew the judge, of course, and the state's attorney. He was quite aware of the particulars. Two of Dasha's Beachside Avenue neighbors had been found dead at their respective homes, two hundred yards from each other, their deaths separated by two highly curious days.

The chief and his detective bureau would be sifting through the evidence and helping the prosecution build its case.

But Dasha Petrov was his friend. She had saved DeFranco and his partner, Tracy Taggart, from a swift and certain end while they were investigating the sea glass murders. Dasha and the chief had traveled some dangerous roads, and they had come to rely on each other's talents. He refused to believe the amazing Mrs. Petrov was capable of cold-blooded murder—and for ill-gotten gain?

Impossible.

Yet his forensic team and the state's attorney had amassed a damning inventory of physical evidence and a compromising timeline. They even had the first, faint glimmerings of a motive—times two.

Chief DeFranco grasped Dasha's elbow and led her out of the guest cottage at Seabreeze, the Gold Coast home she shared with her sister, Galina. The chief's son, Officer Sam DeFranco, was their driver on this fragrant spring evening, the sun still high in the west, resisting the coming night. The chief made sure Mrs. Petrov didn't bump her head when she crouched to get into the squad car's back seat. He closed the car door and went around to enter the back seat from the opposite side, wishing to accompany his dear old friend through every unsavory phase of her coming worries. Dasha's son, Boris, who lived with his family in the manor house, was naturally shaken as he watched his mother being led away in handcuffs. His wife and children were crying, and Dasha told them to buck up. Baba would be back in a wink after she straightened everything out. It was all just a silly misunderstanding.

The chief was unused to the sight lines and perspectives offered by the back seat, where his arrestees first entered the system. The seat was covered by slippery plastic. The steel netting separating the back seat occupants from the driver was so far back it was practically in their laps. Of course, the chief knew the doors locked automatically, and the interior handles had been removed. He could see how some petty criminal—a teenager suspected of a DUI, a housewife shoplifter, a brawling Metro-North drunk fresh off the bar car—might be intimidated by their loss of liberty from the back seat of a patrol car. It made *him* a bit uncomfortable, even though he knew he'd be freed when they arrived at the Jesup Street public safety building.

But Dasha Petrov simply smiled at her distressed loved ones, unperturbed, holding her manacled hands in the air with two thumbs up.

"We need to give the children hope, chief," she said.

"Dasha, I've called Ken Bernhard of Cohen and Wolf," said DeFranco.

"Oh, I love Ken," said Dasha. "But I won't be needing a lawyer. So unproductive. And terribly expensive."

"Dasha, as your friend, I want to remind you that you'll need legal representation," said the chief. "It's not my position to force a lawyer on you. We love it when suspects talk. But I won't let you into that interview room without counsel."

"Well, you're a dear to think of me, chief," said Dasha, "but I have nothing to hide. I am happy to tell you everything I know."

"I have to go by the book, Dasha," he insisted. "I've assigned the case to Ferguson, the head of our detective unit. He's worked with the medical examiner's criminologists at the two murder scenes, so he has a good handle on where the evidence seems to be pointing. It would be wrong of me to intervene. The only thing I can do is make sure it's fair and that they don't bully you."

"You're very sweet," said Dasha, "but I've been bullied by the Gestapo and the KGB. I think I can handle the Westport Police Department. I'll just answer Detective Ferguson's questions, and I'll be home in an hour or two. Will you be in the room?"

"Yes, but I've got to let Ferguson lead," said the chief.

"Chief, I wouldn't have it any other way," said Dasha. "I suppose the state's attorney is sending over one of his minions."

"A newbie named Jennifer," said the chief. "She drew the short straw. Rest of the staff is attending some kind of good-bye party tonight. She'll probably just take notes."

"How about you, Sam?" Dasha called to the younger DeFranco at the wheel. "I'd feel much better if you were in there with me." She smiled at the lad's father, patting his knee.

"Sorry, Dasha," said Sam. "I'm assigned to patrol until midnight. I'm sure it'll be the usual curfew breaks and missing pets."

"Don't forget palpitations, young man," said Dasha. "We of a certain age aren't as spry as we used to be."

"Somehow I refuse to believe that, Dasha," said Sam. The young man was on the lowest rung of the ladder at the Westport Police Department, having just graduated from Connecticut College. But he'd made the grade at the police academy in Meriden, and his father was delighted to bring him aboard, another link in a long chain of DeFrancos who had chosen to serve the town of Westport.

The chief turned to look at the poised profile of Dasha Petrov, one of the CIA's finest, who was slowly learning how to embrace her well-earned retirement. The sun etched her face in the soft light of a day's end, and she was utterly relaxed in the face of charges that would have induced more than a mild panic in anyone else. To the chief, Dasha Petrov was a natural wonder—schooled in all the treacheries of postwar Berlin, the mass death of civil upheaval in Southeast Asia, the intricacies of Cold War spycraft. She'd survived on swift life-and-death decisions, nimble and numerous acts of violence, and an inscrutable knack for escape. She had occupied the fine but crucial gaps in the long path of history and had experienced her adopted country's major milestones from within. But that was only during her professional life.

Upon retirement, Dasha's quick thinking and lightning reflexes had put her between the serial killer Robert Altman and his hapless victims, the chief included. The chief owed her, but he also owed the small Gold Coast town of Westport that paid his salary. His friend, sitting calmly in handcuffs as the light touched her Greta Garbo profile, was being charged with double homicide. All he could do was make sure she was safe, comfortable, and well represented. He also had to make sure he observed his oath to protect and to serve the town he and Dasha both loved. They each viewed Westport from their own unique vantage points, but there was still a common connection—the sheer struggles that had shaped their respective characters. The chief was a local boy who came to embrace his hometown after hard fighting in the Mekong delta of South Vietnam. And when Dasha admired the gated mansions, the cool night air, and the shimmering trees on Beachside Avenue, she beheld her hometown through the eyes of a refugee. As a child, Dasha and her sister, Galina, lived with their mother above the stables at their hideaway in Kaluga, out of sight from marauding Bolsheviks. She barely remembered their family apartment in czarist St. Petersburg. But the memory of the cattle car that had carried them in secret across the Latvian border was seared into her brain. Galina had pressed her nose to the tiny grate that offered only meager ventilation so she could report on the activity at the passport control. Their mother, who had secured their forged documents, had trembled in a corner. After crossing the border, they'd stayed in dormitories and walk-ups and even a few Quonset huts as Dasha and her family made their way west, to America. She wanted to protect her new home-land. That was why she'd transitioned from working in the trans-lator pool of the Allied armies during World War II to become one of the CIA's most talented officers.

Sam drove them around the bend at Burying Hill Beach, up the hill and across the thundering turnpike. Dasha, as usual, admired the waving pastureland at Nyala Farms as the patrol car drove out to the Sherwood Island Connector. She even admired Westport's always thriving Post Road—the Clam Box, Ed Mitchell's clothing store, the saintly spire of Saugatuck Congregational. Soon, the chief's son swung the patrol car into the parking lot on the east side of the Jesup Street station. The DeFrancos, father and son, reversed the little acts that had helped Dasha Petrov get into the car on Beachside Avenue. Sam released his father, and the chief went around to Dasha's door. He opened it with a flourish and solicitously ensured she didn't bump her head when she swung her feet around, planted them with confidence on the ground, and attained the vertical.

The chief wasn't surprised to see a few local newspaper reporters with photographers in tow. The Beachside Avenue homicide victims were known throughout the land. News 12 Connecticut was represented. And off on the fringe the chief saw his stalwart partner, Tracy Taggart, looking appropriately grim at the sight of their friend Dasha being led away in manacles. Duty called. Tracy would submit a bare-bones report that would be beamed by microwave to headquarters at 30 Rock for the six-thirty edition of *NBC Nightly News*. Later on, she would consult the chief on Dasha's prospects for release when she and DeFranco arrived at the home they shared, the last house on the left, on the little dead-end called High Gate Road.

The chief took Dasha to the interview room. It was well lit, spare, and windowless, with a small, Formica-topped table and molded plastic chairs. There were cameras for the closed-circuit television system that would record the interview and a U-bolt embedded in concrete under the chair assigned to the suspect, where the officers could shackle those deemed a risk. Dasha Petrov didn't look like she required this kind of precaution. Her trademark beret was fastened to her old gray head, and her Barbour vest was nicely accented with an Hermès scarf her husband, Constantine, had given her on a whim. He was like that. Presents would just appear, no need for a special occasion.

Ferguson was already in the room with two closed manila file folders in front of him. He rose to his feet when Mrs. Petrov entered. He was joined by a young man in Brooks Brothers gray who introduced himself as Kelly from Cohen and Wolf.

"Ken sent me," he said. "He would have liked to be here himself, but he's home on the couch with a twisted knee after a paddle tennis accident."

"Oh, those paddle tennis parties at Longshore. I admire his vim and vigor, but I worry he'll overdo it," said Dasha. "It's very nice of you to come, but you can go now. I won't be needing a lawyer."

"Dasha, I don't think that's wise," said the chief.

"Why? I haven't done anything wrong," said Dasha. She turned to young Kelly. "I'm waiving counsel. I'm sure you have a family who needs you. Kids with homework? You can go." Kelly didn't know quite what to do with himself, and he turned to the chief.

"She has the right to forgo counsel, but I would like to exercise my rights as a citizen to remain in this room on public property. I will be taking notes," he said. Dasha was a bit flummoxed, and Kelly sensed her irritation.

"Okay. Notes only," said DeFranco. "And I will let you stop the interview at any time, in which case your client will be formally charged and bail will be set."

"I'm not his client, chief," said Dasha, standing her ground. "Let's get on with it."

"Shall we get comfortable?" said Ferguson. "Mrs. Petrov, can I get you some water or coffee?"

"I prefer tea, young man," she said, wishing to push her interlocutor off stride.

"Tea, then," said Ferguson, picking up the phone and dictating an order to the night desk. The chief was a piece of stone, impassive yet embroiled in inner turmoil. He knew what was coming.

"Mrs. Petrov, where were you on the night of April 25?" asked Ferguson.

The chief watched Mrs. Petrov with studied care, expecting the knowing smile, the dancing blue eyes, the deep font of knowledge and experience brimming to the surface. She wasn't one to shout. She would lean into her target and disable them with dash and pluck. But the chief saw Dasha Petrov look down at her wrinkled hands and those liver spots and swollen knuckles and damaged cuticles. Her lips trembled, and when she looked up, the chief saw a single tear slide gently down her careworn face.

Right then, he knew she was in trouble.

2

Just a Few Weeks Ago

Spring was in the air, winter but a memory. Gone were the icy driveways, dirty snow drifts, and banging heat registers. Crocuses were pushing up through the thin skim of remaining snow, and buds were on the trees. Dasha Petrov and her sister, Galina, were making *paska* and *kulich* for their annual Russian Easter gathering, and they thought they could open up a few windows and let in some air.

Soon, it was time for Galina's nap. She'd become overly taxed, and because of her stroke, she tired easily. She mumbled her intentions and took Luna, the cat, into her little bedroom off a back wing of the cottage. Dasha spent a few minutes straightening the great room, placing the piles of Russian-language newspapers and journals into recycling, and taming the dust. She ran a feather duster over the framed photos of her children and grandchildren, spending a bit more time on the photograph of Constantine, her titan. Had it been ten years since he'd passed away? Seems like yesterday he'd been puttering in the greenhouse—just before the aneurysm that killed him before he hit the ground.

"At least it was quick, Con, my darling," Dasha said aloud. She spoke to him every day, asking him what he thought of the state of affairs with that boy Clinton in the White House. And what did he think of Gorbachev and Yeltsin and the drastic upheavals now faced by the Russian people? She asked Con about matters close to home. What was his impression of the new property tax? And where could they save on maintenance? And what of their son Boris's sudden career anxieties, which had come out of nowhere? Yes, she'd come into some money immediately following the home invasion perpetrated by the serial killer next door—bearer bonds, heaps of cash, untraceable diamonds and gold bars. But Seabreeze's needs continued unabated, and now the grandchildren were eyeing expensive schools.

"Con, I wish you were here to help me sort this out," she said, running her feather duster over the photo of Reinhard Tristan Heydrich, the Nazi monster she'd had a hand in bringing down on the Troja Bridge in 1942. Back then, life had been in constant peril. But she missed the clarity—good against evil, the mission and the path unambiguous.

It was time for her walk. She pulled on her Wellington boots and donned Constantine's Barbour coat, which still retained the fragrance of his French cigarettes. She had her Irish fisherman's sweater underneath to furnish another layer and a woolen scarf Galina had knitted one Christmas, back in the days when the poor dear could speak and had two good hands. As was her custom, Dasha took her chestnut walking stick with the knife hidden in the top. As she'd demonstrated when she stopped the murderer Robert Altman, it was a simple matter to withdraw her secret knife and use it as circumstances required. The blade was from a German paratrooper's kit. Constantine had had it handcrafted by a Montana artisan he'd encountered on a prospecting trip for Petrov Petroleum. He brought it home and presented it to her with a smile. "It's for defensive purposes only," Constantine had told his wife, knowing her profession in the field of intelligence might expose her to a certain degree of unpleasantness, to put it politely.

Constantine was right. Dasha had used her secret knife on more than one occasion. She didn't scare easily, but ever since her encounter with Altman, and the attention her intervention had received, she'd embraced the idea of carrying a concealed weapon, even in her retirement.

She stepped out the front door into the garden and immediately made a field assessment. She was armored against the cold. The sky was blue, the air clean, the wind moderate. She could press ahead without much care. She had her Leupold binoculars around her neck. She put out a leg, planted her stick to steady herself, and pushed off.

She was a student of the light. She imagined how a painter might apprehend the changed and changing world that greeted her every time she beheld her beautiful sound. It was always different. A north wind pushed against the incoming waves and folded them back in a dainty spindrift. The scattered clouds carried a tint of gold, set against a vivid blue. The distant shore of Long Island was etched on the horizon in sharp relief. Her swans were paddling toward her, and she took a packet of cornmeal out of her pocket, indulging her beautiful friends, extending a welcome to the Petrov family home. The light would change soon and reshape the scene in an endless tapestry of renewal and transformation.

She walked down the little stone staircase that connected the top of the seawall to the beach. She turned to the west and walked smartly along, trying to elevate her heart rate. She climbed over the groins that extended perpendicularly from her neighbors' seawalls. She looked at the plovers, admired the mallards, inspected the horseshoe crabs, spotted the shells, and, yes, observed a bit of sea glass here and there. Her objective was a large rock in front of the home belonging to her friend Barnaby Jayne.

And lo and behold, there was the man himself. She liked to make it look like she was running into the old boy by chance, their morning walks intersecting on this treasured stretch of beach. But, ever the intelligence professional, she knew the man's habits, having interviewed his housekeepers and of course old Miguel, who worked on Jayne's gardening staff. Dasha knew Barnaby would be leaning against the rock just as she walked up. And there he was, taking in the view of Cockenoe Island to the west. He wore his standard-issue rumpled khakis with the frayed cuffs, the Wolverine wool shirt with a polo shirt underneath, an L.L. Bean puff vest, and his tired old leather driving gloves. On his head sat his trademark Irish woolen hat. The man was handsome, she'd give him that, with those chiseled cheekbones and that manicured gray goatee and the dancing almond-colored eyes that sparkled when he smiled.

"You again," she said.

"That's what you said yesterday and the day before," said Jayne.

"And the week before that and last month, too," said Dasha.

"I'm beginning to enjoy our routine," said Jayne, smiling.

"It's not unpleasant," said Dasha coyly. Was she protecting herself?

"What do you have to report?" asked Jayne.

"Swans are fed. Mallards will become doting parents soon enough. The water looks clean. Not like the tar balls we used to have to contend with—before you moved into the neighborhood," she said.

"Glad I missed that," said Jayne. "Reminds me of the tangent about the shipwreck I wrote into *Crestfallen*, my fourth novel in the Raptor series. Flaming wreckage, bunker oil all around, saboteurs absconding with the lifeboats."

"That's one of the reasons I enjoy our little coincidental meetings," said Dasha. "You'll invoke some reference to one of your novels. I've read them all. I enjoyed *Crestfallen*. But there's something about your debut . . . what was it called?"

"'*Huntress*,'" said Jayne. "I won an Edgar for that."

"The hero was a beagle named Sally who dug up a kerchief that carried the blood types of both the killer and the victim," said Dasha. "It came out before DNA analysis became routine."

"Had to make do. You've got a good memory," said Jayne.

"I have to confess. I reread it the other day, Barnaby," said Dasha. "You're quite good, you know."

"It's been a living," he said with all due modesty, knowing in his bones how correct she was. Few could beat Barnaby Jayne at the craft of writing mysteries. Since he'd started out, the critics had swooned over his deft and nuanced grasp of the sinister. His victims were innocent and unsuspecting, carrying their dark burdens stoically onward, toward their inevitable demise. Jayne preferred the unconventional when it came to murder. It was not uncommon for his books to feature a victim who had been shot through the heart by a bolt from a crossbow, or whose skull had been cleaved by an executioner's ax. One story featured an oafish clerk with a briefcase full of secrets who had been pushed in front a train. Jayne's murders were complex tapestries of doom that left readers breathless—and wanting more.

He'd written twenty-seven novels and seven screenplay adaptations and signed off on massive serializations of his most prized works—while frightening his readership in lockstep with his burgeoning bank account. Foreign rights. Movie deals. Gargantuan advances. The works of Barnaby Jayne were minting money, and Dasha was gratified to see all this output materialize in the form of an imposing Beachside Avenue mansion, a fleet of antique automobiles, a well-heated pool, and Tammy, the fifth—and, Barnaby insisted, final—Mrs. Jayne.

"I can't afford another one," he'd once told Dasha in an unguarded moment.

"But that's what you said after the fourth Mrs. Jayne," Dasha had said.

It was during that exchange that Barnaby Jayne took a liking to the widowed Mrs. Petrov. It was an admiration that grew into a fondness that evolved into love. Dasha felt it, too. They could talk about anything, especially Barnaby's work.

"Does Tammy read your books?" Dasha asked that April day.

"Tammy doesn't read," said Jayne, unable to disguise his discomfort. He knew he'd made another colossal romantic blunder. Why did he keep repeating these mistakes when it came to matters of the heart? The characters in his novels would never fail or falter this way. They were masters of the superficial relationships and the casual sex that naturally accompanied their derring-do.

"Why did you marry her, Barnaby?" asked Dasha. "Tammy is even younger than the fourth Mrs. Jayne, and she comes with a pair of spawn from her last brace of lovers—they don't even have the same father."

"Dasha, I have a reputation to uphold," said Jayne. "How would it look if I were to take the red carpet at these incessant awards ceremonies with a nobody on my arm? Tammy is ravishing. And not to put too fine a point on it, but she looks spectacular in a bikini at the side of my pool."

"Barnaby, face facts," said Dasha, comfortably bringing her friend up short. "She eats like a bird, and her breast implants attest to the skill of her surgeon, not necessarily good genes. She can't form a complete sentence."

"Dasha, she gets her point across," said Jayne.

"In bed? Without a doubt," said Dasha. "But what do you talk about?"

"Usually whether she should wear the pearl studs or the hoops," said Jayne. "I didn't marry Tammy for the intellectual stimulation."

"Or lack thereof," said Dasha. "You married her for the physical stimulation. I understand that. But you reach a certain stage in life, and what you really want is somebody on your level you can talk to."

"That's why I have you," said Jayne, smiling.

"Yes, dear boy, you have me," said Dasha, patting his hand. "Ever since Con departed this world, I have yearned for conversation. But I refuse to be the other woman."

"Neither or us would ever stoop so low," said Jayne. "Besides, you've been seeing Michael, haven't you? You can tell me. I can take it." Michael Aubrey was Beachside Avenue's other mystery writer laureate, to Dasha's east.

"Barnaby, you know a woman has to have some secrets," she said coyly.

"Well, I know something about the life you've led," said Jayne. "Secrets are your stock-in-trade."

"As Othello said in his final speech, 'I have done the state some service, and they know it,'" said Dasha.

"Just before the poor, addled man plunges a dagger into his own heart," said Jayne.

"He was a victim of disinformation," said Dasha. "I had to contend with that in my prior life, as well."

"Your prior life," said Jayne. "I'd like to write a book about you. Fiction, of course."

"Funny, Michael told me the same thing," said Dasha.

"Careful, dear," he said. "No fair playing two sides of the street."

"Barnaby, for the love of God, you're a married man," said Dasha. "I'm not playing any side of any street. I am just enjoying the conversation. I wish for you that your home life could be as intellectually stimulating."

"Like I said, Tammy can be stimulating in other ways," said Jayne.

"And, I'll add, it helps anneal Barnaby Jayne's reputation as an epic swordsman," she said unabashedly. "Starlets, rich divorcées, amorous gilded Hamptonites, sparkling talk show hosts. Barnaby, you're a prolific womanizer. It's who you are, and you shouldn't be ashamed of it. But then there's Tammy. She's beneath you . . . so to speak." They both laughed.

"Aubrey can't match my quantity or, over the long haul, my quality . . . Tammy being the exception," said Jayne. "But my heavens, Dasha. The pink bikini. It's a gift from God."

"Stop it, Barnaby," she scolded. "You're embarrassing yourself. I fear Michael is your equal when it comes to being the prurient schoolboy."

"I will concede the point but not the match," said Jayne. "He's not my equal as a man of letters. And I resent the fact he followed me to Westport. Setting up camp on the same street! It's indecent."

"Free country," said Dasha. "And, like you, money's not the issue."

"I think he's a cad," said Barnaby. "He's been stalking me for years, trying to get under my skin. More awards. Better movie deals. He stole my agent, for God's sake."

"Barnaby, you told me yourself you and your agent had a falling-out after *Chameleon*," said Dasha.

"I think Aubrey snatched him away after that little tiff we had regarding percentages," said Jayne.

"More than a tiff, Barnaby," said Dasha. "You fired your cata-
pult at the man when he came in the driveway. A flaming fagot
landed on the hood of his BMW."

"Man had no sense of humor," said Barnaby. "And *Chameleon*
was a triumph, thanks to you."

"I just provided some plot points," said Dasha. "And the way
you were writing about tradecraft needed work."

"I never really knew about countersurveillance until we had
that chat," said Barnaby.

"Patience, logic, asymmetry, awareness—it's all part of CIA
doctrine. *My* stock-in-trade."

"Until Con came along and spoiled you," said Barnaby.

"Yes, spoiled. He made me feel infinitely loved," said Dasha.

"No man will ever take his place," said Barnaby.

"He'd want me to get out and about," said Dasha. "And Galina
is ill served if I just stay at home moping. I enjoy our little chats,
Barnaby."

"And you also enjoy Aubrey," said Barnaby. "You're breaking
my heart. But let's jump to another subject. I've got two books
bubbling. Starting one in postwar Germany, Berlin in fact, where
you plied your trade. And I'm right in the middle of another
mystery. *Hangman*. That one's farther along. It's about an executioner at a state penitentiary who's racked with guilt when he
executes an innocent man. The only way to right the wrong
is to find the real killer. He manages to get the original victim
exhumed and finds traces of some kind of poisonous plant. What
do you think I should use?"

"Several possibilities," said Dasha. "I would go with *Cerbera
odallum*—highly toxic, impossible to identify postmortem. But
there are also some cardiogenics, like white baneberry, that can
incapacitate someone for a later, more convenient *coup de grâce*."

"You see, you're crucial, Dasha, darling," said Jayne. "I can't
live without you. And I can't let you fall under the thrall of that
bounder Aubrey."

"You're both appalling rakes, and I love the way you both
fight over me," said Dasha. "But Barnaby, we have visitors." She

pointed to two children—a little boy and his older sister—on top of the Jaynes' seawall.

"Jim and Lucy," yelled Barnaby. "Come down here and greet Mrs. Petrov properly." They were Tammy's kids, nine and twelve, and now they had the run of the Jayne estate. Other kids hurled into this moneypot would have become unbalanced, but Tammy's children were eerily polite. They approached the old pair.

"Hello, Mrs. Petrov. So nice to see you," said Lucy. Shy little Jim put out his hand for a shake.

"Nice to see you, too, dear," said Dasha. "What news on the Rialto?" She threw out Shakespeare just to watch people squirm. But Lucy lobbed the ball back over the net.

"Oh, I love *The Merchant of Venice*, especially Portia, the lawyer," she said to Dasha's utter surprise. If this was Tammy's child, her mother was something more than a babe in a pink bikini.

"How about you, Jim?" Dasha asked. "What's your favorite Shakespeare character?" Jim didn't hesitate.

"Puck, of course," he said.

"Ah, the trickster," said Dasha. "I'll have to keep my eye on you." And everyone laughed.

"Barnaby, Mom says the car will be here in about an hour," said Lucy. Barnaby turned to Dasha.

"Taking them to the Big Apple Circus in the city. Hired a car. These little outings cost a bloody fortune."

"But who's counting?" said Dasha. "I'll let you go." She turned and started walking back toward Seabreeze. Barnaby Jayne called after her.

"Tell that damned Aubrey you're mine!" he said, as Dasha smiled and continued her daily constitutional.

3

Aubrey's Turn

Dasha Petrov walked back down the beach and ascended the little stone steps leading to the top of the Petrov seawall. She walked back to the cottage in the garden and found Galina sitting at their Scrabble table in the little bow window overlooking the patio. Luna, the cat, was on her lap. Galina and Dasha had worked out a system to communicate using the Scrabble game's little wooden squares. Galina had already posed her first question.

"Barnaby again?" Galina asked.

"Ran into him on the beach," said Dasha, pulling off her coat. She waited while Galina moved her next comment into position.

"Charlatan," said Galina.

"Oh, I don't think so," said Dasha. "That would imply some kind of intent to do anything to remain in the limelight. He's just a highly imaginative man who has allowed his libido to overrule his sensibilities. Tammy may be all plastic surgery and silicone . . . but her two children are charming. And she's landed a big fish. I think she must be rather clever."

"His last book?" asked Galina, suggesting it had *just* cleared the bar.

"You're right," said Dasha. "Not as riveting as the one before it. He's been functioning at such a high level; he's allowed to stub a toe now and then. Let me make you some lunch." She'd already boiled some eggs and pulled them from the refrigerator. She peeled the shells, chopped the eggs, added some mayonnaise and mustard, and sliced in a bit of onion and olive. She applied the salad to some bread and made sure to cut away Galina's crust, just the way she liked it. She brought the sandwich to Galina's perch at the Scrabble table.

"Do you want to take a walk after lunch, dear?" Dasha asked her sister.

"Tired," wrote Galina with her little squares.

"Not like you," said Dasha. "You've got me a little worried."

"I'm fine," said Galina.

"Ever the stoic," said Dasha. "I'm calling Dr. Altbaum." Dasha and Galina finished their lunch, and Dasha put her coat back on for another beach walk. Of course, the light had changed as the sun arced through the sky, offering another seascape. She walked down the beach to the east and stopped. She heard gunfire . . . and smiled.

Michael Aubrey was shooting clay pigeons from atop his seawall. She walked over a groin and looked up. Aubrey was dressed for the field in his shooting vest and a wide-brimmed hat. He was tall and muscular and narrow waisted, with a handsome square jaw and welcoming eyes. He had his favorite Purdey double gun in the crook of his right arm, and he was addressing a muscular, agitated German shorthaired pointer sitting on his haunches to his left, looking out to sea.

"Cease fire," said Dasha when she got to the base of Aubrey's steps. "I'm coming up."

"Hi, Dasha," said Michael. "I was hoping you'd come. I was missing you." Dasha got to the top, and Prince came dashing over to greet his friend, Mrs. Petrov. Of course, she'd thought ahead and pulled a little wiener out of the plastic bag she had in her pocket. Prince wolfed it down and looked expectantly for more.

"Not too many of those things, Dasha," said Aubrey. "He'll lose interest in his lord and master."

"Impossible, Michael," said Dasha. "You are Prince's alpha dog. Emphasis on the word *dog*."

"You wound me," said Aubrey.

"Just stating facts," said Dasha. "You can't help being a male of the species."

"What's got into you?" asked Aubrey.

"I just had a conversation with Jayne," said Dasha. "The two of you are ghastly libertines."

"Well, one of us is," said Aubrey. "He's a pretender. He's on number five, I believe."

"You're keeping track?" said Dasha.

"Of course. My sweet Del is number six!" said Aubrey proudly. "I've married all my affairs."

"I find that preposterous," said Dasha. "Surely you've had a few that have fallen between the cracks."

"A gentleman never tells," said Aubrey, his captivating smile magnetic. Dasha wasn't surprised the man could boast a long parade of conquests.

"But are you happy?" asked Dasha. "I've been around a long time, but I confess some perplexity when it comes to the male capacity for serial copulation. At least some men. I know my Con was true."

"Of course he was, Dasha," said Aubrey. "He had the filet mignon. The rest of us have had to make do with ground round."

"Now you're being coarse," said Dasha. "I have to stand up for my gender. I don't think Max Gunn would say such things."

Aubrey laughed. "I've lived with Max Gunn in my head and at the end of my pen for forty years," said Aubrey. "But I still don't know the man. He's capable of defending himself with either blade or bullet. And yet he shows great tenderness in a lady's bedchamber."

"Tenderness is highly subjective, Michael," said Dasha. "I wouldn't necessarily call Gunn tender. But he does commit himself to a woman's pleasure. That I will give you. Hamburger! Honestly, Aubrey, what would Del say?"

"Del is the bone-in ribeye," said Aubrey. "My favorite."

Dasha laughed. "You're a cad, Aubrey. And you've made your protagonist into an insatiable satyr."

"Well, in *Penumbra*, my fourth, he fell madly in love with Gwen," said Aubrey, ruminating on the yellowed pages of a book he'd written almost three decades earlier. "Max and Gwen were inseparable."

"But you killed her off in *Freefall*, your sixth," said Dasha.

"Their love was too pure to last," said Aubrey. "Better to have it evaporate like a morning mist, rise to the heavens, mingle with the stars."

"Oh please," said Dasha. "Why can't you give Gunn one true love that lasts? It seems like he's always searching for Gwen."

"He's wounded. Women fall naturally into his orbit, captured by the man's gravity. They become a part of his totality," said Aubrey. "Jayne put you up to this, didn't he? Jayne sent you over to disturb my equilibrium."

It would take a lot to unsettle the eminent Michael Aubrey. He'd made his first million at the age of twenty-seven with *Bludgeon*, the book that began the massively successful Max Gunn series. From the outset, Gunn was outgunned and had to rely on his fists and guts and guile. Gunn's world was awash with extremists—subversive organs out to end the world as we know it. Gunn was the only thing standing between these powerful interests and a peaceful American continuum. Gunn roamed the land, fighting the good fight—dealing, poor man, with the legion of women trying to get him into bed.

Dasha had to hand it to Aubrey. Gunn was the reason she was standing on the verdant, sloping lawn leading up to his dazzling Tudor mansion. Gunn was the catalyst that had conjured that eighty-thousand-dollar Purdey shotgun Aubrey was cradling like a child. Gunn had financed the winter abode in Mustique, the pied-à-terre in New York, the ski house in Deer Valley. It was Gunn who'd landed those movie serializations, rivaling at the box office the one and only Bond.

But Dasha knew Gunn had placed inordinate demands on his creator. Gunn was always in need of a clever getaway, or a more demanding safe to crack. Max Gunn needed trickier couloirs to traverse or a shorter fuse to outrace as it sputtered and smoked toward a bigger, more destructive bomb. Aubrey needed material. And he cultivated the former intelligence operative, who edged around her sources and methods but never revealed her secrets.

"You are who you are," said Dasha. "And Lord knows you're interesting. And no, Jayne didn't send me over here to bother you. Shall we pick up the conversation where we left it last time?"

"You were helping me get Gunn into position in his sniper's nest," said Aubrey. "You were offering me your views on the merits of the .308 cartridge over the standard-issue 7.62mm."

"If you go with the 7.62, you'll have to fall back on the M14, which is not as refined as the options available in .308," said Dasha. "The .308 has more power—fifty-six grains versus thirty-six grains—and you'll want your sniper rifle to be light, with a muzzle brake, a free-floating forearm bed, and adjustable butt and cheek pieces. Bolt action. Because one exercises more care with the follow-up shots if you have to work an action. And don't forget the optics. I prefer Leupold, personally."

"Perspective, Dasha," said Aubrey. "You are one in a million. Gunn's having difficulty with his positioning. Questionable intel. I'll let him have the .308."

"And don't forget the Leupold. But Michael, you're spending too much time on the hardware," said Dasha. "You need to plan his escape. The sniper's nest needs to be on a lower floor. The gun should have a flash suppressor and break down conveniently. And for God's sake don't leave any spent casings."

"Dasha, you scare the hell out of me," said Aubrey. "You know far too much."

"Well, I can talk about it now," said Dasha. "The Vietnam War is over, and the principals are dead. I was assigned to assassinate Ho Chi Minh. It was 1949. The French Quarter of old Hanoi. I stayed on my belly in the steeple of a church for three days . . . waiting. A bad choice, incidentally, for a clean getaway. But you live and learn. If I'd been successful, the war might have turned out differently. He'd be dead. But I'd be dead, too. No way I would have gotten out of there alive."

"What stopped you?" asked Aubrey, fascinated as usual by Dasha Petrov's anecdotes, which she threw out as if she were discussing the weather.

"He came into my field of fire," said Dasha. "He was leading a little troop of schoolchildren. He sat in a park across from the church and read them a fairy tale. I watched his lips move through my Leupold scope. I couldn't pull the trigger in front of those children. That's when I lost my edge. I've taken a few lives in the act of self-defense, Michael. Always in the national interest. But I could never be an assassin on par with Gunn. So, take my advice with a grain of salt."

"I presume you've maintained your skills, Dasha," said Aubrey. "Show me what you've got." Aubrey handed her the Purdey.

"I'm a little rusty," said Dasha. "Nice balance. Boxlock design from the 1880s. It's never gone out of style." She stood at the seawall, and Aubrey dropped two shells into the shotgun's open chambers.

"I've got two launchers hidden in the hedges right and left," said Aubrey. "You can ask for a double, two opposing, or a trap shot going away."

"I think I'd like to start with a double, from the left," said Dasha. "It's been a while. Don't laugh . . . Pull."

Two clay birds flew out from the hedge. She brought the shotgun up, felt the Monte Carlo cheekpiece on her wrinkled face, sighted down the rib between the barrels until she could absorb and internalize the brass bead at the muzzle. She led bird one by a barrel's width and popped off a shot. The recoil felt smart and satisfying as the clay bird shattered in a puff of black against a sky of blue. She led bird two by half as much, squeezed the trigger, and attained a like result.

"Beginner's luck," she said.

Aubrey smiled. "Let's try two coming at each other. The classic skeet presentation," he said. Dasha cracked open the breech and watched the spent shells eject perfectly to the side and rear. Aubrey dropped in two more live shells. Dasha was ready for a wider lead and a faster swing.

"Pull." She led bird one from the right launcher by three feet and shattered it. Then she drew a bead on bird two from the left and squeezed off a shot as it faded low and right.

"Four for four," said Aubrey.

"Let me show you something different," said Dasha. She pulled her Walther PPK .380 semiautomatic pistol from her pocket. It had been a faithful friend since her leader and lover Kurt Bartok had given it to her in 1942, a necessary tool in their work with the Czech underground. She cocked the hammer and brushed off the safety.

"That's James Bond's gun," said Aubrey. "I just bought one."

"I owned mine a dozen years before he owned his," said Dasha. "Walther introduced the hammer-drop safety. Brilliant decocking mechanism. Give me a double from the right."

She racked the slide to chamber a round and used two hands to hold the weapon. She sighted through the rear notch down the top of the slide to the front sight blade at the muzzle.

"Pull."

She loved the feeling of her Walther bucking in her hands, and the first clay bird shattered into shards. Bird two met a similar fate.

"Jesus, Dasha," said Aubrey. "Skeet shooting with a pistol."

"Let Gunn try that in your next book," she said.

"Stay for lunch," said Aubrey. "Del is making a salade Niçoise."

"I really can't," said Dasha. "I have to get back to Galina."

"Well, at least come up to the house and say hello to the current Mrs. Aubrey," he said.

"Happy to," said Dasha. "Won't it be nice to drop the word *current* and say *final* instead?"

"Naturally," said Aubrey. But Dasha sensed a bit of reserve. Aubrey didn't care to commit.

They walked up the lawn past Aubrey's elaborate gazebo. It was fitted with a bar, a television for football games, lounge chairs, and windows that raised and lowered with the push of a button.

"This is the only place Del lets me smoke my cigars," said Aubrey.

"Not an unreasonable request," said Dasha, siding with Mrs. Aubrey.

The Aubreys' gardener, Makita, was meticulously clipping a dancing topiary, and Del Aubrey emerged from one of the French doors leading from the living room onto the stone patio. Dasha sensed Del was taking the stage, appraising the poor old woman who lived down the beach. Certainly, Del didn't regard Dasha—forty years her senior—as a threat. Dasha performed her own assessment. Del Aubrey looked crisp and fresh, wearing neatly pressed slacks and an understated white blouse with a high collar, accented by a chic neck scarf. She wore gold bangles on each wrist, and she'd executed her makeup with precision. Dasha focused on Del's massive wedding rock, a bellowing statement from the current Mrs. Aubrey to any potential competitors. Her brunette hair was pulled back under a stylish hairband, and her high heels on this weekday morning suggested Del didn't care much for the country life. Her shoes were strictly Madison Avenue. Dasha sensed the rift and decided to open the conversation there.

"Hello, Del," she said. "I don't want to interrupt your lunch. Michael was just giving me some instruction in the shooting arts."

"Bah, Dasha," said Aubrey. "You were teaching me." He beamed his appreciation at his inscrutable neighbor, and Dasha watched Del's smile turn to ice. Del didn't care for any rivalries, regardless of their origin. Dasha was no exception.

"Del, Dasha can shoot skeet with her Walther," said Aubrey. Mrs. Aubrey smiled at him and turned to Dasha.

"He loves his toys," she said. But then the smiling stopped, and Dasha sensed Del had her limits when it came to Aubrey's enthusiasm. Dasha couldn't resist a bit of a dig . . . to provoke a reaction. At times it was the best way to learn someone's true self.

"Do you like to shoot, Del?" Dasha knew the answer. Del would never be the shoulder-to-shoulder companion Michael deserved and had spent a lifetime searching for.

"Oh no. Michael is the shooter in the family," said Del. "It's where he gets his best ideas for Gunn."

"I guess Gunn is part of the family now, too," said Dasha.

"We're not quite to the point where we set a place for him at the dinner table, but he's definitely part of the scene," said Del. Dasha flashed on what that might mean in the Aubreys' conjugal affairs. Did Del fantasize about the amazing Gunn? Or would Michael Aubrey do? Maybe she liked keeping it a secret.

"I really must be going," said Dasha. "I don't like leaving Galina for too long. We're coping with her stroke, but the poor dear just seems so fatigued these days."

"Come back soon," said Aubrey.

Del led the way through the living room to the center hall and around a table overloaded with roses.

They approached the massive double wooden doors leading to the porte cochere and the winding drive that accessed Beachside Avenue through stone pillars and iron gates. Michael Aubrey swept open the door . . . and stopped.

There was a seven-inch dart from a blowgun lodged in the carved oak panel below a garish brass knocker. There was a syrupy substance dripping from the dart, leaving a stain in the Aubreys' vestibule. Dasha approached and smelled the substance.

"Batrachotoxin, an alkaloid poison from the golden tree frog," she said.

Del backed away from the door. Aubrey's face turned red. He stepped out onto the stone landing leading to the drive.

"God damn you, Jayne!" he yelled across his wide yard. "I know your game! You can't intimidate me. Two can play at this!"

Dasha stood next to him, her expression puzzled yet unemotional.

Grown men, she thought. *There's no telling what might come next.*

4

Counterattack

The tabloid press would later describe the next two weeks as the Battle of Beachside Avenue. For Dasha, it opened innocently enough. The day after the Aubreys experienced deadly frog venom dripping from their front door, Dasha was walking in the arboretum on the north side of the avenue. The space was filled with trees and trails, and she liked to watch the small birds there going about their industries. Nest building. Egg laying. There was always much ado. She was on the trail of a particularly striking warbler when she heard a grunting sound and a muffled curse. She walked toward the noise, taking comfort in her chestnut stick, her Walther in her pocket. She brushed her way through a copse of evergreens and came into a small glade of maple and hemlock. Barnaby Jayne was hanging upside down with a snare around his Bean boots. The contents of his pockets were scattered on the ground.

"Dasha, it was that bastard Aubrey," said Jayne, trying to catch his breath with airway and lungs inverted. "He's dug a punji pit, too. Watch where you step. God damn you, Aubrey—you'll pay!" Jayne shouted into the woods. Dasha heard footsteps and the rustle of clothing moving through the brush. They were being watched.

"I've got to get you down somehow," said Dasha.

"Don't move too close," said Jayne. "Throw some rocks or branches around here and see if you can find the pit."

"How do you know it's here?" she asked.

"Aubrey told me after he snared me," said Jayne. "Told me I'd be skewered if I tried to get loose. Some kind of plot device from that drivel he writes . . . *White Heat* or something."

"So you *do* read his books," said Dasha.

"Have to keep an eye on what that devil is shoveling out these days. Make sure he doesn't steal from me. Throw something over there." An upside-down Jayne pointed to Dasha's right. She threw a log, and it disappeared into a bed of leaves. She probed with her chestnut stick and found the pit. She looked inside and saw sharpened sticks pointing upward, reminiscent of her time fighting the Viet Minh.

"For God's sake, be careful, Dasha," said Jayne. "There might be more." She found two more, in fact, arrayed in a rough triangle around the gently swaying Jayne, who was finding it hard to breathe. How to get the old boy down?

"I'm going to push you over to that tree behind you," said Dasha. "You can hold onto a branch, and I'll cut your snare. I don't want you falling on that beautiful head of yours."

"Too kind," said Jayne, who managed a chin up while Dasha sawed at the line around his feet with her secret knife. Jayne was once again enthralled by Mrs. Petrov's talents, and soon he was on his own two feet with his blood draining properly in the correct direction.

"Now Barnaby, you've suffered a shock," said Dasha. "I don't want you to get upset. Remember this all started with your blow dart and frog venom. Aubrey had to call the fire department hazmat crew after that. Try to calm yourself."

"I hate him, Dasha," said Barnaby, smashing his right fist into the palm of his left hand. "I want to hurt him."

"Please do me one courtesy," said Dasha. "Go home. Get into a hot tub. Have Tammy fix you some Earl Gray with a dash or two of Glenfiddich. I am going to go talk to Aubrey about cleaning up this mess. He's got to come over here and fill in these pits before someone gets hurt. Otherwise, I'll have to call the authorities, and then there will be hell to pay." Barnaby grumbled and fumed and picked up his hat, his wallet, his pocket change, and other accessories.

"Let's keep this between us, Dasha," said Jayne. "It's embarrassing."

"No, Barnaby, it's attempted murder," said Dasha. "And I hate to stress this point: You started it. Go home and get into a hot bath."

Barnaby Jayne skulked away, muttering. She felt sorry for him as he moved into the brush, favoring a knee he'd injured decades ago when he played tailback at Yale. Dasha turned on her heels and walked out of the arboretum and directly to the Aubreys' front gate. She pushed the button next to the speaker phone. Their maid, Sheila, came on the line, and when Dasha announced her identity, Sheila said, "I'll have to see if Mr. Aubrey is receiving." Dasha was normally buzzed right in.

Soon the clearly displeased voice of Michael Aubrey came booming over the speaker. "Whatever Jayne told you is a lie."

"Michael, open the gate," said Dasha. "We need to talk."

"I'm in the middle of something," he said.

"Well, you give me no choice but to call the police," said Dasha. "You've assaulted your neighbor, and you've left a mess in the arboretum. Someone could fall into one of your pits, and you will be liable."

"How do you know it was me?" said a belligerent Aubrey.

"Tell me it wasn't, and I will report your denial to the authorities when I make my call. They can sweat it out of you. Michael, fix this problem before you're named in a lawsuit, and not just by Jayne. I'm trying to help you." Dasha was imploring him, and her logic seemed to have the desired effect. The gates opened, and soon a fuming Aubrey came down the drive wearing the one-piece dirt-streaked coveralls he wore in the garden. He had a shovel in his hands. The faithful Makita brought up the rear.

"Don't say a word, Dasha," said Aubrey. "Blow darts! God damn that awful man."

"I *will* say a word, Michael. You've both had your fun, and you're even. This has to stop."

"He's hated my guts ever since I landed that Academy Award in '87 for best novel adaptation," said Aubrey.

"It was for *Recoil*, as I recall. Max Gunn is trapped on the Jungfrau in a snow squall and commandeers a helicopter," said Dasha.

"Dasha, you amaze me," said Aubrey. "I'm flattered."

"Jayne's *Harbinger* was also nominated. Came within an eyelash of topping you," said Dasha.

"But he didn't top me," said Aubrey. "He'll never top me. Bastard!"

"Get busy, Michael," said Dasha. "We'll keep this just between us. I have to go home to check on Galina." He took her by the hand and pecked her on the cheek.

"I'll try to behave."

5

Tit for Tat

Dasha should have assumed Jayne was not to be outdone, and the details of his retaliation came in a breathless conversation at their meeting rock the day after the horrible deed was done. The man was not without skill. She'd give him that.

Jayne had gotten up at two a.m., leaving a slumbering Tammy and the softly purring Lucy and Jim. He'd gone into his workshop next to his multi-bay garage and found the black pajamas and black balaclava he'd prototyped during research for his novel *Interloper*. He'd found the diamond-blade disk cutter he used to separate rusty car parts, plus the lockpicks he'd trained himself to use while he was writing *Vagabond*. Last to go into his backpack had been the night-vision scope he was experimenting with for an upcoming screenplay. He'd stolen down the beach on his black espadrilles and mounted the seawall in front of the Aubrey residence. He'd cursed the tree lights Aubrey had installed, then worked his way to the back of the house by the boxwood hedge on the south side of the property.

Jayne described the black, moonless night, the still air, and the terrible fear of waking up Prince and having Aubrey's magnificent hunting dog alert his master to Jayne's well-planned intrusion. He'd gotten to the kitchen door of the house and taken a piece of steak tartare out of a plastic bag in his backpack. He'd embedded three full-strength Benadryl pills in the raw meat and knelt by Prince's dog flap entrance cut into the door. He'd pushed it with one hand and held the steak inside the kitchen with the other. Prince, being Prince, had been far more interested in his stomach than their intruder and had wolfed down the treat, venturing out of the house to see if there was any more where that came from. Jayne had lavished Prince with a good rubdown and soothing "good boys," and soon this stalwart example of canine masculinity was sleeping soundly.

Jayne had then donned his night-vision equipment and walked around the back of Aubrey's house to find the door to the basement. He'd used his lockpick to open the door and slipped inside, not at all surprised to find the boxes and bins and cast-offs that seem to effervesce from basements everywhere. He'd worked his way closer to the stairs leading up to the first floor and found what he was looking for—the circuit breaker panel. He'd found a twenty-amp switch labeled *Security System* and turned it off. He'd gone up the stairs and twisted the doorknob, hesitating for a brief second before proceeding to the moment of truth. Had he found the right circuit? Would he trip the motion detectors? He'd girded against overconfidence but decided the risk was manageable. He'd pushed open the door to the sound of a ticking grandfather clock somewhere in the Aubrey household. Prince's bed was in the kitchen, with a folding gate to keep him out of the rest of the house. There were no motion detectors up in the corners for the dog to trip. He had to assume there were motion detectors—now disabled—in the rest of the house. He'd stepped over Prince's gate and crept on his cloth shoes to Aubrey's study.

He'd found what he was looking for—the glass-fronted gun cabinet. He'd used his lockpick to open the door. Aubrey's prized collection was standing there, mute and stratospherically priced—at least three Purdeys of various gauges, a rare Holland & Holland .10-gauge, a cherished Weatherby elk rifle, and a historically significant German Steyr sniper rifle from the First World War. He'd opened a drawer in a cabinet and seen Aubrey's handguns, an original Bisley six-shooter, his 1911 ACP .45, a German Walther, tiny next to the large-frame American handguns. He'd leave them in the interest of saving time. Concentrating on Aubrey's collection of long guns would have more impact. Jayne had gathered up the rifles and carried them down to the basement. He'd found Aubrey's shop, commandeered one of Del's down quilts from a laundry room, and closed the door. He'd put the first Purdy in Aubrey's vise, wrapped the disk cutter in the quilt, and plugged it in. The quilt had cut down on the noise as the disk tool carved through the Purdey's delicately engraved receiver. Jayne had been surprised at how quickly he could gnash through the gun, and prospects brightened for an early exit. He'd managed to hack through Aubrey's long-gun collection, destroying a quarter million dollars' worth of firearms in thirty minutes. He'd taken the pieces back up to the gun cabinet and stacked the cleavered halves in place, so at first glance it looked like no harm had been done. Pleased with his handiwork, Jayne had gone back to the kitchen, down through the basement door and outside—but not before restoring the circuit breaker switch to the "on" position. Prince was having a bad dream, it seemed, and Jayne had taken the time to comfort the poor beast, who woke up and got to his feet. The dog went outside and peed on one of Del's flower containers, and Jayne had helped this fine canine specimen back through his doggy door. He'd gotten back to his own house at four a.m. and slept peacefully until the sun penetrated his bedchamber through a split in the curtain at around six thirty.

Dasha listened to the details of this crime and tried to unhear them.

"Barnaby, why are you telling me this?" she asked him. "Now I'm a witness."

"Aubrey will be too embarrassed to call the police," said Jayne. "Prideful bugger. Can't stand to lose to me. I've had the last laugh."

"Barnaby, you don't know what you're saying," she said. "Aubrey is highly confident, and, like you, he's got a mean streak. This tit for tat will escalate, and somebody will get hurt."

"I can't let him get the upper hand," said Barnaby. "I need to destroy him psychologically. Reduce him to the pitiful, sniveling fool I know him to be. Eliminate forever the bastard's ability to foist his nonsense on the world. Max Gunn! A peevish little oaf with no skill, no grace, no subtlety. All blunt force. No finesse."

"Well, come on, Barnaby," said Dasha. "Your cast of characters knows how to spill blood with the best of them."

"Yes, but they're just plain more interesting," said Barnaby. "Who doesn't like a Nubian spear showing up at a murder scene in Manhattan? Or moccasin treads at the crime scene disappearing off the side of a cliff?"

"God, man, why are you telling me this?" asked Dasha.

"You of all people can appreciate a fine example of breaking and entering," said Barnaby. "I thought you'd be proud of me." He was preening.

"Barnaby, I've had to pick locks in defense of the nation, not in a petty dispute with my neighbors," said Dasha, appalled by Jayne's false equivalency. "There is simply no comparison."

"But don't you like the way I disabled his alarm?" asked Jayne. "Went right around it. Perfected that in *Damocles*."

"Well . . . I have to admit that's kind of clever, but you got lucky," said Dasha. "Barnaby, I can't condone this behavior—by either of you—and I am bracing for what comes next."

Dasha didn't have to wait long.

She found herself atop the Aubrey seawall the next day, patting Prince and feeding him the little wieners he adored. She'd just asked the dog, "So, where's your lord and master?" when Aubrey came shuffling out of his gazebo and down to the seawall, hands in his pockets and a black scowl darkening his normally merry face. Of course, Dasha knew the particulars, but she didn't want to let on. She'd let the travesty unspool of its own accord, and she braced for Aubrey's inevitable counterattack.

Still, she couldn't resist a dig, just to open the conversation. "No shooting today, Michael?" she asked innocently.

"No shooting for a long time to come," said Aubrey, looking down and dejected. The man had been reduced.

"Neighbors complaining?" Dasha asked.

"No, Dasha. And I think you know the answer," said Aubrey, seeming suddenly vexed at the mere proximity of another human being. It was clear he needed to lash out, and she was in the line of fire.

"Whatever do you mean?" she asked, lying comfortably, understanding what was about to come. He needed to yell at the situation, not necessarily at her.

"It's Jayne again," said Aubrey. "I know you two talk. He broke into my home and destroyed my gun collection." He spit out the ugly deed, shaking in anger. "I went to the gun case to fetch one of my Purdeys, and it came apart in my hands. The Holland & Holland. The old Steyr. All the long guns. Now he's gone too far."

"I presume you've got evidence," said Dasha dryly, touching his arm, trying to sooth a man who was still very much a friend.

"Damned little," said Aubrey. "I don't want the police involved. So, I called a private security firm. They found curious scratches on the lock to the basement door and metal shavings near my vise in my basement shop. Bugger used a cutting tool. They were priceless, Dasha. All three Purdeys were prewar. Hundreds of thousands of dollars."

"What about Makita?" asked Dasha. "Did he hear anything?" The slight, fastidious Japanese gentleman lived in an apartment over the Aubrey garage.

"Solid sleeper," said Aubrey. "You can hear him snoring in Bridgeport."

"This is getting serious, Michael," said Dasha. "What connects Jayne to the crime?"

"No fingerprints," said Aubrey. "Only some shoe soles in the dirt by the basement door, and closed-circuit TV footage showing a figure in black scurrying around the boxwoods. It's Jayne. Do you know he's got a limp?"

"It's from what he calls his 'tailback knee,'" said Dasha, revealing she knew a bit too much. She didn't want to point an accusing finger, nor did she want Aubrey to become more jealous.

"I want to smash his face," said Aubrey.

"It's what Gunn would do," said Dasha. "But I think it's time for a truce. Let me see what I can arrange. Can I send out some peace feelers on your behalf?"

"I will need a full confession and financial compensation," said Aubrey after a pause to reflect. "You're the only one I would trust with this mission. I don't want to get the lawyers involved. The next thing you know, we'll have the press skulking through the shrubbery." He smiled at her through all the clouds scudding across his face, and, as usual, she was drawn to the man. Who could resist the creator of the legendary Gunn?

Del Aubrey came down the lawn.

"I suppose you've heard," she said, managing something short of a smile. Did she enjoy seeing her type-A husband diminished?

"Michael just told me," said Dasha. "It's a terrible violation knowing an intruder has been in your home. I presume, now that the horse has left the barn, there will be more security precautions."

"I thought our security was more than adequate," said Aubrey. "Now everything's under review."

"You say the intruder came through the basement?" asked Dasha, innocently.

"That's what my consultant told me," said Aubrey.

"And so, the intruder had access to the circuit breaker panel?" asked Dasha. Aubrey grew quiet and scratched the stubble on his chin.

"Of course," he said, suddenly illuminated. "Why do I pay these experts when I've got you?" Del didn't take kindly to Aubrey's compliment of his "other woman" and moved closer to her husband, slipping her hand through his arm and pressing herself however lightly against his heavyset physique. Her blouse was crisply laundered, her slacks pressed. Dasha detected a hint of lavender from Del's eau de cologne. Dasha could understand Aubrey's attraction to Del, but why did Del submit to being number six?

"Michael, I am just trying to find the logic in all this," said Dasha. "Isn't it time for you and Barnaby to come to terms?"

"I'll think about it," said Aubrey.

Apparently, he didn't think very hard, because two days later the Battle of Beachside reached a climax and unleashed a rabid press corps—just when Dasha thought she was making inroads with Barnaby Jayne. Tammy had taken her children on an expedition to New York—to FAO Schwarz and the Central Park Children's Zoo, and to see the dinosaurs at the Natural History Museum—and Barnaby invited Dasha on a drive up around the Redding reservoir. It was a beautiful sunny day, and Jayne pulled into the Petrov drive at the wheel of his prize, a 1933 Rolls-Royce Phantom II roadster station wagon. He liked to invest in vehicles of significance—Elvis Presley's Cadillac, JFK's Lincoln convertible, Joseph Stalin's Packard—but his favorite was the stately Rolls with the wood-grain paneled sides and in-line six-cylinder engine. He called the car Gladys, after his mother. He said it was the luckiest car in the world. Gladys's original owner bought it after selling his whiskey business to Hiram Walker—a week before Prohibition was made into law. He took his money to Southern California and found a copper mine on his new property. He then sold the mine and went to Utah, where he discovered gold on his next acquisition. After that, he went back to California and bought property near Santa Barbara, where he struck oil. The Rolls was a gift for the man's wife. After they'd enjoyed it as a sedan, they had it rebuilt into a station wagon at the coach works of Bohman and Schwartz. The owner installed a sliding panel in the roof so he could use the vehicle as a shooting car on safari. World War II interfered with the man's travel plans, and, lucky as he was, he couldn't avoid the final knock from the grim reaper. The car was sold at auction and went through a succession of happy owners until Barnaby Jayne picked it up for his collection. Nothing gave him greater pleasure than using the old Rolls for those mundane errands to the post office, or to take Lucy and Jim for ice cream. He enjoyed being the eccentric.

"Listen to that engine," said Jayne as he shifted through the manual gears on the steering column. He'd slid open the roof to let the sunshine pour in.

"I don't hear a thing," said Dasha.

"That's entirely the point," said Jayne. "It's the quietest car I've ever owned. Even the chassis is lubricated in its own oil system, and no metal part touches its neighbor. Genius." Jayne skippered the Rolls through the countryside as it swayed and heaved like a ship at sea.

"I'm really not a car buff, but I enjoy watching how happy you are," said Dasha. And then, after a pause, "There's something I need to speak to you about."

"You're not going to talk me into surrendering to that fool Aubrey," he said, wrinkling his mouth in distaste.

"Now how did you know I was going to bring up Aubrey?" asked Dasha.

"It makes sense he'd send you out to seek an armistice," said Jayne. "A little shuttle diplomacy. You know the players."

"Barnaby, let's not forget how all this started," said Dasha. "Your blow dart with the frog venom. Now it's out of control."

"I was trying to keep him away from you," said Jayne.

"Don't you think I might have had something to say about that?" said Dasha. "I like Aubrey. And I like you. Why can't we all just be friends?"

"I have some commercial interests at stake, Dasha," said Jayne. "I can't let Aubrey steal any of my ideas."

"Well, you need to know that I don't discuss with Michael what you and I talk about," said Dasha. "Nor do I discuss with you anything I talk to Michael about. I have lived my life keeping confidences, and I don't intend to stop now."

"It's your *experience*, Dasha," said Jayne. "I can't have any of that infiltrating Aubrey's writing."

"Well, I can put a stop to this right now," said Dasha. "Turn the car around and take me home. I am ending my relationships with both of you. I won't be a pawn. And I don't want to be a party to this insane rivalry." Dasha's ultimatum seemed to make an impression.

Jayne fell silent, and then he asked: "So, Aubrey wants a truce?"

"That's what he told me," said Dasha. "He suspects you of destroying his gun collection. I neither confirmed nor denied. I got him to the point where he wishes to sue for peace. It will probably cost you some money."

"Let me think about it," said Jayne. Dasha knew he was prideful. He would want Aubrey to come groveling. They drove through the afternoon, stopping at an orchard for some apples and a pie. There was a coolness to their conversation on the ride home, and Dasha had Jayne drop her off on the avenue at the head of the driveway. She related the gist of their exchange to Galina, who was free and clear with her advice.

"Drop them," she wrote with her little Scrabble squares. Dasha heated up some borscht and poured two jiggers of vodka, and they arranged themselves in front of *NBC Nightly News*. They wanted to know all about their friend Tracy Taggart's latest assignment. The dazzling redhead, the chief of police's girlfriend, was chiming in from an icepack off Newfoundland, where protesters were trying to stop the trade in baby seal fur.

"Ghastly," said Dasha. The miserable lot of the baby seals replaced the challenges of adjudicating a peaceful resolution between her two novelists, and she didn't think about Jayne or Aubrey until the next morning, when she encountered Michael Aubrey on the beach.

"Come see the scene of the crime, Dasha," Aubrey implored her. She agreed, thinking it might be an opportunity to get Aubrey to lay down his arms. He took her into the basement of the house, and they went into Aubrey's shop. She felt as if she were peering into the heart and mind of Max Gunn. On the wall hung ropes, cams, lugs, and carabineers for mountain climbing. A spear gun leaned against a corner, next to a scuba buoyancy vest on a hanger. On a wall peg rested a helicopter pilot's helmet with a dual plug ready to be inserted into an intercom. There was a disassembled H&K nine-millimeter pistol field stripped on the bench next to a suppressor.

"All the tools of Gunn's trade?" asked Dasha.

"It pays to know how things work so my adoring public won't catch me in a misstatement. That idiot Jayne once called a revolver a pistol. Can you imagine? The readers love it when you make a mistake."

There was a flight simulator in a corner.

"I forgot you're a pilot," she said.

"That's a procedures trainer," said Aubrey. "Keeps me pin sharp in my Citation. Let's go up some time."

"And what are these blueprints on the wall?" she asked.

"Plans for a submersible," said Aubrey. "Gunn needs to recover a nuclear trigger off a sunken submarine."

"Lot of work being a novelist," she said with unconcealed admiration. "Imagine what you and Jayne could create if you tried collaborating." She immediately knew she'd said the wrong thing.

"Never," Aubrey seethed. "I enjoy hating that man. Keeps me focused."

"But Michael, someone will get hurt," said Dasha. "You and Barnaby really need to end this."

Dasha looked at the workbench and saw printed circuit boards, a soldering iron, small-gauge wire, and thumb switches.

"Looks like you're making a bomb," she said casually. Aubrey looked a bit startled.

"Trying to augment my security system," he said. "I think I can do a better job than the simpletons who installed it."

It was the way he said it: no eye contact, a moment of hesitation, followed by a quick answer that left out details. Aubrey usually liked to impress her with the broad sweep of his expertise. He was trying to hide this so-called "security system."

He got around to showing Dasha the wood and metal shavings underneath his vise, and he showed her the closed-circuit TV footage of the black-clad ninja limping past his boxwoods.

"It's that fool Jayne, Dasha," said Aubrey. "He can run, but he can't hide."

Dasha withdrew from Aubrey's lair, thinking she'd made some inroads—a hope that was resoundingly dashed the next day. This time she was a witness.

On Tuesdays, Thursdays, and Saturdays, she liked to trudge down the avenue to the Green's Farms post office to pick up her mail. On this particular Tuesday, she was pulling a little two-wheeled grocery cart to haul back any packages and using her faithful stick to keep her balance. She walked down the lane that fronted the train station and noticed Jayne's stately Gladys in front of the post office. The sun was shining on this late-March day, and she didn't think anything could disrupt her reverie. Spring was on its way. As she approached the post office, she glanced to her right and saw Michael Aubrey sitting in the front seat of one of his Corvettes, Gunn's preferred mode of travel. She smiled at him, but he was looking down, and they failed to connect. She reflected on the idea that sometimes it was hard to understand where Aubrey stopped and Gunn began. Her novelists' choice of vehicles made an eloquent statement about these competing authors' psychological makeups. Jayne's characters were throwbacks to an earlier age, while Aubrey's Gunn was right on the bleeding edge of science, technology, and every schoolboy's dream of fast cars and saucy women.

She was getting closer to Jayne's wonderful antique automobile when she heard a *wump* sound coming from underneath the old dowager. It wasn't a bang, and it wasn't a crack. It was a *wump*, the same sound gasoline makes when it suddenly alights and there's an inrush of air to nourish a spark that ignites an accelerant. And then she saw black smoke curling around the running boards. Finally, she saw gouts of flame shooting out of the sliding port in the roof. Jayne came running out of the post office, and all they could do was watch the old girl die a cruel, agonizing death. Jayne went back into the post office to call 911, and when Dasha turned, Aubrey's yellow Corvette was driving slowly away.

She comforted Barnaby as the Westport fire department extinguished the car's final burning embers. He and Dasha stood before the once-glorious Gladys, now a sagging black cinder, tires flattened, headlamps blacked, leather interior reduced to a reeking ooze. Jayne was speechless. Dasha touched his arm, and he shuddered in pain, head to toe.

6

Del and Tammy

Dasha would have to tell Galina how low and tawdry the Battle of Beachside Avenue was becoming. She trudged home with her mail, steaming mad, having remained at Jayne's side while he gave the police a brief report. "Might have been a bad wire," he'd said. "These old cars are quirky. No, officer, it's self-insured. I'll call a wrecker." He clearly didn't want the police involved. They might uncover his own contribution to the skirmish, which had failed, so far, to draw blood.

When the police left to file their report, Jayne turned to Dasha. "I know it was Aubrey." It was the first shot in a fusillade of accusations. Dasha waited for him to calm down.

"Why do you think it was Aubrey?" Dasha asked, fearing the answer. Jayne reached into the charred mass that had once been Gladys and pulled some wires away from the still-hot chassis. They led to a canister strapped with hose clamps to a brake line. He pulled the parasitic anomaly away from the car and held it in his hands.

"Smell that?" he asked as he held the blackened bits in front of Dasha's nose. "That's Jet A, aviation kerosene for the bastard's little jet he likes to show off in. And those wires probably lead to a radio receiver somewhere in here." Jayne reached into the poor dead beast's steaming entrails and pulled out a black box with an antenna on one end.

"He triggered it from off-site somewhere, probably the station parking lot," said Jayne. "So clever. Didn't want to plant a bomb. People could get hurt. That would draw attention. Just a little fire to start things going. Same ploy he used in that dreadful tripe

Deadeye he wrote twenty years ago. You didn't see him, did you?" Dasha was torn. She needed time to think.

"I was so upset when I saw the flames, I didn't pay much attention to anything else," she said. Why was she protecting Aubrey? Was it because she knew both parties shared responsibility? Sending Aubrey off to jail and letting Jayne go free would be an injustice. She was confused, and her head hurt.

"I need to get back to Galina," she told Jayne. Galina was her refuge.

She got back to the house and recounted the tale of Gladys's untimely immolation. She left nothing out, of course. The sisters would always bare, and bear, their secrets. Galina took meticulous care with her Scrabble squares as she moved them around the board. She was putting her foot down.

"No more," she wrote. Being the elder sister, Galina was not to be trifled with. She was the only person—aside from Constantine— to whom Dasha ever really listened. Galina was the rock of sense. Galina always had the clear eye. It was Galina she had turned to when the Bolsheviks were at the door those many years ago, when they'd slipped out the back with their mother and ran for their lives. It was Galina who pulled them through.

"Of course, you're right," said Dasha, quietly, hating to lose her two fascinating but irascible friends. But she also hated being in the middle, and she couldn't go on. She and Galina had a quiet night in front of the television and went to bed early. Dasha lay awake. She reached out at one point to pat her Constantine on the arm and realized for the four thousandth night that her love was gone, never to return. She cried herself to a fitful, friendless sleep.

She woke up late the next morning and found Galina up in her favorite housecoat dusting the pictures and singing something unintelligible. Dasha took her tea and announced she was off to check on her birds. It was late April, and there was a persistent chill. She wore her familiar Barbour coat and moved her toes inside her Wellingtons. She had her Leupold binoculars around her neck and her faithful stick. She wasn't sure why she'd felt the need to keep her Walther in her pocket, but she felt safe knowing it was there. She was actually carrying two concealed weapons if one considered her stick with the secret knife in the handle.

She walked down the beach to the west, past her meeting rock, and felt a pang of loss. Barnaby was gone. She'd trust Galina. Dasha had no interest in seeing him. She made it all the way to Frost Point, where her swans were paddling. She'd find solace in this living link to God. The swans recognized their very own Mrs. Petrov, who had arrived with breakfast, and they made their way into shore. Dasha left them to their sustenance, and she told them out loud, "You're my family now."

She turned back to the east and saw two people coming in her direction. She brought her Leupolds up to her eyes and scanned out to sea, making it look like she was watching a flight of canvasbacks. She then swung the binoculars eastward so she could see her beachcombers—Tammy Jayne and Del Aubrey, dressed inadequately for the chill and absorbed in conversation. Dasha had no idea the novelists' wives were friendly, and she was surprised. A passing acquaintanceship among people on Beachside Avenue was not unusual. But Tammy and Del were speaking urgently and confidentially. Tammy put her hand on Del's elbow and put her lips up to Del's ear. Del turned to Tammy and watched her face, taking everything in. It wasn't a passing chat.

Dasha brought the binoculars down and continued walking east, planting her stick, using it to turn over a crab shell or poke at a mullet pushed up on the beach. She'd let the wives come to her. Later she reflected that this was the moment she'd given them that collective appellation. The wives walked up and delivered their frivolous so-nice-to-see-yous. Dasha knew how much they resented her and the hold she seemed to have on their respective husbands. Dasha was able to engage her novelists on their own intellectual levels, and Dasha knew the wives were jealous.

Del was the first to say hello.

"Dasha, how are you, dear? Chilly day," she said, somewhat coolly to Dasha's trained ear. Dasha's profession rewarded the observant. The successful operative knew how to watch for shifts in tone, telltale glances, the avoidance of eye contact—all the little details that let you know there's a tantalizing secret somewhere in the deep, beating heart of an intelligence target.

"Just checking on my birds," said Dasha. "It's not bad out here if you're dressed for it." She looked at Del's chain link mocs from the L.L. Bean catalog and knew instantly Del's regret. She thought she saw Del looking covetously at her Wellingtons. Tammy was dressed in a light windbreaker and boys athletic shoes. She was shivering, rubbing her arms and jumping up and down.

"Hi, Dasha," she said. "Can't stay out here much longer. It is f-r-e-e-z-i-n-g."

Dasha knew Tammy and Del wanted to keep moving.

"By all means, go get yourselves warm," said Dasha. Del and Tammy both smiled sweetly and then glanced at each other. They had no interest in talking to the old woman.

"Well, it's nice to see you, Mrs. Petrov," said Tammy.

"Please call me Dasha," she said—but then she couldn't resist pushing her boundaries. She was, after all, a spy. "Oh, Tammy," she said as the two were walking away, "is Barnaby home? I'd like to speak to him. I have a theory regarding how poor Gladys met her end." Dasha felt the sudden burning need to penetrate the Jayne household. She wasn't sure why. An instinct, a supposition, the first flickering embers of a theory.

"He's in his study," said Tammy. She looked at Del and shrugged. "Come up to the house." Dasha followed the two socialites down the beach to the Jaynes' seawall. She followed the wives up the narrow concrete steps, past the pool, and then up the sloping lawn to the Jaynes' Cotswoldian mansion. Tammy turned to Dasha.

"I'll take you into the kitchen and go find Barnaby," said Tammy. "Can I make you some tea? Let me take your coat."

"Thanks, dear," said Dasha. "Tea would be lovely, but I really can't stay. I'll just hang my coat over the back of a chair if you don't mind. May I bring my stick inside? It helps me with my balance. I'll be mindful of the furniture."

"Of course," said Tammy, leading the way deeper into the house. Dasha followed, and Del Aubrey came behind her. They were on the threshold of the kitchen when Del let out a little yelp and slipped on a rug. Dasha felt Del grab her shoulders in an attempt to keep herself upright.

"Oh, dear me," said Del. "I am so sorry, Dasha. I slipped."

"Those throw rugs are ridiculous," said Tammy. "They're gone today." Dasha kept herself intact and made it to the table. She took off her coat and draped it on the back of a chair, and Tammy went to find Barnaby. Del and Dasha settled themselves, and Dasha undertook some first delicate thrusts to determine the state of play.

"You and Tammy get along so handsomely," said Dasha. "Can't say the same for our two novelists, can we?"

"Tammy is a dear," said Del. "I've needed a friend on this street. Sometimes it's a bit cold—and I don't mean the weather."

"Michael and Barnaby's professional rivalry not getting in the way of your friendship?" asked Dasha innocently. She was curious as to why these spouses wouldn't be manning the battlements to protect their husbands.

"We think it's better if we try to bring them together," said Del. "They really do have a lot in common. I'm sure they'd be fun at a dinner party."

Tammy came back to the kitchen.

"Barnaby will join us in a minute or two," she said. She rummaged in a pantry and came to the table with a tray of cookies, cups, saucers, and tea bags. The water was near a boil. Dasha continued her conversation with Del.

"Still, that poison dart in your doorway was kind of scary, wasn't it?" asked Dasha.

"We can laugh about it now," said Del.

"Michael certainly isn't laughing about his gun collection," said Dasha. "And I know Barnaby suspects Michael retaliated by destroying dear old Gladys. I wish it weren't so."

"Well . . . ," said Tammy, distant and wistful, "the next thing you know someone will wind up in the hospital." Dasha was trying to place Tammy's accent. Brooklyn perhaps, and not the Heights.

"Well, I have tried to rein in Michael, and it's not easy," said Del. "Keeps muttering, 'What would Gunn do?'"

And where, Dasha mused, had Del come from? Queens, she surmised, and not Forest Hills. Someplace a little more earthy. Possibly Astoria. These two Beachside damsels had landed sunny-side up.

"Not what either of you signed up for, is it?" said Dasha flatly. "I mean . . . you meet, find common interests, fall in love, choose to wed. And then you're knocked off course by these silly spats. Outsiders looking in would guess it's all roses and champagne." Did Del and Tammy know Dasha was probing the perimeter? Dasha looked at Del, done up to the nines, with fresh lipstick, blush, a tasteful hair band, and a shapely figure that would enthrall any man, let alone the prolific womanizer Aubrey. She looked at Tammy, hair piled high, lips injected with some kind of filler, breasts standing proud. Del and Tammy just looked at Dasha, seemingly unable to formulate a response. Dasha pushed further.

"Del, how did you meet Michael?" Dasha asked.

"I was staying with friends on St. Barts," said Del. "Getting over a breakup. Michael came into the harbor in Gustavia aboard a chartered yacht. He was down in the dumps after Cynthia, number five. I was invited to a dinner, and we sat next to each other. Let me just say it was a brilliant night—the first of a lot of brilliant nights."

"It sounds wonderful," said Dasha. "The stars aligned. How about you, Tammy? Where did you meet Barnaby?"

"Miami," said Tammy. "At a film festival. I was there with someone else. We locked eyes from across the room. Of course, I knew who he was because he was on *Donahue*."

"Had you read many of his books?" asked Dasha. Surely, she would have been drawn to the man's inner world.

"Not really," said Tammy. "I'd seen some of the movies. His work is his work. He likes to keep the door closed when he's pounding away on his computer. I know how to stay out of his way."

Barnaby Jayne entered the kitchen. He lit up when he saw Dasha. Tammy noticed this unspoken attention he paid to his other woman and wrinkled her nose.

"Tea, Barnaby?" she asked her husband.

"A drop," he said. "I have to get back to the keyboard. Dasha, it's postwar Berlin. Our hero is trying to evade the Soviet NKVD. He's on foot, and he's trying to get to Checkpoint Charlie, the entrance to the American zone and safety."

"Armed?" asked Dasha, rising to the seriousness of the scenario.

"Only with a switchblade," said Jayne.

"He'll need a gun," said Dasha. "The opposition will have those unwieldy Tokarev semiautomatics, not the refined Makarovs that came later. Give your hero a Browning Hi-Power. Loved mine. And fit it with a suppressor, which means his CIA armorers will have smithed it with a threaded barrel. What's the lay of the land?" Dasha was absorbed. She felt Tammy and Del drifting off into a conversation of their own. Something about pre-theater dinner at the Westport Playhouse. "Try the ravioli," Dasha heard Del say.

"Soviet zone. Pre-wall," said Barnaby.

"Have him exit the train at Ostbanhof and walk away from the Spree on Andreasstrasse. He needs to get away from the water. Limits where he can turn. He needs to get deeper into the city, where he'll have more options."

"I hadn't thought of that," said Jayne. "The Spree is more scenic."

"But Barnaby, the man needs to hide. There's some nice rubble near St. Michael's Church and an open park that leads to Oranienstrasse. And that leads right into Checkpoint Charlie," said Dasha. "But your hero will need to behave asymmetrically: wait, stop, hide, change his appearance. Determine the threat level. See if the threat itself is being followed in a bit of countersurveillance. Your man will be sweating, Barnaby. Why is he running?"

"He's a Yank," said Jayne. "He's just made contact with a Soviet general, his spy. He's got microfilm in his pocket."

"If he's up to his neck in trouble, he'll want to hide the canister in the ruins and come back for it," said Dasha. "He can't risk having it fall into the wrong hands. I suppose the fate of mankind is hanging in the balance?"

"Of course," said Jayne.

"And is there a woman in the picture?" asked Dasha.

"A beautiful White Russian," said Jayne. Dasha blushed. He'd gone too far, but Tammy failed to get the connection.

"Have I helped?" asked Dasha. "I really must be going."

Tammy turned to Dasha. "Didn't you say you had a theory about how Gladys caught fire?" she queried, catching Dasha off guard.

"Oh yes, Barnaby," she said, turning to him, giving herself a few seconds to think. "Something hot dripping from the engine onto some dried vegetation. Couldn't that have been the initial cause?"

"I showed you what caused the fire, Dasha," said Barnaby, irritated. He glanced at Del. He seemed to want to avoid the subject in the presence of the enemy camp.

"Oh yes. I am so sorry," said Dasha. "I am just thinking there has to be a natural explanation. Such a beautiful car."

"There will be others," said Barnaby. "But not if I don't get back to work. My publisher is screaming for this one." He arose with his mug of tea and stalked out of the kitchen.

Dasha got out of her chair to put her coat on, while Tammy and Del returned to their trivialities. Later, Dasha reflected on that moment and realized it was the last time she saw Barnaby Jayne alive.

7

Not to Be Outdone

Dasha walked down the beach, trying to get to Aubrey before Del returned. She didn't think it proper to keep popping up between these two households. Why hadn't she listened to Galina? Wasn't Galina always right? She got to Aubrey's seawall and found the man exercising the adored Prince with a tennis ball thrower. He knew he'd rather be exercising one of his Purdeys, but keeping Prince in shape was the next best thing. The German shorthaired was a bristling specimen of well-defined muscle—a keen, clear-eyed spectacle of canine perfection. Dasha could tell Aubrey loved Prince more than anything, including his panoply of children brought forth from the loins of his various wives. If Aubrey had to choose between Prince and Del, Dasha knew which one would have to go.

"Hi, Dasha," said Aubrey. "Prince missed you." She brought out her little wieners, and the dog's faith in mankind was confirmed.

"I don't mean to impose," said Dasha. "Just want to see how you're holding up after your losses."

"I've got bids in with Christie's on a new collection, better than the last," said Aubrey. "We'll beef up security and go on about our business." Dasha wanted to return to a more settled life on the avenue. Maybe that's why she felt she needed to intercede.

"Michael, I saw you at the station right before Barnaby's Rolls caught fire," she said, looking directly into Aubrey's flinty eyes. She could see why women couldn't resist his penetrating gaze, the square jaw, the high cheeks, the unshakable confidence. "You showed me the igniter you fastened to the chassis, and you sat in your Corvette and pushed the remote control. You caused the fire."

"Nobody got hurt," said Aubrey.

"Is that a confession?" asked Dasha.

"To you and you alone," said Aubrey. "I know you'll keep my secrets."

"Only on the condition that it ends now," said Dasha. "I like you both. I admire you both. But I simply can't go on playing Kissinger between you two. Stop it, Michael. Before something happens you'll both regret."

"I guess you're right," said Aubrey. "We've had enough amusement."

"And I'll work on Barnaby," said Dasha. "Galina wanted me to walk away from both of you. But I have to try one more time."

"We'll look back on it and laugh," said Aubrey, patting Prince on the head.

Later, Dasha would look back on that brief exchange and long for those curious spring days, when Barnaby Jayne and Michael Aubrey were alive and thriving and having their innocent bit of fun.

8

Hawkes Talks

Adrian Hawkes had a somewhat ambivalent attitude toward travel. He loved the Concorde on his frequent trips back to London, especially the first-class lounges at JFK and Heathrow, where the drinks flowed freely. When the Yanks lured him across the pond with promises of money and freedom, he'd put company-paid first-class travel in his contract. But Hawkes positively loathed the local public transportation in and around his adopted New York City. The taxis were hard to get in and out of, the subways were packed and dirty, and there was nothing even remotely enjoyable about Metro-North, the commuter line serving nearby Westchester County and Connecticut. The seat backs weren't adjustable, the overhead pantograph failed regularly, and the conductors were dour and surly, lacking in that clever London bonhomie.

And now, as his Metro-North train clacked and heaved through the Bronx toward Westport's Green's Farms station, he somehow felt every crack in the rails transmitted upward through the squealing wheels into his thinly upholstered seat and thence to his spine, his bowels, his cranium . . . only to be finally dissipated through his bloodshot eyes.

Once again, Hawkes was riding the blurry edge between last night's drunkenness and this morning's hangover. He'd gotten back to his Murray Hill studio apartment at two a.m., staggering through the door after fumbling with his keys and landing facedown, fully dressed, on his Murphy bed. At six a.m. the sun was beginning to make an appearance through the dusty slats of his venetian blinds, and Hawkes pried open his spongy eyelids. He'd sensed the rancid, gravelly taste in his mouth after too many cigarettes—and, damn it, that seventh martini offered by the PR flak that he didn't want to drink but drank anyway because, well . . . he liked to drink.

As his Metro-North car lumbered north of the Harlem River bridge, past the graffiti and the smoldering trash, he couldn't decide if he wanted to throw up or release his bowels. Either way, he'd have to make it to the train's rolling travesty of a loo, and if it was anything like the last time, there'd be no toilet paper. He took his copy of the *New York Post*, which he'd grabbed out of the spoilage bin the night before as he was leaving the *Post*'s newsroom, and swayed down the aisle toward the toilet. It was occupied, naturally. He spent the intervening minutes in abject discomfort, rereading his deft, daring, and at times breathtaking copy from his column, Hawkes Talks. It was gossip, pure and simple, and to Hawkes it was the coin of the realm.

BLOCKBUSTER NOVELISTS WAGE WAR ON THE GOLD COAST

We have it on good authority that literary titans Barnaby Jayne and Michael Aubrey are at it again. The two masters of mystery are known for their mutual loathing. Having competed for years at the peak of the publishing food chain, these two tale spinners have sniped in the past over agents, awards, Hollywood contracts, and even women. Who can forget that unfortunate fiasco five years ago when the Rockette dancer Shirley D'Angelo was seen on the arm of both novelists twenty-four hours apart? Shirley was promptly cashiered, only to wind up dating the chairman of Sony Pictures and living happily ever after.

Now it seems our naughty novelists have been trading not just barbs but damaging hijinks in an ever-escalating feud that has left some of their Beachside Avenue neighbors aghast. The latest spat saw Aubrey having to call a Westport fire department hazmat team to deal with deadly frog venom delivered to his front door by Jayne's blowgun. The rivalry has not, as yet, resorted to actual fisticuffs, but charges are flying of wanton destruction to each other's property. Details are coming in. There's a lot of finger-pointing, but no criminal charges . . . yet.

Sources say they are fighting over the affections of a secret Beachside Avenue grand dame who has become a private muse to both of them. Her name is Dasha Petrov, widow of the late oil magnate Constantine Petrov. Mrs. Petrov has made headlines herself in recent years following her retirement from the CIA. Two years ago, she stopped a Beachside Avenue serial killer with the timely application of a knife that, for Mrs. Petrov, always seems readily at hand. Sources report Mrs. Petrov is capable of even more derring-do, but details await confirmation.

The Aubrey-Jayne entanglement now finds Mrs. Petrov squarely in the middle. As of this writing, passions continue to flare on the storied Gold Coast. Stay tuned.

~

The toilet became available, and, as predicted, Hawkes couldn't find any toilet paper. That day's edition would have to suffice. Restored to some semblance of order after this alimentary interlude, Hawkes worked his way back to his seat, folded up his sport coat to form a pillow, and leaned his head against the window. His head felt like a hatchet was repeatedly crashing down between the hemispheres of his brain, still intact after years of accumulated misbehavior. He'd told himself inhabiting bars and imbibing at all hours was real work. That's where he nourished the plantings that bore the fruit. He was also a gifted craftsman, able to weave precious threads into tapestries of gold that sold newspapers. And that, he liked to say, was the name of the game. To achieve this critical economic underpinning, there was, at every hour of every day, at least an ounce or two of alcohol coursing through his veins. Through this self-inflicted delirium, he managed to pour out brilliant, scintillating, even titillating copy. His masters upstairs in the *Post* building were happy. And his readers couldn't get enough of his stories about the seamy underbelly of wealth and fame, where Hawkes shined. It's not that he preyed on the upper crust—he was known to inhabit crack dens, morgues, and precinct houses in the city's lesser districts—but reporting on the crimes and peccadilloes of the rich and famous was always more lucrative, according to his champions in circulation.

He awoke when the conductor announced their arrival at Green's Farms station. It was a Saturday morning. There was a slight chill in the early April air, but the sun was shining. He donned his tortoiseshell Ray-Bans to shield his bloodshot eyes. He shambled forward to the door and braced for what he knew was coming . . . fresh air. He knew the inhalation of anything devoid of carbon monoxide, stale cigarette smoke, Korean kimchi, and other city smells would give his system a brutal shock. The sliding doors opened, and as expected the fresh air assaulted his lungs. He looked at his watch. He had twenty minutes to get to the meeting with his first informant, who had inside knowledge of the internecine squabbles between Aubrey and Jayne. He gave himself a frisk to make sure everything was in order, lingering over the number-ten envelope in his right front breast pocket, which contained ten crisp hundred-dollar bills.

Hawkes had made this trek before, but knowing the way to the meeting point didn't make it any less disagreeable. The birds were singing, the buds were popping on the trees, and he saw waterfowl paddling placidly in the wetlands to his left, Green's Farms Academy, the former Vanderbilt estate, just a golf shot away. To his eye it was too pretty, too serene, too comfortable. Hawkes was all city, through and through, and the countryside made him anxious. No cabs to hail, no streets in numbered grids, no Blarney Stones appearing down the block, neon signs beckoning. Having no place to pop in for a bracer caused Hawkes to tremble. He did have his flask, thank God, so he stopped by the side of the road and gulped down a healthy glug of Jim Beam, America's gift to the world.

He walked down the drive leading to Burying Hill Beach, past the shuttered, preseason guard shack and out to the little parking lot leading to the groin jutting into what the locals called the sound. He waved to his source—the one who'd written him that note and started the ball rolling—and was immediately set back on his heels.

She wasn't alone.

"Hi, Mr. Hawkes," said Lucy. "This is my brother, Jim."

The lad extended a hand, presumably the way his mother had taught him, and Hawkes reciprocated.

"You're not one to talk, now are you, Jim?" asked Hawkes of the little boy.

"I know how to keep quiet," said Jim. "Tell him, Lucy."

"You don't have to worry about Jim," said Lucy.

"So why is he here?" asked Hawkes.

"He wants in," said the girl.

"Only if he can get the goods," said Hawkes. "What have you got, Jim?"

"Barnaby knows Mr. Aubrey burned Gladys to the ground," said Jim. "I heard him muttering about it in the basement. He's mad. He thinks Aubrey planted a bomb under Gladys and made her catch fire."

"Pretty serious charge, Jim," said Hawkes, intrigued. "Do you have evidence? What's in the backpack?"

"First let's talk price," said the little boy.

Hawkes turned to Lucy. "The more I give him, the less I've got for you. You understand that, don't you?"

"I'm okay with that," said Lucy. "Jim and I work together."

"Show me what you've got, Jim. I'll give you ten dollars," said Hawkes.

"Not enough," said Jim. He started to walk away. He'd heard from his Grandpa Mario, Tammy's dad, that in a negotiation you should always be prepared to walk away.

"Wait," said Hawkes. "I can pay you more. I've come all the way out here. Just give me a peek so I can see what I'm buying."

Jim stopped, turned, and walked back toward Lucy and the newspaperman with the foul-smelling breath. Jim looked him up and down, the way Grandpa Mario had taught him. Hawkes's clothes were a mess, his tie askew, his hair on end. His face was thin to the point of being gaunt, with a long, dripping nose. Jim couldn't see the man's eyes behind those Ray-Bans, but he could smell the alcohol and could only imagine the jaundiced eyeballs and red-rimmed sockets. Jim knew he had the upper hand, and he would allow a cool reserve to do the talking. The boy opened up his backpack and pulled out the burned radio receiver, fuel canister, and wires Barnaby had extracted from Gladys's blackened cadaver.

"It's a bomb," said Jim. "Aubrey planted it. He could go to jail."

"Looks like a bunch of burned-out junk to me," said Hawkes, mindful of the price. He'd have to get it evaluated. "Fifty bucks." Jim knew Hawkes could go higher. Lucy had told him about the crisp hundreds he'd withdrawn from his pocket the first time she'd met him.

"A hundred," said Jim. Hawkes frowned.

"You're a little thief," he said, taking out his envelope and peeling off a banknote. "I can connect this to Gladys, but how do I connect it to Aubrey?"

"Ask Mrs. Petrov," said Lucy.

"Ah, Mrs. Petrov," said Hawkes. "And how do I locate the famous retired intelligence officer?"

"She's usually on the beach feeding her swans," said Lucy. "Mrs. Petrov is the only one on the street who has a relationship with both Barnaby and Mr. Aubrey."

"Why is that?" asked Hawkes.

"She has experience that Barnaby and Aubrey both want to understand, for their books. I listened to Dasha speak to Barnaby the other day about a scene in one of his spy novels. Barnaby later told me Dasha offers something he calls 'verisimilitude.' He says it's rare."

"So, both Barnaby and Aubrey look to Dasha for inspiration?" asked Hawkes. "Is she in line for royalties?"

"I wouldn't know about that," said Lucy.

"What else have you got for my C-note?" asked Hawkes.

"We need an advance," said Jim. "We're about to go deeper, and it's risky." He could hear Grandpa Mario whispering in his ear.

"Bollocks," said Hawkes. "I only pay for what you can deliver. Your risk is your risk."

"We're done, then," said Lucy. "Nice knowing you." She and Jim turned to walk back down the beach toward Frost Point.

"Wait," said Hawkes. "How deep did you say you can go?"

"Barnaby puts all his important papers in a file cabinet in a closet. He locks it, and I know where he keeps the key," said Lucy.

"Could be just a bunch of pro forma, like everyone's personal papers," said Hawkes.

"Could be tax returns, last wills, angry correspondence with his agents, editors . . . maybe even women. We know our mom is not the first," said Lucy.

"Are you hoping she's the last?" asked Hawkes, getting too personal for Jim, who covered his ears.

"Our mother is always changing," said Lucy. "Her clothes, her jewelry, her houses . . . "

"Her men," piped up Jim.

"It's who she is, and she's the only mother we've got," said Lucy, "so we love her."

"We *do* have a few dads," said Jim, offering his sister encouragement.

"Including Barnaby?" asked Hawkes.

"Of course," said Lucy. "If not Barnaby, then another one. Give us another hundred, and we'll look through his papers. He's got a copier. We'll get you duplicates of the good stuff." Hawkes took out his envelope. He was ready to go five hundred for the girl. The arrival of the boy complicated things but was not unwelcome. He'd get away with only two hundred for these two. There would be a surplus at the end of the day, and his favorite watering hole, Blarney Stone, was right across from Grand Central on Lexington Avenue. He peeled off another hundred.

"I want to see how and where he spends his money," said Hawkes. "Bastard children, opium dens, a string of harlots, fiddling with his will. I'll only pay for the dirt. You've got my private line at the newspaper. Off you go."

His other appointment had just pulled into the little parking lot. He called after his prepubescent informants, "Don't get caught." He watched Lucy and Jim begin their trek down the beach under the seawall belonging to a Beachside newcomer, a film producer named Harvey Weinstein.

Hawkes turned around and approached the driver's side of the idling Chevrolet pickup truck. The driver rolled down the window.

"Hi, Makita," said Hawkes.

"Get in," said Aubrey's Japanese gardener. "I don't want anyone to see us."

Hawkes walked around to the passenger side of the Silverado. Tidy was Hawkes's immediate impression. An American gardener would have had dirty tools behind the seat, soil drifting on the floor mats, a dash filled with receipts for mulch and whatnot. Not Makita. The bed of the pickup had a pristine plastic liner. Makita had built a tool rack behind the seats for saws and pruners and dibbles. Hawkes had first encountered the talented Makita only two weeks prior, after he'd followed the gardener from Aubrey's estate and pulled his rented Corolla next to the Silverado at Gault's nursery on the Post Road. Hawkes quickly learned that Makita admired the portrait of Benjamin Franklin on the hundred-dollar bill; he wished to be a collector, in fact. At their first meeting, Hawkes learned Makita had been trained at the Shinto shrine in Kyoto, where a certain reverence always accompanied one's horticultural exertions. That's where Aubrey had met him a decade prior and later imported him for his Beachside Avenue estate. But Makita had elderly parents, and he needed to send money home. He was too proud to ask Aubrey for more—but he was not above stealing Aubrey's secrets. Makita believed espionage to be an art form, every bit as cultured and well-mannered as a bonsai tree.

Makita had purchased some take-out sushi. The pair sat in Aubrey's truck in the parking lot of Green's Farms Congregational Church, juggling their chopsticks and soy sauce with wasabi and talking things over. Hawkes got straight to the heart of the matter.

"Can you confirm Aubrey firebombed Jayne's Rolls-Royce?" he asked. n

"I watched him put together his device," said Makita. "Handed him his tools."

So, Hawkes thought, *little Jim was right.*

"Did you see him attach the bomb?" asked Hawkes.

"It wasn't a bomb. It didn't explode. It just caused a fire. We snuck into Jayne's garage, which he leaves unlocked. His gardener, Miguel, told me," said Makita. "Aubrey did the work of attaching it underneath the car. I just assisted." Makita was covering his tracks.

"Did you try to talk him out of it?" asked Hawkes.

"Certainly," said Makita, "but Mr. Aubrey told me no one would get hurt, so I went along."

"Would you testify to this under oath?" asked Hawkes.

"I am not familiar with this term *under oath,*" said Makita.

"In a legal trial in front of a judge, would you repeat what you just told me?" asked Hawkes.

"No," said Makita. "I wouldn't want to get fired."

"So, you would lie to a judge and jury?" asked Hawkes.

"Oh yes," said Makita. "I am only telling you these things so you have confirmation. You will have to ask someone else to be quoted in your newspaper. And I would never talk to a judge."

Hawkes let the matter rest. "What else has happened between Aubrey and Jayne?" he asked.

Makita trotted out the full tit for tat. He had helped Aubrey dig the punji pits, whittling the sticks to deadly points. And he had helped Aubrey fill the pits after Dasha intervened. Jayne was suspected of having destroyed Aubrey's gun collection. How he gained entry was still being investigated.

"What's next in Aubrey's bag of tricks?" asked Hawkes.

"He wants to put deadly piranha in Jayne's swimming pool," said Makita. "He's talking to a company in Iquitos, Peru, about shipping them up."

"Is he giving any thought to calling it quits?" asked Hawkes.

"Mrs. Petrov is trying to get them both to stop," said Makita. "I overheard her and Aubrey talking."

"So how do I get to talk to Mrs. Petrov?" asked Hawkes.

"The best way is to run into her on the beach while she's feeding her swans," said Makita. "If you like birds, she'll like you."

"That's helpful," said Hawkes. "I have a job for you."

"Haven't I given you enough?" asked Makita.

"There's money in it. Here's a camera," said Hawkes, handing him a little Minox. "I want you to find his tax returns for the last three years. Front page of his 1040 showing adjusted gross income, but more importantly his Schedule C. I want to see what he's deducting. Has to be a lot of unrelated personal stuff in there."

Makita frowned. "I'm sure he's incorporated—C or S," he said. Makita was not unsophisticated in these legal and accounting matters, Hawkes mused.

"Still has to list his expenses," said Hawkes.

"He'll say it's all part of 'research and development,'" said Makita. "I've heard him use that language, from the alcohol he drinks to the food he eats to maintaining all his properties. He says it's all to keep Gunn 'in beer and kippers.'"

"I hear he keeps a jet," said Hawkes. "That takes a gusher of money. Does he write it all off?"

"I understand the question," said Makita. "Let me see what I can do."

"Drop me off back at Burying Hill," said Hawkes. "I want to see if the swans are hungry." Makita held out his hand, and Hawkes gave him five hundred-dollar bills. "There's some extra in there. Consider it an advance on quality product."

The day was unseasonably chilly, and Hawkes's attire was at best unseasonal. As soon as he stepped onto the beach on his way to Frost Point, he got sand in his wingtips, but he pressed on. He could keep the battle of Beachside Avenue going for a full week at this rate, so the investment was worth it. Circulation, and the mandarins upstairs, would approve. The tide was mercifully low, and he could make his way around without getting his feet wet. He was standing on Frost Point, looking east, when he saw a pair of swans paddling toward shore a hundred yards down the beach. There was a green-clad figure in a beret carrying a stick approaching them, and the swans were undeterred. He started walking in their direction, and as he got closer, he could take in a more detailed picture. She wore a Barbour coat, a black wool beret, a colorful scarf, and Wellies on her feet, and she carried a rugged walking stick. She was pulling foodstuffs from a pocket, which the swans accepted with pleasure. She was smiling, but her look turned to annoyance when Hawkes approached, scaring away her feathered friends.

"So sorry," Hawkes said, recognizing he'd given offense. "I was just out for a walk admiring the ducks. I didn't mean to frighten your swans."

"Mates," said Dasha. "There will be cygnets soon. I don't want anything to upset them as they begin this journey together."

She appraised him up and down, and Hawkes could feel the weight of her disapproval. "You couldn't tell a mallard from a merganser. Where on earth did you come from?"

"The city," said Hawkes. "I like to come out here on the weekends . . . to get some air."

"Well, you're not dressed for it," said Dasha. "I suggest you turn right around and get back on your train and go back to the city. Don't come back until you can handle this wind chill."

"Seems like a nice day to me," said Hawkes, shivering a bit but undecided if it was because of the weather or the need for another pull on his flask. "Is this beach private? Sorry if I've trespassed."

"All citizens enjoy riparian rights from the water up to the mid-tide line. Above that, the beach belongs to the property holders. You can certainly walk here if the tide cooperates, but I would ask you not to disturb my swans," said Dasha.

"I understand better than most," said Hawkes. "Where I come from the Queen owns all the swans. God help you if you disturb one."

"England, then," said Dasha. "What brings you to this side?"

Hawkes wanted to lie, but he knew it would be unproductive. She would read his byline soon enough.

"My name is Adrian Hawkes. I'm a reporter for the *New York Post*," he said. "And you must be Mrs. Constantine Petrov." He wanted to get on her good side by using a formal name.

"I have an intense dislike for the *New York Post*," said Dasha. "It's a tawdry scandal sheet. I know the name Hawkes. You're on Page Six."

"Looks like you read the *Post* well enough to know my byline," said Hawkes, congratulating himself on the swift rejoinder.

"I skim . . . in the supermarket checkout," said Dasha, who seemed unused to being bested. "What do you want?"

"Aubrey and Jayne are fighting over you," said Hawkes. "It's a wonderful story. Two grown men. Successful beyond measure. Dueling for the affections of a retired spy."

"Retired intelligence officer," said Dasha. "I recruited the spies that have helped protect this nation." Her story was out in the open. Nothing could be done about it. Hawkes looked at her closely, wishing to confirm key details of her *curriculum vitae*.

"My LexisNexis search tells me you were born in the time of the czar. You and your family escaped the Bolsheviks, only to wash up in all the trouble spots in Eastern Europe. You fought the Nazis, had a part in the death of Heydrich, architect of the Holocaust, tried to blow up the V-2s before they could do any more damage to London," said Hawkes. "Might have saved my life when I was a boy growing up in the East End."

"A cursory overview," said Dasha.

"But you've raised your head above the lip of the foxhole in your retirement," said Hawkes. "You helped local law enforcement stop a killer right on this street. You've been busy, Mrs. Petrov."

"And now that my activities have raised my profile, unfortunately I have to contend with the likes of you," said Dasha, who seemed to sense that Hawkes was the kind of person who reveled in verbal jousting.

"Aubrey and Jayne have been infatuated with you, Mrs. Petrov," said Hawkes. "They both want to absorb your fascinating life story into their novels. They're fighting over you."

"Nonsense," said Dasha. "All of us on this street enjoy our privacy, especially when it comes to fending off reptiles like you. Be gone."

"Jayne started it with that blow dart, didn't he?" asked Hawkes, looking Dasha in the eyes. She blinked and looked out to sea.

"Thought so," said Hawkes. "And Aubrey retaliated by blowing up Jayne's car."

Hawkes observed the retired intelligence officer and knew she was trying to steel herself. He knew she was concealing what she knew about the punji pits, the snare, the destruction of the gun collection. He didn't have all the details, but he had enough to cause Dasha some discomfort. Her home and neighborhood were about to come under the klieg lights.

"Oh," Hawkes continued. "I have it on good authority this open warfare has involved the loss of Aubrey's gun collection and a bit of reckless endangerment across the street in the Audubon Society arboretum."

"What do you want?" asked Dasha, perturbed.

"Just an interview," said Hawkes. "I want to sit down with this aging lady spy and go through her life story. My readers will be enchanted. Your star will be elevated. I'll reign triumphant. It's not asking much."

"It's low and unseemly," said Dasha. "Aubrey and Jayne are my friends."

"I didn't make myself clear, Mrs. Petrov," said Hawkes. "I'm going to write the story. I have more than enough to go on. I would prefer to get your views. I am sure you can add the necessary brushstrokes."

"I find this conversation tiresome," said Dasha.

"My readers will be particularly interested in how you resolved the case of the sea glass murders, Mrs. Petrov. Your serial killer met his end right in your living room, according to the local press. Fell under the spell of your knife. Word has it you had a license to kill during your heyday," said Hawkes.

"Odious man," said Dasha.

"I've been called worse," said Hawkes. "It will be easier on you if we can figure out how to cooperate."

"Unlikely," said Dasha, turning to walk back up the beach to the little steps leading to the top of her seawall. She turned to Adrian Hawkes and said, "Come back, and I'll have you arrested for trespassing."

9

A Dose of Murder

Chief Anthony DeFranco took the call from Jameson, the responding uniformed officer, on the morning of April 26. Miguel, the gardener, told Jameson he had found Mr. Jayne sitting in a lounge chair by his pool, thoroughly dead and already an ashen shade of blue. He was dressed for the chill in his down vest and heavy khakis. He had his trademark Irish woolen cap pushed low on his brow, and he was wrapped in a quilt. For all the world it looked to Miguel like his employer had been enjoying a bit of nocturnal stargazing and had fallen asleep in his chair. Two days before, Mrs. Jayne and her children had taken advantage of the kids' school break and jetted off to Turks and Caicos, leaving Jayne alone in the big house and Miguel, as usual, occupying his apartment over the garage.

DeFranco jotted these particulars on a pad and told Jameson to secure the scene—no one was to leave or come onto the property—and to put some crime scene tape in a twenty-foot perimeter around the body. For DeFranco, there was no telling how the famous Mr. Jayne had met his end, but for now he would treat any death not under the supervision of a physician as unnatural and therefore suspect. He walked down to Stanley Ferguson's cubicle and tapped on the detective's shoulder. Ferguson looked up from his phone call, and DeFranco delivered a quick, knowing nod to the left.

"Honey, I have to go," said Ferguson, hanging up on the missus, who had called for some advice about what color to choose for their living room curtains.

"Body on Beachside Avenue," said DeFranco. "Get your coat. And bring your crime scene kit. We can roll the medical examiner with a call from the car."

"Natural causes?" asked Ferguson.

"Won't know until we get there," said DeFranco. "Decedent was found in a lounge chair next to his pool. Nobody around. Could be cardiac arrest."

DeFranco and Ferguson got into the chief's unmarked Ford Crown Victoria. Ferguson drove while DeFranco called the ME, ensuring a criminologist was on the way. There was no need to hurry. The chief put in a call to his partner, Tracy Taggart, who was on leave after a whirlwind trip to Israel and the West Bank for her employer, *NBC Nightly News*.

"I'll be a little busy," said the chief, "but I pulled two fillets out of the freezer, and we've got that leftover root vegetable mélange you like. If I'm not back by six, start the grill, and I'll check back in."

Their domestic duties attended to, the chief and Detective Ferguson rode in silence up Green's Farms Road past Nyala Farms and took a right across the I-95 overpass to access Beachside Avenue. The Crown Vic swooped smoothly around the curves by Burying Hill Beach and moved sedately up the avenue to the Jayne residence, third house on the right after the J. C. Penny mansion. DeFranco knew the street well.

They pulled into the drive and found Miguel pacing by the massive double front doors. The medical examiner had not yet arrived. Miguel was twisting his ball cap in his hands, a knot of worry, and he led them around the side of the house to the pool area. As instructed, Officer Jameson had strung the crime scene tape in the prescribed twenty-foot circle—lashed around a picnic table and some beach chairs—and was standing at a distance.

"Good work, officer," said the chief. "Can I assume no one has approached the body while you've been on site?"

"You assume correctly, chief," said Jameson. DeFranco needed to establish the hygiene of the crime scene and note any discrepancies in evidentiary custody.

"Call for backup, and search the house," said DeFranco. "We have to make sure everyone's safe. Have someone sit with Miguel in the kitchen, and calm him down. Get Graciela to come over. She speaks Spanish."

"On it," said Jameson, turning on the heels of his patent leather shoes, apparently delighted to have something to do other than watch the slowly decomposing Mr. Jayne.

A criminologist named Oliver Snell arrived, followed by two techs with a gurney. Oliver, DeFranco, and Ferguson stood together just outside Jameson's yellow tape and discussed next steps.

"Just a suggestion, chief," said Oliver, "but let me start the investigation in a forty-foot circle around the body. I'll be looking for blood, shell casings, footprints, stains, and identification. Then I'll move closer, and we can see what befell this gentleman. Can you and Detective Ferguson check the beach? We'll be interested in footprints, articles of clothing, anything weird. When we get settled, I'll have one of my techs go over it with a metal detector."

"Sounds reasonable," said DeFranco. "Make it so."

Oliver took out a Nikon and started his inspection, and DeFranco and Ferguson moved in a wide arc around the body to the steps leading to the beach. They both scanned the grass on either side of a stone walkway, looking for signs of trauma, like blood spatter or weapons. They stood on top of the seawall and looked down to the area of beach directly in front of the steps. There were numerous footprints in the sand. DeFranco produced a handheld radio while Ferguson rummaged in his toolbox for some small flags on wire standards. The two seasoned police officers were reading each other's minds.

"Oliver, we'll need a tech down here with the dental stone to take some castings," said DeFranco into the handheld radio. He received an acknowledgment and went back to his scan.

"I see at least four good ones," said Ferguson. "But sand is a bitch for this kind of thing. Too loose. Give me some moist mud every time."

"We have to deal with what the good Lord giveth," said DeFranco.

"You're not getting all religious on me, are you, chief?" he asked. DeFranco thought for a minute. *You're not a praying man,* he mused, *but you're the luckiest bastard alive.*

"Figure of speech," said DeFranco, moving carefully down the steps and eyeing his footprint candidates. He put flags next to three. Ferguson voted for two. Oliver's tech arrived with the necessary tools, and the chief and his lieutenant went back up the steps.

"Jameson, say status," said the chief into the radio.

"Attic is clear. We're working our way down. Graciela, Peter, and Sam are here to help."

DeFranco would have to take his son aside at some point and invite him over for a steak dinner. So far the management of the scene was orderly and sterile. Isolation of the witness had commenced, and Graciela was no doubt getting an earful the chief could tap later. No persons had been found, as yet, hiding in the house, so safety was uppermost. And Oliver was turning his attention to the fatality resting in the lounge chair, wrapped comfortably in a quilt. He was ready to approach the decedent.

"Chief, I've covered this area pretty carefully. No blood, weapons, shell casings, or foreign objects. And unfortunately, nothing we might be able to lift a print from, like a cocktail glass. Looks like time and manner of death will have to wait till we get back to the office. Gentleman looks like he just decided to expire."

DeFranco, Ferguson, and Snell put on their rubber gloves and approached the corpse. There were flies beginning to swarm, and DeFranco had to wave a few away. What might the insect population and behavior say about the state of decomposition and therefore the time of death? He'd discuss it with the medical examiner, his eminence Dr. Samuel Goldberg. Oliver slowly pulled back the quilt from around Barnaby Jayne's Irish wool hat, and the first indication DeFranco thought they might have a situation on their hands was a slight "hmm" from Oliver's highly professional lips.

The criminologist went to his own tool kit and pulled out a headlamp and a pair of tongue depressors. He got down on one knee and swatted at a pair of persistent flies while he looked right into Jayne's dead face. The novelist's eyelids were slightly parted. The chief got down behind Oliver to have a look, and he could see Jayne's pupils fixed and dilated. Oliver pried open the dead man's mouth with one of the tongue depressors, and a welter of black blood spilled out and ran down Jayne's puffed vest. Oliver made it seem like he'd seen worse and kept prying open Jayne's jaw.

"Some teeth are missing, and there are black powder burns," said Oliver. "We've got a GSW fired from low and upward into the man's soft palate."

Ferguson let out a long, low whistle at the mention of a GSW, a gunshot wound, while the chief maintained strict discipline in the presence of a dead man who had just now been identified as a possible crime victim. He was always struck by the enormity of that transition.

"You can see the powder burns inside his mouth," said Oliver. "Muzzle went right in, and the trigger was pulled."

"Okay, let's rule out suicide," said the chief. "Take a look at his hands."

"We'll get a paraffin lift back at the morgue to see if this guy has fired a weapon lately," said Oliver. The wax would pick up any trace of powder residue. "But it's been my experience that if the guy had done this to himself, he'd still have the gun in his hand. Sometimes they can't let go. Rigor mortis."

"Any idea how long he's been sitting out here?" asked the chief.

"Quick guess? Eight hours maybe. Just looking at the early decomposition and the lividity in the lower extremities," said Oliver, lifting the decedent's pants leg and pulling down his socks.

"Puts the time of death around one in the morning," said Ferguson. "I'll walk up to the house and let Graciela know. Maybe the gardener saw something around then."

"When Jameson and his team have cleared the house, have them look in any outbuildings and get them started on canvasing the neighborhood," said the chief. "Sights, sounds, unusual activity."

"Right," said Ferguson. The detective turned, and DeFranco reflected on how fortunate he was to have good people on his team. Back when he was in Ferguson's position, he wasn't the pro he needed to be. Changing that had taken some strong women suddenly coming into his life.

Oliver continued to pull away Jayne's quilt and had unbuttoned his shirt down to the diaphragm. "No additional wounds that I can see," he said. "I think we're going to find the preponderance of blood loss from the head wound in the man's lungs and stomach when we get him on the table."

"It'll play hell with the content analysis, but we'll just have to see," said the chief. "Take his hat off."

Oliver complied and stood back.

"Jesus," he exclaimed, and even DeFranco was inclined to invoke the deity. The top of Jayne's head was a sodden mass of blood, bone, and brain matter. The back of his vest was black with blood, and it had started dripping off the body onto the pool deck. Oliver and DeFranco were crouching now, trying to get a better look at the avulsed and eviscerated tissue.

"Chief, right here," said Oliver. "Base of the skull. Top of the neck. Two entry wounds."

"A double tap," said DeFranco, suddenly seizing on the implications. "Is the mouth wound a separate entry point?"

"I think so," said Oliver. "And look at those holes." He held up a small ruler for scale. "Three-sixteenths in diameter, exactly one inch apart in a neat line."

"This was a goddamn hit," said the chief, fighting to maintain his professionalism and keep his utter amazement in check. It was a wonderful April morning. The sun was making its daily, sanguine climb to the heavens. The birds were singing, and the chief looked up and around the scene, feeling as if the world was crashing in.

"Stanley," said the chief into the radio. "We need to bring in at least two more uniformed officers to tour the neighborhood. Release Jameson and DeFranco. Tell them to come over to the pool, please."

His officers gathered around him; the chief conveyed the unsettling news that murder was most assuredly the cause of death.

"Jameson, you take the beach on the west side of the property," he said. "Sam, you'll be on the east side. Get down from the neighbors' access, and stay well away from the front of the property. We're trying to harvest some shoe imprints. We need to keep the neighbors away from the scene until we've cleaned things up. It's going to be a long day. I'll get you relief when I'm able." The young officers nodded their salute and went about their duties.

"We've got us a first-class shit show," said the chief. "What did Graciela get out of the gardener?"

"Last time he saw his employer was about nine p.m. in Jayne's study. He said the man of the house was working on his computer. Really leaning into it. They talked about reshaping a rose bed on the west side of the house today, and Miguel went back to his apartment."

"Do we believe him?" asked the chief.

"He said he made a call around one a.m. to his mother in Guadalajara. About the same time Oliver said Jayne got whacked. Easy enough to check," said Ferguson. "He's in there shitting his pants. I don't think he's our hit man."

"Agreed," said the chief. "What's his status?"

"He's a naturalized American," said Ferguson. "Mr. Jayne sponsored him. Miguel showed us the plaque. He can't stop crying."

"He'll have to remain close and available," said the chief.

"I'll have Graciela communicate that to him," said Ferguson. "Want me to call the state's attorney?"

"Yep. And also state CID," said the chief. "Let's let Miguel go back to his quarters and task Graciela with crowd control. We need tape all across the front of the property. Media will be here soon." The chief knew the newsrooms kept radio scanners going throughout the day. There was no way they could avoid hearing about unusual police activity on Beachside Avenue. He could feel the gravity shifting under his feet. DeFranco could see the neighbors peering over the hedges into the Jaynes' yard. One guy had a television camera with a long lens. DeFranco recognized him—Tracy Taggart's old sidekick from her News 12 Connecticut days. DeFranco strolled over to him, moving with a slow, confident walk that belied the swarm of butterflies in his gut.

"Danny," said the chief. "Long time. How have you been?"

"Great, chief," he responded. "What gives?"

"Gentleman next door expired," said the chief. "We're trying to get to the bottom of it. As long as these neighbors don't object, I don't mind you shooting B-roll across the hedge. But I can't let you on the property, and I won't have a statement until I get back to the station. It's going to be a while. I'll have Madge in media relations call you." He wanted to keep it nice and friendly until he could figure out what was happening.

And he needed to talk to Tracy. One of America's preeminent literary masters had been murdered. She would need to cover this story, and he would need to help her. He well remembered her patience and decency when they had both been tasked with smoking out the killer behind the sea glass murders. They had pushed the boundaries of their professional obligations, and they had survived some pretty significant conflicts of interest. But he didn't want to put either of them in that situation again. She was his partner.

His team was assigned and busy. Oliver and his techs were preparing Mr. Jayne for transport. There were obviously some people he'd need to notify. Turks and Caicos? It was time to stroll through Jayne's inner sanctum. He took his gloves off, put them in his pocket, and donned another pair. No use mixing his prints with the victim's. Just a waste of time for the criminologists. He would concentrate on the more intimate features of the house—a desk in the kitchen where household business was attended to, reading material in the downstairs powder room, a bar area with half-consumed bottles of very fine scotch. There were glasses in the bar sink he'd want Ferguson to examine for prints. He walked by Jayne's study. He'd leave that for last.

The chief walked up the floating double-helix staircase and cataloged the bedrooms in his mind. There was a hers for one stepchild, festooned in pink, and a his for another kid, decorated in a Power Rangers motif. There was a guest bedroom overlooking the lawn, and DeFranco looked out the window. He saw the remains of Barnaby Jayne fill out a body bag strapped to a gurney as Oliver and company made their way toward their van. He tried to be the hard-bitten cop, but it saddened him to see a man depart his pride and joy for the last time in such a manner.

He found the master. The California king was made, and he remembered that Jayne had never gone to bed, according to Miguel's recollection. Did the Jaynes have a housekeeper? A maid who cooked, cleaned, and made up the beds? He'd have to look into that. Another question for Miguel.

He went downstairs and into Jayne's study, where he knew he'd have to spend some quality time. There was a tiny green "on" light on the keyboard of Jayne's IBM computer. Jayne had never switched it off. The chief hit the space bar, and the screen came to life.

Too easy, he thought. Was that intentional? Did Jayne intend to come back to the keyboard? Was the man interrupted, lured outside to investigate?

The chief sat in Jayne's creaky leather chair and rolled himself closer to the desk. Now the computer was asking for a password, another rock in the road. He'd have to get one of his IT guys on it. He started opening up drawers and saw the typical profusion of notes, paper clips, postage stamps, cheap ballpoint pens, and a flurry of dust balls. There was a checkbook with a register where DeFranco noted the man had eighty-seven thousand dollars in available cash. There was a file drawer for bank statements, household utilities, payroll for staff, trusts he'd established for various offspring, and a folder marked *Crawford*, from which DeFranco gleaned statements for a brokerage account with a current balance of $57 million.

DeFranco couldn't begrudge the man. "You earned it, Barnaby," he said out loud. He would have to call Mr. Crawford and let him know the bad news.

The chief glanced around the desk, looking for anything pertaining to Mrs. Jayne's trip to Turks and Caicos, and finally found a slip of paper with the words *Paradise Lodge, T&C*, and a phone number written in a fine, female hand. He steeled himself for a minute before picking up the phone to dial. He waited a few minutes while the hotel operator put him through to Mrs. Jayne's cabana. She failed to pick up. She was likely cavorting on the beach with the kids. The operator came back on, and he asked for the number of the local police department. He dialed the number and spoke to a duty officer who responded compassionately, in a lovely West Indian accent. These sorts of notifications were not uncommon in tourist destinations, he said. They would find the guest Mrs. Jayne, deliver the bad news about her husband's death, leave out the grisly details, and figure out how to get the lady and her children packed off to the airport. DeFranco would need to remember this act of grace and civility on the part of his fellow officer of the law.

He looked into Jayne's *Trusts* file and found names, birth dates, addresses, and phone numbers for his various offspring—four, in total, that he could see. The chief started calling them, and the conversations went just as a wretchedly as expected. Shock, anger, grief, tears—the full gamut of human emotion. He registered his sorrow at having to convey such awful news, listened to them express their pain—and cocked an ear for any indications that one of the Jayne children might have had anything to do with their father's murder. A pregnant silence, an absence of surprise, the critical white space around the picture that gave the work true meaning. He didn't catch any of the children in any verbal missteps and knew he'd have to interview each one of them as the investigation continued. With Turks and Caicos law enforcement assisting with Jayne's wife, he considered the man's next-of-kin notified.

Tracy.

He used his personal flip phone and got her on the second ring.

10

Partners

Tracy Taggart was lounging in the bath at their little house on High Gate Road, last house on the left. She had gotten back on an El Al flight from Tel Aviv the previous afternoon, and she was exhausted. It had been a whirlwind trip to interview the prime minister of Israel and to meet the Palestinian leadership on the West Bank. She wasn't sure what she'd accomplished—both sides were dug in hard—but she'd made some vital contacts, got a sense for the changing geography, and sampled the region's fascinating history as a cultural crossroads. She was appalled at the massive concrete barriers the Israelis had erected to hem in the Palestinians and just as angry at the suicide bombers who had compelled the Israelis to take this drastic, dreary step. Over three days, she and her crew fed four eleven-minute news pieces to the home office, the full hour-long interview with the prime minister, and a wrap-up analysis from the fabled stone walkways of Old Jerusalem.

For fun, some officers in the IDF had taken her to a shooting range and shown her how to field strip and fire an Uzi. Her crew shot some interviews and B-roll of armed Israeli civilians for a piece on the realities of home defense in the Jewish state that she would pitch when she got back to the office. Her Marine Corps dad in far-off Indiana would approve. Right now, she was glad to be back under the roof of the house she shared with the chief of police, where she could keep her Kimber .45 in the secret compartment in her purse. Her dad had given her the handgun as a parting gift when she'd left the land of the Hoosiers for far-off godless Connecticut, which was to Mr. Taggart the dark side of the moon. She was a Marine Corps veteran herself—trained as a medical corpsman with a duty assignment on an amphibious assault ship. She'd had some exposure to all kinds of firearms, but she'd wondered if her management at NBC would allow one of their journalists to carry legal firearms—maybe not on assignment or during office hours, but on her own time. She didn't ask, and she didn't tell.

For now, she was in her delightful element—lavender suds up to her chin, the toes of her left foot turning the spigot to let in more hot water, a classical guitarist demonstrating stunning dexterity on a stereo downstairs. As instructed, the chief's fillets were out of the freezer, and a quiet dinner at home was eagerly contemplated. Thence to bed, to catch up on some things, as it were.

Her cell phone rang, and she saw the number for the chief's private line. She stood up to allow all those delicious suds to slide down her sinewy form and wrapped herself in a terry cloth robe.

"Hi, sweetie," she answered, just the way the chief liked it.

"I've run into a bit of a situation," he said, employing a reserve that suggested she pay close attention. "The author Barnaby Jayne is dead."

She took in a sharp, clean breath and let it out in a gasp.

She was going to work.

"How? And where?" she said, thoughts spinning: her film crew, her assignment editor, B-roll, stand ups, Jayne's obit, historical footage, on and on. The news was like a breaking wave that crashed onshore and then spread over everything it touched.

"He was murdered, Tracy," said DeFranco. Another sudden intake of breath and a quick exhalation that came out like a low growl. "The body has been moved to the medical examiner's office. But I can get you and your crew on the property. How fast can you get over here?"

"Twenty minutes," said Tracy. "Jesus, Tony, this is huge."

"Yes it is, dear," he said. "I saw Danny shooting the Jayne property over the hedge, so it won't be long before more media shows up. You've got an exclusive for about an hour. This is payback for all the crap I put you through during the sea glass murders."

"Okay, I'll be right over," said Tracy, rubbing a towel through her flame-red hair, cut in a bob.

"I'll tell my officers out front to let you through," said DeFranco. "Come to the front door. If your camera team gets slowed down, maybe you can cut a deal with Danny."

"Love you, Tony," said Tracy. "But while I'm talking to you, I'm not getting my tail over there."

"Don't break any laws," said the chief.

Tracy jumped into khaki slacks, a white blouse, and a light powder-blue cardigan sweater. She put a jacket on over that, checked her purse for her wallet, keys, sunglasses, phone . . . and handgun. She was technically on assignment. She took her Kimber out of her purse and locked it in the steel box in the closet where she and the chief kept their firearms. In the basement they had a larger strong room with steel doors for their shotguns, ammo, and other accessories. But in the first-floor coat closet, their handguns rested in quick-access steel cabinets—his and hers. She thought it was cute. She got herself into her VW Passat and aimed it toward Beachside Avenue. Driving with one hand, she defied the chief's orders and dialed her cell phone with the other. She got Grimes on the assignment desk. Grimes had covered wars, assassinations, deadly hurricanes, and political calamities, so he didn't ruffle easily. But the murder of Barnaby Jayne caused even old, grizzled Grimes to let out a low whistle before he got his ancient gears to turn.

"I'll get a producer going on the obit and the footage," said Grimes. "There's a camera crew in New Rochelle that can be at your location in about forty-five minutes. See what you can do about access. Which department took the call?"

"Westport PD," said Tracy, causing Grimes to emit a barking laugh.

"Know anyone over there, Tracy?" he asked, tongue firmly in cheek.

"I'll see what I can do," said Tracy. "Just so you know, the chief called me first."

"He by God better have called you first if he wants to enjoy all the comforts of home," said Grimes. Tracy laughed and rang off. Enough chitchat.

She pulled her Passat into the Jaynes' drive, waving to Graciela, who had recently given Tracy her mother's tamale recipe. Tracy drove up to the front doors and took in the tableau. There was a crowd gathered outside the iron fence; police were standing strategically to protect the scene. And it was a glorious day on the Gold Coast. One expected murder to arrive on a wet, gray dawn. But murder always seemed to follow another plan.

She used the big knocker on the front door, and after a few seconds it opened, and the love of her life was standing in the Jaynes' grand vestibule. She took in the whole of the man right there. He'd slimmed down from the time she'd first met him, when even he would have to admit he'd been smacked around by the ravages of life. Now he wore a trim Brooks Brothers' blue blazer, cut a trifle full to accommodate his Glock in a shoulder rig. He had gray flannel slacks, a white shirt with a businesslike collar, a striped tie, and kerchief points in his left front pocket. The diet she'd enforced had taken the slack out of his cheeks, and that gut, inevitable for a man approaching fifty, was beginning to recede. His short black hair had flecks of a distinguished gray, and when he smiled, his cheekbones and dimpled chin flashed their greeting right along with his straight teeth and upturned mouth.

She wanted him—right then and there—and remembered they were both on duty.

"Hell happened?" she asked, and the chief stated the gruesome pattern of facts, or as much as could be known at that point.

"I need to get over to the ME," said DeFranco, "but we have time. They won't start without me. Wanna go?"

"Depends on how much I can get done here when the team arrives," she said. "Can you take me out to the scene?"

After a simple tour of the surroundings, they stood next to Jayne's lounge chair by the pool. There was a bloodstain that was now a glistening black. There were flies swarming in a haphazard circle.

"The techs from the ME have what they need, so I have ServPro coming over to deal with that mess," he said. "Excuse the flies."

"Tell me again why you think this was a hit?" asked Tracy.

"Three shots to the head, caliber undetermined," said the chief. "Two at the base of skull, top of neck, an inch apart in a perfect horizontal line. One through the mouth into the soft palate."

"The tabloids call that a 'gangland-style' killing," said Tracy. "How much of that am I allowed to report?"

"Let's dicker a little," said the chief. "You can report that sources indicate it might have been a professional job. Put in plenty of fudge to give me maneuvering room. But leave out the detail on shot placement. I will probably be able to fill that in on the second day."

"So now you've become versed in the second-day lede," said Tracy.

"I know a famous journalist, and I'm a quick study," said DeFranco. His radio crackled, and his son, Sam, was apologizing.

"She wouldn't take no for an answer," said Sam. "She's coming up to the pool."

It could only be Dasha, thought the chief, watching his old friend approach just as the thought vanished . . . to be replaced by the living embodiment of Dasha Petrov before him. His dear old friend, to whom he owed so much, was moved to tears.

"Where is Barnaby, chief?" she asked, looking at the pool of blood, the milling police officers, the gathering of a catastrophic momentum.

"Dasha, Barnaby Jayne is dead," he said, holding her by the shoulders and looking into her sad old eyes. He knew he'd have to hold her up, and as predicted, she sagged and shuddered at the delivery of this diabolical news. Tracy took her to a chair by the pool and sat with her, holding her hand.

DeFranco, Tracy Taggart, and Dasha Petrov were now comrades-in-arms, having survived an armed intrusion by the serial killer Robert Altman. Tracy sensed that the loss of her friend Barnaby had dealt Dasha a devastating blow. She and the chief watched their friend stare into the cool blue sound. A terrible reality had suddenly intruded on Dasha's simple life of caring for Galina, and feeding the swans.

Detective Stanley Ferguson came up to the triumvirate. He knew Tracy, of course, and he had more than a passing acquaintance with the remarkable Mrs. Petrov. Tracy could tell he was a trifle disturbed to have civilians at his crime scene, but Dasha Petrov was a neighbor of the decedent, and her presence could be justified as part of the ritual neighborhood door-knocking. But Tracy was media, and to Ferguson media always spelled trouble. She sensed Ferguson was trying to navigate these troubled waters.

"How is Alice?" Tracy asked, referring to Mrs. Ferguson. "Didn't she sprain something recently?" Ferguson was obviously pleased to have NBC's high-flying reporter take a personal interest in his family.

"She's fine," said Ferguson. "Thanks for asking." Ferguson turned to the chief and permitted himself a first, tentative theory: "Bullet fragment analysis will be the whole ballgame."

Dasha was pacing. Tracy knew she was watching a deep well of frustration.

"Motive, gentlemen," Dasha finally said. "Who would want to kill Barnaby Jayne? And who would have the opportunity? Those questions are every bit as consequential as your bullet fragments, assuming you can find them."

Tracy looked at Ferguson, who was looking at Dasha, and she could feel the test of wills—like static electricity—ignite the air between them.

"We'll get to that, Mrs. Petrov," Ferguson said, "in time."

The chief allowed this interplay to run its course. He'd survived the receiving end of Dasha Petrov's penetrating insight and analysis. The woman was impulsive if not impetuous. But she leaned directly into the fight, and that had its advantages.

"While you're looking for bullet fragments, evidence of the killer or killers might be in plain sight right on this property," she said.

"Okay, Mrs. Petrov," said Ferguson. "Where would you start solving this murder?"

"Let's get out of the sun," said Dasha. "Tammy and the children are in Turks and Caicos if memory serves. Let's use Barnaby's study."

Dasha led them inside, and Tracy wasn't surprised she knew where she was going. Dasha turned to Ferguson.

"I presume you've interviewed Miguel," she said.

"We have," said the chief, "but Dasha. Do the Jaynes have any other domestics?"

"Yes, but this is Felicity's day off. She's the maid. Comes from the Philippines, if I'm not mistaken. Island of Cebu."

"Do you know how we can reach her?" asked the chief.

"Her home number will be in Barnaby's address book," said Dasha. "You *have* found that, haven't you?"

Dasha swept into the study and sat down at the great author's desk. She rummaged around the loose papers, clearly frustrated. "Did you check his pockets? Slender blue book with all his contacts. He was in the process of moving everything over to his computer, but he always needed to have his contacts in his little book."

Ferguson left the room, muttering "I'll call the ME. Maybe it's still on him."

"Have them check the floor of the van," said the chief to Ferguson's retreating figure.

Tracy looked up at the walls of the author's study. Jayne's collection of bludgeons, axes, and daggers was a testament to man's inhumanity to man. In a bookcase were thumb screws and shackles and peculiar devices of curious origin and dubious utility. His crossbow collection spanned the arc of history, from an ancient Greek device called a *gastraphetes*, according to an engraved identification card, to a fifteenth-century German *wallarmbrust* used for "siege defenses." Jayne's fascination with this ancient device included a DaVinci sketch of a crossbow from the fifteen-hundreds and concluded with a modern composite hunting crossbow with articulating cams, a carbon fiber stock, and sophisticated optics. Jayne clearly was a man of deep enthusiasms. Dasha noticed Tracy's wandering attention.

"Only part of Barnaby's collection," said Dasha. "He was a student of the macabre. I helped with his research. I don't see his address book here."

"What about a calendar?" asked the chief. "We need to know who he was meeting, or planned to meet."

"Turn on the computer," said Tracy. "Maybe he'd made some progress porting things over." The chief found the "on" switch, and they all gathered around Dasha, who remained seated. A window came up, asking for a password.

"Name of his first dog, best friend in kindergarten, favorite English teacher?" said the chief. "Where do you even begin?"

Dasha pondered the dilemma.

"Barnaby had a thing for his mother," Dasha said. She hunted and pecked until the word *Gladys* was typed out, represented by anonymous little dots. She hit the return key, and the air seemed to leave the room when the password was denied.

"Passwords usually need a number and a special character. An uppercase letter and a lowercase letter," said Tracy.

"Helpful, dear," said Dasha. "How about Glady's birth year?"

"Worth a try if you can figure it out," said the chief.

"Barnaby told me earlier this year she'd be 98," said Dasha. "That means she was born in 1893. And I'll toss in an exclamation point." Dasha typed in *Gladys1893!* and the computer came to life. There were folders for novels written, novels in progress, and novels scarcely contemplated. There was a folder for finances, and it appeared as though Jayne had been making the transition between paper statements and online statements. Tracy swooned when she saw the balance of his brokerage account, but Dasha didn't seem fazed. "I'm sure he had more than one."

"How about a date book?" asked the chief. One folder looked promising. It was a calendar template, but all the cells were blank.

"He didn't trust this thing," said Tracy. "He preferred ink and paper."

"Like a lot of us, darling," said Dasha.

One folder was marked "Family," and when they peered inside, they encountered a cascade of subfolders and files. "Can I get a copy of that?" the chief asked.

"Tracy, you better take over," said Dasha, and Tracy assumed the chair. She ransacked a few desk drawers and found a floppy disk still in its wrapper. She put it in the drive, initialized it, dazzling Dasha with her technical skills, and performed a copy function with a few keystrokes.

"I think my guys are probably here," said Tracy. "Sweetie, can you have Graciela let them in? I'll eject this disk in just a second."

The chief raised Graciela on his handheld radio, and she acknowledged the NBC camera team was on its way.

"Any other media out there will be ticked off," said the chief, "but it can't be helped. I'm biased." Tracy handed the disk to the chief, who put it in his pocket. He jotted down the password, and Tracy hit the shutdown key.

Ferguson came back into the room, only to hear Dasha request attendance at the autopsy. The chief caught Ferguson rolling his eyes. "She needs to give us positive identification," he winked, and Ferguson relaxed the furrow in his brow.

"Does Mr. Jayne have a fax machine?" asked Tracy. "I need to get a backgrounder sent out from my producer in New York." The chief pointed to a closet, where Tracy found a printer and a fax machine. The look on Ferguson's face suggested the detective was none too happy with the drop-by-drop contamination of his crime scene. Tracy was on the phone with her assistant, and soon, five double-spaced pages were rolling off the fax.

Barnaby Jayne's office machinery rested on a two-drawer wooden filing cabinet. While Tracy waited for her backgrounder, she tried the drawers. They were locked. She made a mental note, picked up her papers, and went back out to the front of the house to issue instructions.

11

Lingering Aura

After Tracy had left the room, Dasha Petrov scanned the space and the possessions that had belonged to her fascinating friend. She thought of Barnaby's archrival Michael Aubrey. Could he have perpetrated this wretched crime? She pushed the thought out of her mind. Preposterous. But the thought took on a measure and a meaning she found difficult to quell.

The chief left to get ready for his interview. Ferguson was trying to roust Miguel so he could contact Felicity. Dasha was left alone with Barnaby's lingering aura. He was a streaking meteor that had arced across her sky, and now he had suddenly become enveloped by the night. Her sadness was palpable—the same grief she'd experienced when Constantine died, or when she'd lost dear Marcus Willoughby, her mentor in the field of intelligence, who had changed the course of her life. And yes, she'd lost friends on the field of battle—she was a witness to the destruction of her secret cell, Marigold, during the Pilsen bombardment—but somehow the depth of caring one experienced as one grew older compounded the magnitude of her mourning. In the back of her mind, she heard Barnaby ask, "Dasha, how shall we set the stage?"

The secret to finding Barnaby's killer was in that room. She was sure of it. A note, a scribble, a document . . . something. And she was drawn to the locked drawers in that wooden filing cabinet in the closet. Where was the key? Tammy might be able to help when she and the kids got home. She went outside and listened while Tracy and DeFranco went about their professional duties. She thought Tracy's talents were worth a brigade in the field when one considered the way she could marshal public opinion.

And she would have DeFranco on her team any time. He had strengths and instincts driven by that elusive quality called heart. She listened as Tracy eulogized Barnaby Jayne while the camera rolled.

"Barnaby Jayne, one of this century's leading mystery writers, is dead, the apparent victim of gunshot wounds suffered in the early morning hours today at his Gold Coast mansion in Westport, Connecticut. He was found by his gardener seated in a chair by the side of his swimming pool. His body has been removed to the Fairfield County medical examiner's office, where an investigation is underway. His wife, Tammy, and his stepchildren were out of the country at the time of the shooting.

"Beginning with his highly acclaimed debut novel, *Huntress*, in 1946, before he turned thirty, Barnaby Jayne dominated the competitive field of mystery writing. Each book took on a character of its own but always returned to the dark themes of torture, dungeons, medieval weaponry, and long-lost love. His heroes—both men and women—always triumphed as they stood against Jayne's never-ending parade of villainy.

"*Huntress* was the beginning of a remarkable career spanning nearly fifty years. He wrote twenty-seven best-selling novels, numerous film adaptations, seven original screenplays. It's been estimated that Jayne's literary output now exceeds three hundred million copies when you include foreign rights and translations."

Her editors would sort out the details. She needed to bring in the official version of the crime.

"We talked to Chief Anthony DeFranco of the Westport Police Department. Chief, what do we know about what took place last night on Beachside Avenue?"

"Tracy, this is what we know so far: The body of Mr. Jayne was found at eight a.m. sitting in a chair next to his pool at his home. He suffered gunshot wounds to the head. We have found little physical evidence at the crime scene, but what we do have will be evaluated. His wife, who is on vacation out of the country, has been contacted, as have his children from previous relationships.

We know this is a high-profile case, and we'll have more as it becomes available."

"Chief, you mentioned head wounds. Can you give us more information about the cause of death?"

"All I can say at this point is Mr. Jayne appeared to have suffered multiple gunshot wounds. The body has been transported to the medical examiner, and the investigation is continuing," said the chief.

"At this point do you have any information about Mr. Jayne's associations that might shed some light on this murder?" asked Tracy. She expected him to punt, and he did so.

"Well," said the chief, "the investigation is just starting and will continue for several days before we can find and process all the evidence. Contacting Mr. Jayne's associates will be a normal part of that process."

"Thank you, chief," said Tracy. "The literary world is reeling today from the news that mystery writer megastar Barnaby Jayne has been found murdered at his Gold Coast mansion. For *NBC Nightly News*, this is Tracy Taggart reporting from Westport, Connecticut."

Dasha approached Tracy's standup—distant, despondent, disbelieving. She had to hold out a hand and grab a chair, and the chief helped her sit. The chief waited for the cameraman to put his machine down and made sure their microphones were off. He'd witnessed public officials embarrassed by hot mics in the past—saying something flagrantly stupid for all the world to hear.

"Can I get you some water, Dasha?" Tracy asked. "Maybe we can get Sam to take you home."

"No, dear, I'm all right," said Dasha, looking away toward the sound. "I just saw him yesterday. He was enjoying the quiet and was getting a lot of work done. He was in that euphoric state when the words were coming quickly and laying themselves down on the page. He described it to me. He said the first hundred manuscript pages were an uphill climb, but when he reached the crest he could schuss down the mountain and wind up in the ski lodge with a drink. Delightful man."

"Dasha, Tracy and I need to go to the medical examiner's office," said the chief. "I'm sure I'm breaking a few rules, but you can come if you want. You're a close associate. It might jar some things loose."

"I'll go," she said, "for Barnaby. But I need to check on Galina first. Can you accommodate that?"

"Of course," said DeFranco. He called for Ferguson on his handheld and issued instructions to continue with photography, inventory, and interviews, especially Felicity. He also gave his detective the number for the police department in Turks and Caicos. Westport PD would need Mrs. Jayne's arrival information, and he wanted to send a car to pick her up.

"Stanley, make sure the ServePro people get the stain off the pool deck," he said. "I want the house shipshape when she walks in the door."

"On it," said Ferguson, and the parties sauntered off in their different directions, hoping to reconvene with more, and better, information as to who might have wanted Barnaby Jayne dead. With the chief at the wheel of the Crown Vic, Dasha and Tracy sat quietly in the back seat as the car rolled sedately down the Jaynes' driveway. There was a crowd outside the iron gates, mostly late-arriving media. Dasha made eye contact with that odious man from the *New York Post*, Adrian Hawkes. His sunglasses were removed, and she noted his squinty, piglike eyes and the sagging pouches that indicated too much alcohol and not enough sleep. He gave her a knowing smile, brought his hand up with index finger extended to look like a gun, then moved his thumb to signify the discharge of a firearm. He aimed directly at her.

He was taunting her.

What does he know? she asked herself as the chief's car moved down the street and pulled into the driveway at Seabreeze. Galina was napping with Luna the cat, so Dasha left her a note and a plate of food she could put in the microwave. She moved toward the back door, ever-present stick in hand, and patted her coat pocket to make sure her Walther was safe. The chief took the back way over Sasco Creek, and soon they were driving westbound down I-95. At one point Tracy took Dasha's hand, and she held it all the way to the medical examiner's office.

They went through the back door and reached the domain of Dr. Samuel Goldberg, who was maneuvering his powered wheelchair around the stacks of books and journals drifting inside his lair. The doctor had been the victim of childhood polio, but his disabilities only seemed to fuel his considerable mental talents in the field of forensic science.

"Chief DeFranco and Tracy Taggart!" he bellowed, and they all shook hands and hugged as appropriate. Goldberg had helped crack the case of the sea glass murders. "And this must be the amazing Mrs. Petrov. You're more beautiful in person than you are on television."

"Flattery will get you everywhere," said Dasha, "but we're here on very solemn business."

"I know," said Goldberg. "The eminent Mr. Jayne. Was he a friend of yours?"

"One of the best," said Dasha. "I saw him practically every day for ten years. We had ongoing discussions about his various literary projects. We were intellectual soulmates."

"Will you want to attend the autopsy, Mrs. Petrov?" asked Goldberg. "If the chief agrees, I can admit you and Miss Taggart as part of the team. After all, I run this place."

"Maybe at a distance," said Dasha. "I can make an initial identification for the record and make myself available for questions. Tracy, is that all right with you?"

"Yes, Dasha," said Tracy. "I'll be with you."

"Let's go," said Goldberg, taking the lead down the hallway with the institutional linoleum and light-mauve tiles. It was designed to be easily maintained, not to be pretty. The medical examiner used his powered throne to kick open the double doors leading to the examining room, and there was poor Barnaby, naked, laid out on the table with the gutters down the sides leading to a slop sink at the foot. His skin was an ashen blue, darker on the bottom where the blood had settled, and his pear-shaped girth had collapsed into a saddle of fat that was woefully unbecoming. Dasha grieved anew, more for this lack of privacy, and steeled herself, knowing they were doing their best for a man whose life had been cut short. She tried to protect him even now.

"Can't you cover him?" she asked the doctor, and Goldberg nodded to an assistant, who found a paper sheet to lay over most of Jayne's body, leaving the head exposed.

"Mrs. Petrov, for the record, this man is Barnaby Jayne?" asked Goldberg, speaking into an overhead microphone.

"It is," said Dasha. She wanted to look away, but she couldn't. She had to really see him, to sear into her mind how he looked at the end of his life—mouth a black hole, top of head a ragged mess, sightless eyes slightly parted. Seeing Barnaby Jayne this way would motivate her to give her friend his well-deserved justice.

"Thank you, Mrs. Petrov. Let the record show positive identification of the decedent, Mr. Barnaby Jayne, was established at 1:37 p.m. April 26, 1991. This postmortem is being conducted by Dr. Samuel Goldberg, assisted by criminologist Mr. Oliver Snell and assistants Mr. Claude Blakeley and Ms. Marjorie Cummings. It's also being attended by Chief Anthony DeFranco of the Westport Police Department, Miss Tracy Taggart, and Mrs. Dasha Petrov. Now that we have the preliminaries out of the way, Oliver, why don't you bring us up to speed."

"Thank you, Dr. Goldberg. I received the call from Westport Police at approximately 8:15 a.m. on April 26 that there was a possible deceased person at the Beachside Avenue estate of author Barnaby Jayne. Upon arrival, we were met by the chief and Detective Stanley Ferguson, who took us to the pool deck, where we found Mr. Jayne sitting in a chair wrapped in a quilt, which we have taken into evidence. We also have the chair.

"I made a concentric search in a forty-foot ring around the decedent, looking for weapons, identification, spent casings, fabrics, threads, shoe prints, blood spatter, all the usual and customary items that normally accompany a homicide, although the cause of death at that point was undetermined. The chief found footprints on the beach that might be of evidentiary interest, and a total of five stone castings were taken.

"I approached the decedent and determined he had suffered a gunshot wound in the soft palate of his upper mouth. Powder burns indicate the muzzle of the firearm that produced this man's wounds was shoved into the oral cavity. Dental impressions are being taken, and we are reaching out to his dentist to get the latest X-rays. We may find tooth marks on the weapon that killed him when it can be located. I also found two side-by-side wounds on the back of the dead man's head at the top of the neck and base of the skull. These wounds appear to be through and through, exiting out of the top of his skull and causing considerable avulsion of blood and bone."

"Oliver, have you made a thorough inventory of any other signs of injury?" asked the doctor.

"No other wounds," said Oliver. "He appears to have had an appendix removed at some point, and there is a Y-shaped scar on his left shoulder, indicating an open rotator cuff repair. They do that sort of thing laparoscopically now, so this looks likes older surgery."

"Angle of entry of the head wounds?" asked the chief. Dasha was about to ask the same question; the chief beat her to it.

"You've been studying that book I gave you," said Goldberg. He turned to his assistant. "Oliver, I have to question your assumption on what made that exit wound," said Goldberg. "I think the mouth shot probably passed through his palate, pituitary, and medulla, and then veered upward. Those neck shots had more material to pass through—the thickened trapezius muscles of the neck, for instance, and then into the suboccipital triangle."

"What does the angle tell you, doctor?" asked Dasha.

"It tells us where the gun was in relation to the victim," said Goldberg. "It might give us some indication of the height, strength, and capability of the shooter."

"What about shot placement?" asked the chief. "The job looks professional to me. Nothing haphazard about two neat holes in a horizontal line. This wasn't an accident, and it wasn't spontaneous."

"Agreed," said Goldberg. "Oliver, get the eighth-inch rod and insert it into one of the wounds at the back of the head. Claude, can you and Marjorie help Oliver turn the victim?"

Goldberg's three assistants went about their assigned tasks, and Dasha tried to remember it was all for Barnaby, poor man. Oliver inserted the rod into one of the wounds, and it passed without obstruction up to the eight-and-a-half inch mark.

"You can see it's aligned roughly with the orbit of the left eye," said Goldberg. "See how the rod is angled slightly upward? If the victim was standing when he was shot, I would guess the shooter to be a bit shorter. If the victim was seated, the shooter would have had to be almost in a kneeling position to get that shot placement and wound angle. At this point, I am strongly suggesting the victim was standing when he received the two neck wounds. Oliver, you said the area around the seated victim was clean?"

"As a whistle," said Oliver. "No blood, no spatter, no shell casings."

"Go back over that area with luminol," said Goldberg, referring to the chemical that caused blood to shine under ultraviolet light. "And chief, consider the possibility he was shot elsewhere and then planted by the pool."

"I can handle that," said the chief. "And if he was moved, that would indicate more than one shooter—people with sufficient strength to lift him."

"That is correct, chief," said Goldberg. "We might have two or three people in on this."

"Can we presume Barnaby was sitting in his chair, wrapped in a quilt, out by the pool, waiting for someone to come up from the beach?" asked Dasha.

"That suggests he knew his murderer," said Goldberg, warming to the theory. The ME turned to his assistant. "Oliver, we need to see if we can find the bullet fragments. Please remove this man's left eyeball." Claude and Marjorie settled Barnaby back onto the slab and placed his head on a stone tablet to stabilize it. Oliver retrieved an extractor from work bench, and the victim's eyeball was out in seconds and hanging by the optical nerve. Dasha and Tracy looked on, bracing themselves, yet fascinated.

"Dr. Goldberg, I am noting some swelling and some cracks in the orbit of the eye," said Oliver.

"Use your Dremel to cut away the bone, and see if you can find the other end of your wound channel. The bullet will likely be on that pathway somewhere," said Goldberg. He turned to the chief. "It's unpleasant, but it beats pawing through his brain."

Dasha, Tracy, and the chief watched Oliver slice through bone, ah-ing and hmm-ing. He reached for a tweezer and, smiling in triumph, extracted a jagged piece of metal and placed it in a metal pan.

"Measure that, Oliver, and tell me what we've got," said Goldberg. Oliver reached for a caliper.

"Nose of the bullet has expanded on impact, but I don't think it's a hollow point," he said. Back end is roughly three-eighths of an inch in diameter, which equates to a nine millimeter."

"But we don't really know that until we can match the bullet's striations with the rifling from the weapon that fired it," said Goldberg. "It could be a .380, also known as a nine-millimeter short, or 'corto' in Europe."

"A lot of guns to consider," said Tracy.

"Hundreds," said Goldberg. "But let's be glad it's not thousands. Chief, bring me that firearm, and we will have something to work with."

"What is your opinion of the mouth shot?" asked Dasha. Goldberg turned to her.

"Idle speculation," said Goldberg. "In the Mafia hits I have investigated, a shot through the mouth is a sign of disrespect. The victim was a loud mouth, talked too much, broke ranks—a stool pigeon."

"Could the mouth shot have been made to make us think it's a Mafia hit?" asked Tracy. "To lead us down the wrong path?"

"Always a possibility," said Goldberg.

"Could also be a force of habit," said Dasha. "The shooter has a method, and this is a calling card."

"So, Dr. Goldberg," said the chief, "we need a hypothesis. Later on, we'll come to a theory, because it's a little early. Three shots, two placed perfectly to within a fraction, one through the mouth. No bullet casings left at the scene. Nine millimeter, or a .380. Pick one. Is this a professional assassination?"

Dasha spoke. "Don't be afraid to get this wrong," she said. "Like the chief said, it's early. We just need a place to begin."

"I would say the person who killed Barnaby Jayne had certainly killed before," said the doctor. "And I would say he was shorter than the victim. Five-five to five-eight in stocking feet. Mr. Jayne is six-one, hence the slight upward angle of the neck shots. The shooter was accompanied by one large, maybe two same-size individuals who could help get Mr. Jayne into his chair."

"Could the shooter be a she?" asked Tracy. And everyone in the room turned in her direction.

12

Suspicion Falls

Dasha needed to speak to Aubrey.

She wouldn't allow herself to make the leap that Jayne's literary nemesis had killed him. But Aubrey might know something, or at least have a notion that would point her toward the killer. She allowed the chief and Tracy to drive her home. There were more crowds in front of the Jayne residence, and now bouquets of flowers were being piled against the fence. Barnaby's fans had been alerted, and they were coming to the Gold Coast in droves. The chief pulled into Dasha's drive and solicitously exited the driver's side so he could open her door and take her by the arm to see her safely inside. Tracy carried Dasha's stick, and they all gathered in the great room, where Galina was noodling over her Scrabble board and petting Luna.

Dasha gave Galina the bad news in Russian. Galina emitted a short scream, followed by a welter of tears and trembling lips. She had no great love for Barnaby Jayne, less for Michael Aubrey, but to have murder haunt the avenue gave Galina a start. The chief and Tracy left the sisters, and Dasha suited up for a walk on the beach. Galina knew where she was headed and moved her Scrabble pieces into position.

"Stay away from Aubrey," she wrote. And Dasha responded impatiently to her elder, all-knowing sister.

"He's a suspect, Galina," she said.

"Let the chief handle it," Galina wrote, while Dasha stood next to the door, arms folded, coat zipped, beret lashed to her head with her Hermès scarf. It wasn't often Dasha defied her sister.

"The chief is still processing the scene, Galina," said Dasha. "I can be of use. I'll report back. I promise. Don't worry." And she was gone, hating that she and Galina were quarreling, but shaking off any misgivings by moving smartly across the lawn, resolutely planting her stick—feeling Constantine guiding the way. She got to Aubrey's property and found the man himself sitting in his gazebo smoking a cigar and nursing a glass of port. Prince ran up to Dasha, and she had his wiener out of her pocket and in her hand. Aubrey spoke first.

"I didn't do it, Dasha," he said in a steady, even voice. "I'm as shocked as anybody." Dasha looked at him and tried to summon years of instinct in order to gauge whether or not the man was telling the truth. She'd been led astray by superiors, spies, fellow agents, even her own children. The petty liars would look away, change the subject. The practiced dissemblers would look you right in the eye and spin their untruths into great tapestries of deceit. The truth tellers were not without passion, but they were calm, steady, unblinking, wishing to ally themselves with the side of right. Dasha would knock him back a bit.

"You had motive, opportunity, and means," she said calmly.

"Let me pick that apart," said Aubrey. "Yes, Jayne and I had our professional differences. And yes, it's escalated into silly games-manship. But I have all the money in the world, a house on the water, a spiffy new wife, a jet that can get me around the country on a whim. Why would I risk that, Dasha? Come on. I want to find Barnaby's killer, too. If nothing else, to remove suspicion from me."

"Well argued, Michael," she said, "but be prepared for the chief, who will want to interview you. Where were you last night?" she asked.

"Del, Prince, and I were in front of a fire watching a baseball game on television," said Aubrey. "Red Sox at the Mariners. Seattle won four to two. Randy Johnson beat the living hell out of Roger Clemens. I got bored after the fifth inning and went to bed."

"Okay, Michael," said Dasha. "You had me at motive. Removing Barnaby Jayne would not directly benefit you. In fact, it casts you in an unfavorable light if your chicaneries become known."

"Too late, Dasha," said Aubrey. "Did you see this? *New York Post*, early edition. Page one. Hawkes Talks column. That ass Adrian Hawkes. He was at the scene. He must have phoned this in." The despicable Hawkes was now trumpeting her friend's murder, and seemed to revel in it.

Mystery Man Murdered
Hawkes Takes the Gold Coast

A leading light in the world of literature was extinguished today with the cold-blooded, gangland-style murder of mystery novelist Barnaby Jayne, whose bullet-riddled body was found at his Gold Coast estate. Jayne enjoyed a half-century career at the pinnacle of the highly competitive realm of mystery writing.

His agent, Bea Aldwich of the Aldwich Agency, decried what she called "an incalculable loss." Holding back tears, she said of her client: "He stood on Everest. He'd attained the heights, and he had so much more to give. I'm shattered."

Attention now turns to finding Jayne's killers. Anonymous sources in the Fairfield County medical examiner's office allege the noted novelist suffered three gunshot wounds to the head. Caliber and precise shot placement suggest a professional hit, according to these sources. Attention now turns to any Jayne associations that might offer a clue to this who-done-it, an ironic ending for a man who described unnatural death in all its morbid, and at times creative, manifestations.

Recently, Jayne is reported to have been engaged in a tit-for-tat competition with Michael Aubrey, another hugely successful and prolific author who writes the Max Gunn mystery/thriller series. Jayne and Aubrey are Beachside Avenue neighbors, and lately they've taken to trying to best one another in an increasingly dangerous game of one-upmanship.

Jayne is alleged to have fired a poison dart at the Aubrey front door. Aubrey retaliated by snaring Jayne in a trap while Jayne walked in a nearby arboretum. Jayne is said to have counterattacked by destroying Aubrey's prized gun collection, and Aubrey exacted his revenge by fire-bombing Jayne's antique Rolls-Royce.

It's said these two story-tellers were fighting over the attention of Mrs. Dasha Petrov, a Beachside Avenue resident who enjoyed a storied career as an officer in the Central Intelligence Agency. It's said Jayne and Aubrey looked to Mrs. Petrov for inspiration and realistic anecdotes they could weave into their novels. Thus ensued the petty competition that today may have led to the death of Barnaby Jayne.

It's unclear what the police will be looking at to solve this high-profile mystery, but Aubrey, and even Mrs. Petrov, are not without motive, sources say.

Hawkes Talks has decamped to the suburbs, where we'll be reporting on the drama as it unfolds.

～

"Balderdash," said Dasha, throwing the paper on the floor. "I loved Barnaby the same as I love you, Michael. We're friends. Hawkes is naming us both as suspects. It's actionable."

"I'm lawyering up," said Aubrey. "I suggest you do the same, Dasha." Del Aubrey appeared in the doorway to the patio and called to Michael.

"Bring Dasha in for a glass of wine," she yelled, and Aubrey said, "Join us." Dasha wasn't in the mood, but her work of intelligence gathering required it. Del Aubrey was open and smiling when she greeted Dasha but quickly turned dark and serious—the human emotions one might expect when murder came this close. And Del was well aware of the villainy of Adrian Hawkes.

"It's shocking what that man is allowed to publish," she said, aroused. "But what can we do?"

"Defamation is difficult to show if you're a public figure," said Aubrey. "He's hiding behind that. Have some of this white Bordeaux, Dasha." Aubrey poured her a glass. Dasha had removed her coat, and Del hung it in a closet, where she'd placed Dasha's stick. The threesome bantered on, and Aubrey lapsed into earnest praise for his fallen competitor.

"He made me a better writer," he said. "I would never admit that while the man was alive. But in the back of my mind, I always tried to elevate my game to get up there on the pedestal with Barnaby. I mean, I'm good . . . but I have to say Barnaby was great."

"You shouldn't compare," said Dasha. "You have different styles, approaches, audiences. You are both exceptionally talented."

"I hated that running spat you were having," said Del. "It was beneath both of you."

"He started it," he snapped. Clearly, Aubrey didn't like his sixth wife bringing him up short.

"Listen to yourself," said Del. "You sound like you're back in a schoolyard. You're both grown men." She stopped, becoming more somber. "I don't know how Tammy is dealing with this."

"Have you spoken with her?" asked Dasha.

"She left a message on the answering machine," said Del, just as the phone rang. "That might be her. I'll take it in the study." She left the living room, and Dasha looked over at her friend Michael. He was resting his wineglass on his belly, looking dejected, Prince trying to offer a bit of cheer with his head on Aubrey's knee.

"Del is going to our place on Mustique tomorrow," said Aubrey. "She needs to get out of here. Can't say I blame her. It's going to be pretty sad for the next few weeks."

"You were furious with him, Michael," said Dasha. "Now you're sad?"

"I never wanted him dead, Dasha," said Aubrey. "In a way, I enjoyed the competition."

"This finger-pointing will get very rough," said Dasha.

"You have to help me find a way out of it, for both of us," said Aubrey. "Why would Hawkes suggest you might have had a motive? I can see him leveling these accusations at me. But not you."

"No clue," said Dasha, "other than the desire to stir the pot with these calumnies. It's how they sell newspapers."

Del came back into the room.

"Tammy's back, and she's a mess," she said. "I have to go down there. It's too dark to walk. I'll take the Benz."

"Del, can you drop me at my drive?" asked Dasha, eager to get Del alone, if only for a moment. "I have to check on Galina."

"Certainly," said Del. "I'll get your coat and stick." They walked out of the house and entered Aubrey's Mercedes. While Del maneuvered down the drive, Dasha asked a question that had been on her mind since her encounter with Del and Tammy on the beach those many days ago, when the world was more or less right-side up.

"You're Tammy's first call," said Dasha. "She's lucky to have such a good friend at a time like this."

"Yes, we're married to superstars," said Del. "It can get a little rocky. It's nice to have support."

"You seem so close," said Dasha, rising to make a crucial point. "Did you know each other before you arrived on the avenue?"

The question was fired like an arrow, and it seemed to strike Del right between the eyes. She hesitated, looked straight ahead through the windshield, and started to respond but held her tongue. Dasha didn't think the question was all that complicated, but Del had a hard time forming a response.

"Oh no," said Del finally. "We just had some common ground, and we clicked. You know. The sisterhood. We've helped each other get through some tough moments. Like now. Is this your stop?" It was clear Del wanted to end the conversation, and she pulled up at the Seabreeze driveway.

"Good night, Del," said Dasha. "Tell Tammy everyone on this street is appalled. We're pulling for her and the children." Dasha got out of the car and walked up the drive. She entered the guest cottage and made sure Galina was safe. Dasha's sister had micro-waved some soup, deployed a TV table one-handed, and was watching the news. The face of Barnaby Jayne filled the screen. Dasha kissed her sister, found her Leupold binoculars, and went right out the door to the patio toward the seawall. She turned west and started walking down the beach toward the Jayne estate for a bit of tawdry spying. She didn't always take joy from her line of work, but it was the life she chose. She was finding facts, chiseling away at the rock of deception to find the sculpture of truth within. Just as she'd once taken up the sword and shield of intelligence for her adopted country, she now pursued the truth for Barnaby.

When she got to the Jayne seawall, she was relieved to see Chief DeFranco and Tracy Taggart standing hands on hips, looking down to the beach. The chief was wearing a headlamp, and Tracy was holding what looked like a fluorescent lamp plugged into an extension cord that ran back to the pool cabana. The chief looked up, and his headlamp shined in Dasha's eyes.

"It's just me, out for a stroll," said Dasha. "I'm coming up."

"We're following up on the ME's luminol request," said the chief. "It reacts with the iron in hemoglobin and starts to fluoresce. We're trying to figure out where Barnaby was shot and how he was moved."

These were vital questions, of course, but Dasha really wanted to get a sense for the comings and goings in the Jayne residence, now that his eminence was no longer in situ. She could see clusters of people gathered in the living room, no doubt offering their sympathies. Del was talking to poor Tammy. Lucy and Jim were sitting in the kitchen, and Felicity had arrived like the cavalry.

"We know it wasn't the chair on the deck," said the chief. "We'd see the mess pretty clearly."

"But moving him to the chair shows Barnaby had more than one assailant," said Dasha. "What does the luminol reveal?"

"We just started," said the chief. "Tracy, shine the UV light over the top of the seawall where it meets the grass."

"Use your imagination, chief," said Dasha. DeFranco didn't mind Dasha's inevitable lecture. "The evidence is telling you he was shot, then moved. Probably not too far. And he certainly wasn't killed in the house or the outbuildings. They've been examined carefully all day. We'd see evidence. So how could this happen? Visualize the scene. Barnaby is sitting by the pool wrapped in a quilt, watching the stars . . . "

"Or waiting for someone," said Tracy.

"Or waiting for someone, dear. You're right," said Dasha. "The someone arrives along the beach, calls up to Barnaby, and he approaches the seawall. Another party—or parties—approaches from behind and shoots him in the back of the head, and he falls face down with his head hanging over the wall. They turn him over, put the gun in his mouth, and fire one more time. At least that's what a professional might do. They pick him up, carry him back to his chair, wrap him in the quilt, and put his hat on his head. They leave him for Miguel to find when the sun comes up."

"Why doesn't he have his hat on when he approaches the seawall?" asked Tracy. "Why doesn't his hat have a bullet hole?"

"Not sure," said Dasha. "The theory is couched in certain assumptions. He took it off? His killers put it back on?"

"Wouldn't we find evidence of the shooting on the beach?" asked the chief. "Blood spatter, brain matter? We went over the area pretty carefully when we took the shoe castings."

"Barnaby's killers are fastidious, chief," said Dasha. "They used that hose coiled on the side of the pool cabana to wash down the area. Maybe cover the evidence in sand. Let's use the luminol on the beach."

They walked down and stood under the spot in alignment with where Miguel had found Barnaby's moldering corpse. Tracy found a child's beach toy in the pool cabana and was scraping away the sand in layers an inch at a time. Every time she removed a layer, the chief sprayed more luminol, and Tracy shined the ultraviolet light on it. They found evidence of blood on the sixth layer, and a steady glow on the seventh. Now the chief also saw bits of brain and bone. The chief wielded his trusty Nikon to record the evidence. He took samples with tweezers wielded by a gloved hand and put them in a plastic bag for Dr. Goldberg.

"I have to get this over to the ME for blood typing and serology," said the chief, who appeared unsettled at having to handle Jayne's mortal remains.

"And I'm still jet-lagged," said Tracy. "I'm going to have you drop me at home. Dasha, can we give you a ride?"

"No thank you, dear," said Dasha. "I can walk home. There's a lovely moon." DeFranco and Tracy smiled and gave Dasha a kiss on the cheek. They moved up the Jaynes' lawn, and Dasha lingered by the pool, where Barnaby Jayne had made his last stand. When she knew she was alone, she brought the Leupold binoculars up to her careworn eyes on this sadly momentous day. She thought she recognized Bea Aldrich, Barnaby's agent, talking to a gentleman. Bea had been the subject of a profile in *Vanity Fair*. There were some Beachside neighbors paying their respects. Lucy and Jim were passing a tray. And Tammy and Del were sitting on a couch talking—heads together, listening carefully to each other, nodding in agreement.

"The sisterhood," said Dasha Petrov, to no one in particular.

13

The Lad Shows Promise

Adrian Hawkes had hope for little Jim. Adrian had been bribing sources for more than thirty years. And most of the scallywags with whom he'd conducted business didn't give a fig for quality control or timely delivery. It was all cash on the barrelhead, no service after the sale. But this new generation of thieves charged appropriately, paid attention to detail, and could get the goods into your hands, Bob's your uncle. Of course, Adrian knew Jim was a clean slate—free, so far, of the dust and rust of corruption. And yes, adding more years would certainly destroy the lad's sense of honor, you could be sure of that. Give him time, and he'd wallow in the depths of depravity with the rest of the pathetic fools who'd coughed up information for money. Right now, as Jim sat in the passenger's seat of Adrian's rented Toyota, the lad could not have been more accommodating. But Jim was in a bit of a hurry. He needed to get back to social studies class at Coleytown Middle School.

"I copied what I thought were the important papers," said Jim. "There was some pretty boring stuff about insurance, car registrations, the deed to the house. The papers with the blue wrapper from Scopes, Sneed, and Belding seemed more interesting, especially this one called last will and testament."

Adrian scanned the photocopy, bypassing the Whereas, the Be It Known, the long list of chattels, and got down to the meat—the who gets what. Barnaby had splintered off a few million here and there for his biological children and even acknowledged Lucy and Jim with college tuition assistance when the time came. But the bulk of his estate was going to Tammy, including the brokerage accounts and the Beachside Avenue property.

Curiously, he appeared to have attached an addendum that acknowledged the enormous contribution Mrs. Dasha Petrov had made to his literary works. He was giving Dasha $10 million. The addendum appeared to be signed by Jayne, but it wasn't notarized or witnessed.

"I have to get back to class," said Jim, breaking Adrian's trance.

"Right," said Adrian. "You can go. Call me when you get more."

"You're forgetting something," said Jim.

"Oh right," said Adrian. "Your filthy lucre." He peeled off a crisp hundred.

"You said five hundred last time we spoke," said Jim, flickers of indignity breaking into a flame. "This is Barnaby's will, for fuck's sake."

"Hey watch your mouth," said Adrian. "What would your mother say?"

"Where do you think I learned it?" said Jim, holding out his hand. Adrian peeled off four more hundreds, knowing the higher-ups would understand the need to prime the pump.

"Here you go," said Adrian. "You've got my number. Give Lucy my best." They parted company, still friends.

Adrian went back to reading Barnaby's most intimate legal document. So, Mrs. Petrov was in line to get a cool ten million. She was the only trained killer on Beachside Avenue. Snuffing out the life of Barnaby Jayne would be all in a day's work for this CIA femme fatale. He needed to research more of Mrs. Petrov's history and start to connect the dots that would lead to the killer of the talented Mr. Jayne.

14

Paw Prints

Dasha Petrov was heading out on her daily beach walk. A blue sky was studded with puffy white clouds, and a brisk northeasterly wind chilled the air. Her heart was empty at the prospect of an absent Barnaby. She couldn't quite believe he was gone. She was waiting to wake up from the nightmare—which became far worse when she stood on her patio to start her morning trek. Aubrey's Prince came bounding up to her without his collar, which carried the receiver for the electric fence Aubrey had had installed around his property. Prince was happy to see Dasha, and of course she'd remembered his treat. She pulled a wiener out of a plastic bag in her pocket and gave it to the dog—reeling back in horror when she took another look. There was blood on Prince's paws and rear haunches. She bent down and saw more blood on his face and nose, but he didn't appear injured.

"Let's go find your master," Dasha told the dog, and the pair walked resolutely toward the beach. Every step caused more panic as she approached the Aubrey seawall. There were bloody paw prints on the steps leading down to the beach. Prince bounded up the stairs, and Dasha used more treats to buy Prince's affections. She needed to reunite Prince with his collar and determine the source of the blood.

She was frightened.

She hadn't been this scared since the war, when life was cheap, dispensed with, and discarded by the freight-car load.

Prince ran up to Aubrey's gazebo and sat down to wait for her. She finally made it up to the door and looked inside. Michael Aubrey was sitting in a chair. His throat had been cut, and his head was cocked off at a freakish angle, fresh blood oozing from the gaping wound in his neck. His shirtfront was completely red with blood, his chest gurgling up multiple stab wounds. The color of his face was that ashen blue she'd come to know and hate.

She couldn't cry or scream. She could barely move.

She had to reach the chief. She enticed Prince into the garage with more treats and closed the door. The dog was confused and upset and started to bay, but she couldn't have him romping through the crime scene. She entered the Aubrey household and called out for Makita. The gardener's truck was gone, so he must be gone with it, she surmised. She got to the phone hanging on the wall in the kitchen and dialed the chief, who picked up after being patched through with help from Madge.

"Chief. Michael Aubrey is dead," said Dasha. She heard the chief emit a long, disbelieving "Nooooo," on the other end of the line. But his police instincts soon kicked in, and he counseled next steps.

"Where are you, Dasha?" he asked.

"I'm in the Aubrey kitchen, using the Aubrey phone," she said.

"Where is Aubrey?" asked the chief.

"His gazebo in the front yard," said Dasha. "He appears to have been stabbed."

"Where is the Aubrey staff?" asked the chief.

"Uncertain," said Dasha. "Makita's truck is gone. It might be Sheila's day off."

"Stand by," said the chief. Dasha sensed him turning in his chair, keying a microphone. She heard him get one of his patrolmen on the line without alerting unwanted listeners like the media. She could hear him on her end of the line, and her faith in the chief blossomed anew. "Cruisers in the vicinity of Green's Farms, call my mobile line." Seconds later, Officer Sam DeFranco dialed the chief, and the chief gave him the barest outline. "You're going to have to clear that property before backup arrives. Get your shotgun out. Remember Dasha is in the kitchen. No friendly fire."

"Roger, chief," said the stalwart Sam.

"Dasha," said DeFranco. "I've got Sam coming over to you right now. I want to make sure you're alone, and we need to clear that house. Stay on the line with me."

Dasha heard a door slam on an upper floor and feet running down stair treads.

"Chief, there's someone in the house," said Dasha. She heard a siren in the distance. It must be Sam, she thought. She heard another door slam and more feet moving quickly through the front of the house. She saw a dark form moving from the den to the living room. She pulled her Walther out of her pocket. She heard a slow, heavy walk moving in her direction. The siren grew louder. She would stand her ground—like she always had.

"Stop," she said in a firm voice. "I've got a gun."

The chief heard her through the phone. He got Sam on the radio to urge him forward. The next few seconds were a blur. The dark form wore a long, black duster coat, a black felt fedora, and a mask depicting Edvard Munch's *The Scream*. He was coming toward her with a knife raised in his right hand. Dasha fired her Walther into his chest, but he kept coming, and she immediately thought, *Body armor*. He seemed to shake off Dasha's first bullet, and when he lunged for her, she fired again. This time her shot went wide and entered a doorframe. She pulled the trigger once more, but the slide was open, and her seven-round magazine was empty.

Impossible! she screamed at herself. There should be three more rounds.

Patrolman DeFranco pulled into the Aubreys' drive, and Dasha's attacker fled out the front door. Dasha decided to chase the masked man, and that's how Sam DeFranco found her—trying to make her way across the lawn doubled over and cramped—with her stick in one hand and her pistol in the other.

"Dasha!" called Sam.

And Dasha pointed toward the beach and screamed, "He's getting away!"

Sam bolted into action and was yelling into the radio clipped to his epaulet. "Shots fired 206 Beachside Avenue. Requesting immediate backup."

The chief was in the front seat of the Crown Victoria with Ferguson seated to his right when he heard his son make the call. Sam ran up to Dasha, who was bent over, breathing hard.

"Don't let him get away, Sam," said Dasha.

He ran down to the seawall and scanned the beach east and west. There was no one there. And when he turned around, Dasha was flat on her back in a heap on the lawn. When he got back to her, her eyes were closed, her Walther was in one hand, her stick was in the other—ready to take on all comers but stopped in her tracks by nothing more than her long, momentous time on earth.

The last thing she'd felt was a pain in her chest, and then her world went black.

15

Here We Go Again

Tracy Taggart was seated at her desk in her cubicle at *NBC Nightly News* on the forty-third floor of 30 Rockefeller Plaza. She no longer had to pinch herself when she walked through those massive lobby doors and through the three-story art deco lobby. But she knew how lucky she was to be occupying a foreign correspondent's chair on one of America's preeminent television networks. The job had taken her around the world five times—but today she was working on the second-day follow-up of the murder of Barnaby Jayne. She'd lead with the tributes and encomiums, the elaborate funeral and burial arrangements, with interwoven B-roll showing mounds of bouquets at the Jayne estate and tearful man-in-the-street footage decrying this towering loss. Jayne was a giant, and Tracy's coverage was expansive, encouraged by her managing editor and the anchor, who'd been a Jayne fan from a young age. He allowed Tracy to sit at the anchor table during the nightly news, an honor and a privilege.

She was thinking, *What could possibly go wrong?* But two events transpired in rapid succession to answer that question most definitively. First, her love, partner, and helpmate, Chief DeFranco, called her out of breath from the estate of Michael Aubrey.

"Michael Aubrey is dead, Tracy," he said in his clipped, highly stressed professional voice. "And Dasha was transported to Norwalk Hospital. Collapsed with chest pains in hot pursuit of Aubrey's killers. You better get out here."

"Killers plural?" Tracy asked, astonished.

"She claims there were two," said the chief.

"I'm on the roll, sweetie," said Tracy. She walked briskly down the hallway to see Grimes. The assignment editor was wrapping up a conference call with bureaus in Paris, Moscow, and Hong Kong. He looked like he didn't appreciate the interruption, but that was life in network television news.

"What's the crisis du jour, Tracy?" he asked.

"Michael Aubrey, Barnaby Jayne's Gold Coast neighbor, has been murdered," she said in an even tone. Grimes didn't really care for expletives embroidering the normal fast-paced tempo of the newsroom. He always said a good vulgarity was only cheapened through overuse. He counseled his team to keep their voices down for the normal trauma, and leave the verbal fireworks for big things, like the fall of Saigon. But he couldn't help himself.

"Holy fucking shit!" he said. "Call the break room and put together a team. I'll get you a truck from the motor pool. Get your ass out there."

Tracy saluted, unshaken, having heard just as much or worse from her Marine Corps dad.

She piled into the truck with a driver, who doubled as a sound man, plus a cameraman and a director, who would operate the console and transmit the material back to home base by a microwave link. As they were leaving, a resourceful intern named Betty handed an early edition of the *New York Post* through the passenger-side window. It landed on Tracy's lap, and the second cataclysm of the day slapped her to attention. The page 1 story was bylined Adrian Hawkes, and there was a graphic slug that announced she was holding a special edition of Hawkes Talks. The headline screamed: What Is She Hiding?

There was a photograph of Dasha with a heavy, bold blurb in fifty-two-point type: "Jayne's Gold Coast neighbor, ex-CIA spy Dasha Petrov, stands to gain millions by his murder. Details page 3." Tracy turned the page while the sound man turned right onto the West Side Highway and headed north.

CIA-TRAINED KILLER NAMED IN JAYNE'S WILL

Who would want Barnaby Jayne dead? It's normally the first question police ask when conducting a murder investigation, especially a cold-blooded killing like the one that stalked the glittering Gold Coast yesterday morning. A landscaper found literary lion Barnaby Jayne shot to death on his pool deck. Officers in the Westport Police Department are wetting themselves trying to apprehend Jayne's killer. But they've failed to establish a motive—until now.

In a *Post* exclusive, we've obtained a copy of Barnaby Jayne's last will and testament. His widow, Tammy Jayne, stands to inherit the bulk of the Jayne fortune. But his neighbor, Mrs. Dasha Petrov, is in line to garner a cool ten million, according to an addendum to the will Jayne drafted recently. Let's not forget that Mrs. Petrov was the muse Jayne and literary heavyweight Michael Aubrey were fighting over in recent days. Their rivalry amounted to little more than penny ante stunts and other tomfoolery, nothing rising to the level of reckless endangerment, let alone murder. Even so, when Jayne's body was discovered, suspicion initially fell on Aubrey.

The provision for Mrs. Petrov in Jayne's will turns our attention in her direction.

And just who is this mysterious Mrs. Petrov? She's the widow of Petrov Petroleum chairman Constantine Petrov. Mrs. Petrov was born in czarist Russia and fled the Bolsheviks in the great White Russian diaspora, winding up in Prague, Czechoslovakia. She joined the anti-Nazi underground at the beginning of the Second World War and was a key player in the assassination of Nazi Rudolph Tristan Heydrich, the so-called architect of the Final Solution.

The multilingual Dasha Petrov was snapped up by Allied intelligence after the war, which was turning its attention to our new Soviet adversaries. It's said that Dasha Petrov was tasked with stopping Soviet hit squads from ending German reconstruction through any means available. Sources say Mrs. Petrov was influential in Operation Paperclip, which transported German rocket scientists to this country to start America's space program.

She also worked for many years nurturing spy rings in Moscow. Needless to say, Dasha Petrov is not alien to the violent removal of anything that gets in her way. Let's not forget a knife-wielding Dasha Petrov was the person who stabbed and stopped—permanently—the serial killer Robert Altman during the case we now know as the sea glass murders.

Should we worry this massive case with international implications is being overseen by a sleepy Westport Police Department? When will the State of Connecticut send in the cavalry? And how about the FBI? Stay tuned.

Hawkes Talks is on the case.

～

Tracy wanted to throw the newspaper out the window, but the crew in the back wanted to read Hawkes's unsubstantiated tripe. She was worried about Dasha, but she also knew she had to go to the crime scene first and get her spot news piece in the can. After that, it was the "dead famous author" routine all over again—an obit, interviews, historical footage, movie clips. She called her production unit and got them started on assembling background material.

An hour went by, and her truck pulled into the Aubrey drive. Graciela once again did her utmost to accommodate Ms. Taggart, the chief's famous friend. But this time there was more media on scene. She waved to Danny of News 12 Connecticut, and he acknowledged her without a smile. Somehow the second high-profile killing in less than three days took away the media's lust for the lurid—unless you were Adrian Hawkes. Tracy saw the little weasel out by the gate, and he shot her a dirty look when she used her special pass to drive into the scene. They parked the truck down by Aubrey's garage, and she took in the situation. Criminologists or, as they used to call them in the Old World, dieners, had arrived from the ME's office, and several Westport PD cruisers were lined up, along with an ambulance and a fire engine. Right up at the front of the queue was the chief's Crown Vic. He'd been one of the first responders—leaning into the fight, as Dasha would say. She walked around the side of the house and got to the gazebo, where she caught the chief's eye. He walked over, still wearing his latex gloves.

"We haven't moved him yet," he said. "But Oliver and his team will take him back to the ME's office in about five minutes. You guys can get B-roll, but try to be respectful of the decedent."

"As always," said Tracy. "How is Dasha?"

"Not sure," said DeFranco. "They transported her, and I let her son know. He's with her now. She had all kinds of things to say before the doors closed. Two assailants in the house. A description of at least one of them. She claims she shot him in the chest, but he didn't go down. Suggests body armor—and a higher caliber of killer."

"Did you see the front page of the *Post*?" asked Tracy.

"I can't even imagine," said DeFranco.

"Hawkes says he's seen Barnaby Jayne's will. Says Dasha is in line to inherit $10 million," said Tracy. "Bizarre."

"Okay, we'll have to get into all that," said the chief. "Are you going to weave that into your standup?"

"No way," said Tracy. "It's unverified."

"Good. Hate to feed that monster. It's going to be another very long day," said the chief.

"Can I set up on the lawn and shoot back toward the house?" Tracy asked. "Gives the shot some context."

"Don't see why not," said DeFranco. "But don't transmit anything just yet. I still need to make my notifications. Apparently Mrs. Aubrey left for the Caribbean yesterday. I still need to reach her."

"Just thinking out loud, Tony," said Tracy. "Two high-profile murders and two spouses conveniently out of the country. I see a pattern."

DeFranco looked at her and saw the rare beauty he cherished—and the deeply probing mind.

"Tuck that away," he said.

16

Knife Play

While Tracy and her team went about their work, DeFranco went up to the Aubrey house, found the great man's study, along with a number for their Mustique residence, and finally raised Mrs. Aubrey, who screamed in all the right places. She would whistle up the chartered Piper Seneca the Mustique residents used to hop over to Barbados, then catch the milk-run six o'clock United flight to Kennedy. DeFranco asked about other Aubrey kin who needed to be notified and also cautioned Mrs. Aubrey that, while Mr. Aubrey's body would be moved to the medical examiner's office, the gazebo was still being processed and cleaned, which would take some time. Best not to go in there.

Del thanked the chief through her sniffles and tears, and he set about the work of finding and calling Aubrey's far-flung issue, begat of various former Mrs. Aubreys. Satisfied next-of-kin had been notified, he walked out to the front lawn, gave Tracy the thumbs-up, and went back to the gazebo, where Oliver Snell, dressed in a one-piece Tyvek hazmat suit, was photographing the corpse. Claude and Marjorie were taking blood samples.

"We've got some good footprints, chief," said Oliver. "Killer or killers tromped around in here for a while."

"Any ideas if they match the castings at the Jayne scene?" asked the chief.

"I'll know when I get back to the office. It's early," said Oliver.

"Looks like it would take a couple of people to finish this guy, no?" asked DeFranco.

"Maybe. Maybe not," said Oliver. "Anybody he knew and was comfortable with could get behind him while he was seated and cut his throat. He'd pass out in a hurry and offer little resistance.

Then it's just a matter of sticking the knife under his rib cage and nicking an artery or two before finding the heart muscle itself. He pretty much bled out."

"Sounds like it would take some skill," said the chief.

"And training," said Oliver. "Commando stuff." The tech turned to his subordinates. "I think we're done with the scene. Let's bag him and tag him."

"All right," said DeFranco. "I'll get ServPro over here. Seems like I should keep them on speed dial."

Stanley Ferguson came to the door of the gazebo.

"I checked the house top to bottom," he said. "No sign of intruders. I did see where Mrs. Petrov said she shot into the doorframe between the kitchen and the front hall. Oh, and his landscaper, Makita, came back. He was at Gault Nursery buying lawn fertilizer. He's got receipts, and I called over there to check his story. I think he's okay."

"Can we get Makita to check on the dog?" asked DeFranco.

"Already done," said Ferguson. "He gave the hound a bath and tucked him in in his apartment over the garage."

Scratch that off the list, DeFranco thought.

"Any news on Mrs. Petrov?" asked the chief.

"She's out of the ER, and they've admitted her," said Ferguson.

"I'll get over to see her, but the ME comes first," said the chief. "Where is Dasha's firearm . . . and her stick?"

"Sam has secured them both in his cruiser," said Ferguson. "We can transfer them to Oliver. Gun takes a .380. Knife is clean. Pains me to say it, but they'll need to be processed, chief."

"Right," said DeFranco. "We'll get them both under the scope at Goldberg's office."

"Just to rule things out," said Ferguson.

"Yes," said the chief, pained. "Always good to rule things out."

There was a stir; Oliver and his team were heading out. DeFranco witnessed for the second time in three days an exceptionally talented man being removed from his estate in a body bag. He went back out to the side of the house fronting the sound to give Tracy her exclusive. As she and her team were packing up, he went out to the front gate to deal with the rest of the media, which arrayed itself in a semicircle around him with boom mics and shoulder-mounted TV cameras. Hawkes pushed himself into the front row, and DeFranco braced for his question.

"Chief, Adrian Hawkes from the *New York Post*," he said. "Aubrey's neighbor, Dasha Petrov, formerly of the CIA, stands to receive millions of dollars from the Barnaby Jayne estate. Is she considered a suspect in these crimes?"

"What you are alleging awaits further investigation," said DeFranco. "For now, I am not going to accept that as fact."

"Will you be questioning Mrs. Petrov?" asked Hawkes.

"We will be talking to a lot of Mr. Aubrey's neighbors," said DeFranco.

"Will your investigation include an examination of Mr. Aubrey's will?" pressed Adrian.

"No doubt," said the chief, turning to a young woman from the *Westport News*. "Mary?"

"How, where, and when was Mr. Aubrey found?" DeFranco was glad to get off the subject of Dasha. He gave the broadest outline.

"How was he killed?" asked Tracy's replacement on News 12 Connecticut, an up-and-comer named Sandra.

"Mr. Aubrey died from injuries sustained from a knife," said the chief, somehow preferring the longhand for "stabbed."

Soon the questions seemed to peter out and the chief said, "Thank you" and turned to go back up the Aubrey driveway to find Stanley, regroup with Tracy, recover his vehicle, and head to the ME. After that, the hospital. As he expected, Adrian Hawkes shouted one more question to the chief's backside as he moved away from the huddle of press.

"When will Dasha Petrov be questioned, chief?" he asked, more like a taunt. DeFranco didn't dignify the question with a response and just kept walking. He found Tracy, who was helping her team pack up their van.

"Next stop, the medical examiner," said the chief. "Ride with me and have your guys follow. We might be able to do another standup."

"Thanks, chief," said Tracy. "But I don't want too much access. The rest of the media won't like it, unless I can work out a pool arrangement."

As they drove down Aubrey's driveway, Tracy saw Adrian Hawkes conferring with Makita. She'd have to give Hawkes some credit. The man was a digger, and he didn't like relying on official statements.

"Nothing we say will satisfy Hawkes," said DeFranco, who'd witnessed the same exchange. "He's defaming Dasha as far as I'm concerned. He'd love to have me name her as a suspect."

Fateful words as they assembled later around the slab at Dr. Goldberg's examination room. Michael Aubrey was naked, obviously fit, and profoundly dead. The red gash under his chin stretched from ear to ear, and his chest and midriff suffered at least five gaping stab wounds.

"He was rendered unconscious after the first stroke that sliced his carotid artery," said Dr. Goldberg. "A blessing. Poor man. He bled to death rather quickly. But the throat cut isn't all that interesting. You could get that result from a kitchen knife. The stabbing injuries in the chest offer more of a clue."

"How so?" asked DeFranco.

"Oliver, why don't you explain," said Goldberg.

"Sure," said Oliver. "A knife actually has a lot of parts. A bolster to help keep the user's hand clear of the blade. A quillon that hangs down and assists with grip. A spine, a thumb rise, a tip. All kinds of things that separate one kind of knife from another. Most knives have a cutting blade on the bottom only. The blade that produced Mr. Aubrey's injuries had two sharpened blades top and bottom. This is characteristic of what we call a dagger. It can cut backhanded or forehanded."

"So that means the killer could have drawn the blade across Aubrey's neck and then produced a slashing wound without having to change hands or reposition the knife," said Tracy.

"Precisely," said Oliver. "It's not a knife you're going to cut onions with. It's a killing instrument."

"The shape is kind of a flattened rhombus, if I remember my eighth-grade geometry," said the chief. "In cross section, it's a parallelogram with four equal sides and no right angles. What kind of stabbing injury does it produce?"

"It basically cuts two sides of the wound going in," said Oliver. "You can see that in these chest wounds." They all leaned in. "A regular knife creates a wedge-shaped cut. With a dagger you get a cut on both sides. But there's also a ridge here in the middle."

"What produced that?" asked Tracy.

"It's what we call 'fluting' in the blade," said Oliver. "It's an indentation that promotes blood loss. So, we're looking at a blade that's six to seven inches long, perfectly sharp all the way around, with a blood groove down the middle."

"Show them Mrs. Petrov's knife, Oliver," said Dr. Goldberg in that dispirited way a parent uses to express disappointment in a child.

"Detective Ferguson brought us this," said Oliver. "Also Mrs. Petrov's firearm, but I'll get to that."

"Wait," said DeFranco, "what was the state of this knife when it arrived? Did it have Aubrey's blood on it?"

"It was perfectly clean," said Oliver. "But it's possible the person who used this knife rinsed it off in the sink, towel dried it, and put it back in Mrs. Petrov's chestnut stick she uses as a scabbard."

DeFranco immediately thought, *How did Dasha's weapons leave her possession?*

"What about the shape of Dasha's knife, Oliver?" asked Tracy.

"That's the interesting thing," said Oliver. "It matches Aubrey's wounds very closely, if not precisely. It has a double blade, the right blade width, the right length, and that fluting groove I described."

"You have her Walther?" asked the chief. "Are you sure it's hers?" He didn't want to hear what he knew was coming.

"Patrolman DeFranco recovered Mrs. Petrov's firearm at the scene of the Aubrey murder," said Oliver. "It was in her possession.

It had scratches on the muzzle consistent with marks from Jayne's dentition. The patrolman also recovered her stick with the concealed knife. He gave these items to Detective Ferguson, who logged them in with us. Detective Ferguson also went to the hospital and retrieved Mrs. Petrov's Wellington boots."

The chain of custody.

The chief and Tracy were bracing for the building windstorm the evidence was creating. Could Dasha Petrov be their killer?

"Did you fire the weapon and recover a bullet?" asked the chief.

"We have a bullet trap for that purpose, and we put the recovered bullet in a comparison microscope with the bullet fragment we pulled from Barnaby Jayne's brain," said Goldberg. "Striations in the known bullet match the striations in the butt end of the fragment. There is no doubt Mrs. Petrov's gun fired the shots that killed Jayne."

"And now we've got evidence Mrs. Petrov's knife could very well have produced the wounds that killed Michael Aubrey," said Oliver.

The chief and Tracy were appalled and sickened. They simply couldn't believe it.

"There's more, chief," said Goldberg.

"Over here we have a shoe impression from the beach in front of the Jayne estate, and over here we have a photo of a footprint in blood taken at the Aubrey murder. The same Wellington boot belonging to Mrs. Petrov created both the impression and the footprint," said Goldberg. "You see that nick in the third tread line? It makes it unique."

"Well," said Tracy, "it will come down to custody. Dasha's gun and Dasha's knife might have caused these murders. And Dasha's boots might have been at both scenes of the crime. But did she pull the trigger? Wield the knife? Wear the boots?"

"I understand from this morning's *New York Post* there might be a motive," said Goldberg. "Something about Jayne's will bequeathing millions to Mrs. Petrov. What's in Aubrey's will?"

"We'll have to get to that," said the chief.

"Will you arrest Dasha Petrov?" asked Goldberg.

"Not today," he said. "She's not a flight risk. She's in the hospital with a heart problem. We'll keep you advised." DeFranco and Tracy Taggart left the examining room. Whereas it had been DeFranco's predilection to go slow with what they could reveal during the sea glass murders case, now it was Tracy's inclination to hold back on what she should tell the mob of media waiting on the front steps of the medical examiner's office. She'd already agreed with a few locals to use her access to assist the gaggle.

"Damn it, Tony," said Tracy. "I'm just not ready to throw Dasha under the bus. There has to be an explanation."

"Think it through," said DeFranco. "Hawkes is the only one so far to point the finger at Dasha, although I'm sure there are some reporters—the lazy ones—who are repeating the allegation. It's not untruthful to say the investigation is continuing."

"I'm getting ready to deliver to the pool the same BS I hate," said Tracy.

"Let me deliver it," said Tony. "We just need to know more about these murders before we can level charges."

"They'll want details," said Tracy.

"Slash to the neck. Stab wounds to the chest," said the chief. "We don't need to get into anything of an evidentiary nature."

In the end the chief made the basic official statement, and Tracy stood with her fellow press members. The press took it in and got ready to dole it out. They gathered around Tracy after the chief was finished, wanting to know more. She fielded the questions with some generalities, and only Adrian Hawkes pushed a theory that seemed to fit his reporting.

"Is the medical examiner matching Jayne's and Aubrey's wounds with Dasha's Petrov's Walther PPK, or her dagger, which she keeps in her chestnut walking stick?" said Hawkes.

It was the crux of the case. Where did he get his information? Tracy knew other media would pick up the storyline.

"Too early to say," said Tracy, her mind reeling. Talk of Dasha's knife, which she'd used to subdue Robert Altman in the case of the sea glass murders, was probably all over town. But how did Hawkes get wind of her Walther?

"We've got a mole," said DeFranco later, when they drove toward Norwalk Hospital and their interview with Dasha Petrov. An early afternoon edition of the *New York Post* was already calling Dasha "The Gold Coast Viper."

17

Mounting Evidence

DeFranco's placard on the dash of the Crown Vic afforded premium parking at Norwalk Hospital, and his badge got them through security and into an elevator leading to the upper floors. They found Dasha in bed, wearing a flimsy hospital gown and an oxygen mask. The machinery by her bed noted Dasha's EKG and blood oxygen level, or pulse ox. There was something dripping into an arm and a tube from a catheter leading into a jug strapped to a pole. Predictably, she was beyond perturbed at her predicament. "Mad as a wet hen," the chief later described it. She brightened when DeFranco and Tracy entered the room.

"Oh, thank God you're here," she said, and Dasha's visitors drew up chairs at her bedside.

"Did you get the man?" she asked.

"I'm afraid we didn't, Dasha," said the chief. "We scoured the beach up and down but couldn't find anyone matching the description you gave Sam before you were transported."

"Oh dear," said Dasha. She looked away, toward a window streaked with rain.

"Dasha, let's talk about you first," said Tracy. "What are the doctors telling you?"

"I'm being held 'for observation,'" said Dasha. "My heart is fine. I just suffered what they call 'orthostatic hypotension,' brought on by exertion. Basically, I fainted. I have to get out of here."

"Dasha," said DeFranco, "let's slow down a little. Your gun and your knife. Did they ever leave your possession?"

"Absolutely not," said Dasha, irked at the very idea.

"Let me tell you what's shaping up here," said the chief. "You need to help me explain this. It's been proven by the ME that your

Walther fired the shots that killed Jayne. It's also been shown that a knife very much like yours produced Aubrey's fatal wounds."

"And Dasha," Tracy added, "your boots match footprints found at both scenes."

"Of course my footprints were at both scenes," said Dasha, anger rising to the surface. "I've walked up and down that beach in front of Barnaby's house for years, and I was at the Aubrey's on a regular basis."

"But Dasha," said Tracy, "the ME has photos of your boot soles in Aubrey's blood. Your boots were at the scene of Michael's murder."

"Plus," said DeFranco, "there's talk that Jayne's will shows you receiving $10 million upon his death. It's a motive, Dasha."

"I know nothing about any of that," she said. "I'm being framed. The real killers are out there, chief. You need to help me find them." Just then, a nurse came in and adjusted the machinery over Dasha's bed.

"Your heart rate is elevated, sweetie," said the nurse. She turned to DeFranco and Tracy. "I'm afraid she's a little upset. I think it would be a good idea for you to leave."

"Wait," said Dasha. She reached for the chief's hand as he rose to go. "My PPK carries seven rounds. I fired two with Aubrey when we were target shooting off his seawall. That leaves five. I fired one into the chest of my attacker inside the Aubrey house. I think he was wearing body armor. Another shot went wide, and my gun was empty. That's four. Where did those three extra rounds go, chief? Somebody used my gun to kill Barnaby." She was agitated, and the nurse was growing impatient.

"We'll come back to talk about it tomorrow," said the chief. They left her as the nurse put the oxygen mask back on her face. She was composed, and her eyes were closed, but the chief and Tracy knew Dasha Petrov's mind was working furiously.

They returned to the chief's car, and Tracy asked the pivotal question: "Do we think she really saw someone in the Aubrey house?" she asked. "In a *Scream* mask?"

"I want to believe it," said the chief. "And don't forget, Sam said she was muttering about a man in that black duster and told him she heard someone upstairs at the Aubrey's. Dasha wouldn't just make it up. You and I know that, but try telling Ferguson."

"Stanley is just doing his job," said Tracy. "Let's stay on the evidence pointing to Dasha. If we can poke holes in it, maybe it will lead us to the real killers."

"Either that, or reinforce the State's case against Mrs. Petrov," said DeFranco. "We've got to be objective, Tracy."

"Let's start with this provision in Jayne's will," said Tracy. "Hawkes is the only one calling it a motive. I would like to see that for myself and talk to the lawyer who drafted it."

"Wouldn't hurt to knock on the widow Jayne's door," said DeFranco. "It's not too late. Means a late supper. Do you mind?"

"Of course not," said Tracy, and the chief aimed his unmarked cruiser toward Beachside Avenue. When they arrived, the gates were closed, and the chief got out to use the intercom. He got back in the car as the gates swung open.

"Mrs. Jayne is a bit testy tonight," he said. "Says we're intruding."

"We won't be long," said Tracy.

"As long as she cooperates," said the chief. This was the part of police work that people seldom saw or appreciated: the late nights, the strained interviews, the devotion to hard physical evidence, not hearsay. The chief used the massive knocker, and they were greeted by Lucy and Jim, Tammy's offspring from her "priors," as Barnaby called them.

"Mom is tired and wants to know if you can come back tomorrow," said Lucy.

"We have just one question for tonight," said DeFranco. "And yes we'll have to come back tomorrow, too. Tell your mom we need to see Mr. Jayne's will. It's very important." Tracy was studying the kids, and she watched little Jim turn visibly red and look to his sister for some kind of guidance. Lucy's face was an impassive blank. She was older, Tracy mused, and more inclined toward the preteen deceptions that kept parents off balance: the petty thievery, subtle lies, and incomplete information that allowed kids to navigate the shoals toward adulthood. Lucy could see the chief and Tracy weren't going anywhere.

"I'll go tell my mom," said Lucy. Jim was more than happy to follow her, and soon Tammy Jayne appeared at the top of the staircase wearing a flowing sheer bathrobe. The chief and Tracy somehow expected puffy eyes and tear-streaked mascara, but Tammy looked like she was in pretty good shape for someone who'd entered widowhood just three days ago.

"How can I help you?" she asked in a nasal accent that Tracy placed somewhere near Flatbush. "It's late."

"Forgive the intrusion, Mrs. Jayne," said the chief in that smooth, confident way that Tracy loved. "We're trying to find the person or persons who murdered your husband. We would like to see his last will and testament."

"Talk to his lawyer," said Tammy. "Scopes, Sneed, and Belding. They can help you. I think he uses Joshua Belding."

Tracy noted her use of the present tense.

"I'm sure he kept a copy here," said DeFranco. "It's highly material to the case."

"All right, but in the future you can't just come barging in here," said Tammy.

"I can get a search warrant," said the chief, adopting a very direct tone. "But we only do that if we think someone is hiding something. I was expecting more cooperation." He was so smooth that Tracy wasn't sure if Tammy realized she was being brought up short.

"He keeps his important papers in the filing cabinet in his closet," said Tammy. "Come this way. DeFranco and Tracy followed her to Barnaby's by-now familiar study. She went to a glass-fronted bookcase, found a Wedgewood box, produced a key, went to his closet, and unlocked his file cabinet. Lucy and Jim were standing in the doorway, watching their mother comply with a request from law enforcement. They seemed to be accustomed to their mother running the show, and now the tables were turned.

"There's a file marked 'Will' in there," said Tammy. "Suit yourself."

The chief moved to the cabinet and found the manila folder. It was empty. He held it up for Tammy to see.

"Oh Lord," said Tammy. "I know it's in there somewhere." Tracy had her eyes on Lucy and Jim. Lucy poked Jim in the ribs, and Jim slapped her. They were acting up and acting out at the wrong time and place.

"You two, cut it out," said Tammy, while the chief continued to sift through the files.

"I think this is it," he said. "It was misfiled under 'Watering System.' Still in the *W*s, though."

The legal-length document was folded thrice and stapled to a blue outer protective sheet. It was thick and refused to lie flat. He fanned through it and got to the money part. Tammy would receive the bulk of the Jayne estate. There was no mention of Dasha Petrov. He went to the signature page and found provisions for a notary, two witnesses, Jayne's signature, and a raised seal created by an embossing stamp. There was a final page interleaved behind the signature page. It was unstapled, not notarized, and not witnessed. It read:

Witnesseth,

Being of sound mind and body, I would like to amend my last will and testament by subtracting $10 million from the bequest granted to my now wife Tamara Garcetti Jayne and give said $10 million to my dear friend and collaborator Dasha Petrov, without whom many of my literary accomplishments would not have been possible.

Signed
Barnaby Jayne
November 12, 1990

"It looks like Mr. Jayne added this addendum without the aid of counsel," said the chief. "Is that his signature?" He held the document up for Tammy.

"It is," she said. "You can compare it with the signature on the previous page."

They were a match as far as the chief could tell.

"This doesn't seem right to me, Mrs. Jayne," said the chief. "You could probably contest this addendum."

"I've already talked to Belding," said Tammy. "He doesn't have a copy of that page and wants to know where it came from."

"You looked at this recently, then," said the chief. "Did you misfile it?"

"I guess so," said Tammy, put off by the chief's challenge.

"Can happen to anybody," said Tracy, trying to play the so-called "good cop."

"One last thing," said the chief. "I want to print out a record of copies made on this machine going back thirty days. Do you mind?"

Tammy looked a bit quizzical, and Lucy was standing her ground, but Jim turned on his heels and ran up the stairs. The chief stroked the correct keys, and a single sheet came out of the machine, listing everything that had been copied during the requested period. There was a line devoted to a photocopy made on April 27, twenty-seven pages. The chief counted the number of pages in Barnaby Jayne's will, and he wasn't surprised the number totaled twenty-seven, including the strange addendum.

"Did you make a copy of this the day after Mr. Jayne was found?" he asked Tammy.

"No, I didn't," said Tammy. "Didn't need to. Belding has everything."

"Curious. We'll be going, then," said the chief. He noticed Lucy couldn't make eye contact. He put the will in the correct folder and closed the file drawer. They watched Tammy lock it and restore the key to its little hiding box—the one that everyone in the household likely knew about, especially Lucy, who absorbed with interest all the actions and reactions of the players in Barnaby's study. When DeFranco and Tracy got to the front doors, the chief turned to Mrs. Jayne.

"I'm afraid you can expect calls from me or my department from time to time in the next few weeks as things come up," he said, "until we find the people who did this."

"Sounds to me like Dasha Petrov tops that list," said Tammy. "I never liked that woman."

The feeling was mutual, thought Tracy.

"Let's check on Galina before we go home," said Tracy as they drove away from the Jaynes' waterside palace, and DeFranco aimed his cruiser toward Seabreeze, the Petrov pile. Satisfied Dasha's sister was comfortable—and after giving reassurances her sister would be coming home soon—they headed toward High Gate Road, last house on the left.

"I'll call Belding in the morning and express my curiosity about that addendum," said the chief. "Looks to me like it was slapped on last minute. It would be easy to contest. I don't think Tammy is in any danger of losing $10 million."

"The addendum achieves the goal of pointing a finger," said Tracy. "That's what it was designed to do, as far as I'm concerned. And while we're looking at Dasha as the potential killer, we're not looking for the people who really did it."

"A proper conspiracy, love," said the chief.

"We have to start somewhere," said Tracy. "Like Dasha says. You have to begin with a theory. And how about that photocopy made on the twenty-seventh? Somebody in the Jayne household did that."

"Who then got it into the hands of Adrian Hawkes, so he could play the hero at catching the Gold Coast Viper," said DeFranco. "It would be interesting to see Aubrey's will. If Dasha's named as a beneficiary . . . "

"A fake beneficiary," said Tracy.

"We'll know we're onto something," he said. "What does Grimes have you assigned to this week?"

"The Gold Coast mystery," said Tracy, "until it's solved. Grimes hasn't had this much fun since the Claus von Bülow case."

They arrived at the home they shared. Tracy dropped her generous sack that carried all her essentials, from lipstick and blush to a little NEC laptop she used to hammer out copy in the front seat of the news team van. She watched the chief remove his Glock and his ankle snubbie and place them in the lockbox in the front closet. They poured a glass of wine, cooked a red snapper fillet they'd caught from the decks of *Paisano, Too*, and talked about Sam's new girlfriend and Tony's daughter Angelica's professional accomplishments. And at the appropriate hour, they climbed the stairs to luxuriate under the covers. DeFranco turned off the bedside lamp, and Tracy folded herself around him like a cat. Five minutes went by in this dark, peaceful bliss, far removed from the intrigues of Beachside Avenue, when Tracy sat bolt upright, turned on the light and said with urgent worry: "Tammy's a Garcetti."

18

Sources

They were at Dasha Petrov's hospital bedside at nine a.m. the following morning. Dasha had perked up a bit. She was enjoying coffee, some orange juice, and a bite of toast. She took a special interest in DeFranco's recap of their visit to the Jayne manor the night before.

"So, a copy was made," said Dasha. "And somehow the pertinent addendum got into the hands of that scoundrel Hawkes. The natural question is, who had access?

"Tammy, of course," said the chief. "And maybe Miguel and Felicity."

"I would rule out the Jaynes' domestic help," said Dasha. "It's been my experience on that street that people toiling in the scullery or the garden are honorable, hardworking individuals with families to support. They would never want to jeopardize their jobs. Having said that, I was never sure about Aubrey's Makita. Bit of a cipher."

"We'll get to the Aubrey home. Let's stick with Jayne. How about Lucy and Jim?" offered Tracy.

"They're certainly clever enough to have a little something going on the side," said Dasha. "And Hawkes is low enough to offer some bribe money to minors in exchange for information."

"In this case, it's the key to the whole case," said DeFranco. "It indicates Mrs. Petrov had the means, the opportunity . . . *and* the motive."

"Always a key ingredient," said Dasha.

"So that leaves the question, how did they get your firearm and your knife?" asked Tracy.

"Let's not leave out the boots," said DeFranco.

"Well . . . it's just a theory," said Dasha.

"Let's hear it," said Tracy.

"Begin with the big picture," said Dasha. "Barnaby and Michael hated each other. And their dirty little tricks had progressed far beyond innocent fun. They wanted to break each other's will, destroy each other's concentration—cause something so dreadful they couldn't work."

"Had it gotten that bad?" asked the chief.

"I think so," said Dasha. "Try as I might, I couldn't get either of them to cease and desist. I mean Aubrey had firebombed Barnaby's car, for heaven's sake. Things were escalating."

"Where was it leading?" asked Tracy.

"I think Barnaby wanted to steal Aubrey's wife. There's no better way to hurt a man," said Dasha. "That's why Barnaby was sitting by the pool on the night of the twenty-fifth. He was waiting for Del to come up the beach. Tammy and the kids were in Turks and Caicos. Barnaby could satisfy his urges and stick it to Michael, so to speak."

"Only way to prove that would be to get them on the witness stand," said the chief.

"For now, it works as a theory," said Dasha. "It sets the stage. And Del had to have had an accomplice. Someone came up behind Barnaby while he was greeting Del down on the beach. This person put a gun to Barnaby's head. Maybe the same someone in the *Scream* mask I saw at the Aubrey residence, chief. I've had my doubts about Tammy and Del. I've seen them kibitzing in the background. They know each other too well. It's like they had a prior life . . . before they landed in clover on the avenue."

Tracy was following Dasha's thread.

"They made a deal to kill each other's husband?" she asked.

"Why not?" said Dasha. "They'd both stand to gain. And they can cover each other's tracks."

"Explains why the wives were out of the country when their husbands were murdered," said the chief. "Ironclad alibis."

"Dasha, let's think," said Tracy. "Gun. Knife. Boots. Your possessions are clearly linked to these crimes. How did that come to pass?"

"I'm not entirely sure, dear, but I know there's an answer," said Dasha. "I need to get out of here so I can get busy."

"The nursing supervisor says you've got one more day of complete bed rest," said the chief. "Tracy and I will get moving and report progress."

"Thank you, chief," said Dasha. "We're the three musketeers." A tear ran down her old cheek.

"Let's visit Mrs. Aubrey," said Tracy as she and DeFranco rode down the elevator . . . and into the unknown.

19

Too Perfect

Tracy Taggart could never quite explain it to the chief, but most women had a strange sixth sense when it came to evaluating members of their own gender. Men would look, admire, and move on to the box scores or the need for an oil change. But women could tell when a fashion accessory was a half season out of date, or when someone's eau de cologne had been applied with too much enthusiasm, or when the telltale bulge around the bra line meant too much time with the cookie dough and not enough time in the gym. Tracy Taggart took one look at Del Aubrey and decided she was a bit too perfect. Most of the well-to-do she'd met in Connecticut preferred country chic, but Del was crisp, creased, powdered, and braced for a new day when she answered the chief's knock on the door.

"We're sorry to bother you, Mrs. Aubrey," he said in that endearing, somewhat bashful, but clearly direct way Tracy loved. "There's a lot of follow-up, and this investigation is nowhere near complete." Tracy thought she detected a slight scowl darkening Del's comely visage. The widow Aubrey wanted it to be over with.

"I want to help," said Del, poised and appropriate, but somehow not altogether pleased. She looked directly at Tracy. "How can I know that what I say isn't going to appear on *NBC Nightly News*?"

The chief responded before Tracy could return the opening serve.

"Miss Taggart is functioning as a consultant to the department, a role she's taken on before," he said.

Tracy knew he was back-pedaling.

"I'm quite happy to remove myself, Mrs. Aubrey, if that will make you feel more comfortable," she said. "And believe me, any journalist will tell you that respecting confidences is a vital part of the job. I am here on deep background."

Del seemed mollified and nodded toward the chief.

"It's all right," she said. "I'll trust you."

"We need to see Mr. Aubrey's will," said the chief.

"I don't know anything about that," said Del, a statement Tracy found laughable.

"I'm sure he kept a copy," the chief persisted.

Del smiled and asked the chief and Tracy to come in. "Where are my manners? It's been a rough few days, as you can imagine. Let's see what we can find in Michael's study," said Del.

The chief had been all through the house as Del was making her way north from Mustique, so he knew the rough layout. But Tracy was seized by the thought and care that had gone into the furnishings. There were old prints and richly hued wallpapers and wide-plank floors. The window treatments and drapery matched perfectly, and the whole package somehow reflected Del's carefully tailored appearance.

"Such a beautiful home, Mrs. Aubrey," said Tracy. "You've obviously put your heart and soul into it."

"Michael's vision and my eye for detail," said Del. "We were a team."

It was the first time Tracy and the chief had detected any outward sign of mourning. Tracy looked outside, saw the yellow police line tape around the gazebo, and wondered if Del yearned for the moment she could restore it to some sense of normalcy. They went into Aubrey's study, where the chief had placed his call to Mrs. Aubrey, notifying her that she was a widow. Del went to a low two-drawer filing cabinet behind Aubrey's desk. She pulled out a drawer, went to the *W*s, and expressed some frustration when she couldn't find the relevant file.

"Try *L* for last will," offered the chief, and Del found the document. To a skeptical Tracy, this fumbling was all for show.

As expected, Aubrey was a man of property, vast wealth, a fleet of vehicles, and a $2 million jet—and it was now all hers. The chief was looking for the telltale addendum, and he found it after the notarized and witnessed signature page. In language and form, it closely matched the Jayne addendum, and it stood out similarly as a piece of legal patchwork that could be contested and tossed out quite easily. It was intended to cast Dasha in the least favorable light as a money-grubbing killer. The chief noted the figure. Mr. Aubrey's friend and mentor Mrs. Petrov was in line to receive another $10 million from her neighbor to the east.

"Were you aware your husband was bequeathing money to Dasha Petrov?" asked the chief.

"I had no idea," said Del, her face a mask, her tone even, her inflection barely surprised. Tracy didn't believe her.

"We heard a lot about the rivalry between Mr. Aubrey and Mr. Jayne," said Tracy. "Is this the case where the famous gun collection once stood?"

"It is," said Del. "Michael was rebuilding his collection. It was sad what took place between Barnaby and Michael."

"Barnaby is suspected of having destroyed his shotguns and rifles. Is that correct?" asked the chief, picking up on Tracy's trail of inquiry.

"Yes, that's right," said Del. "Michael and Barnaby were two of a kind. Always trying to best each other."

"Can we see his handgun collection?" asked Tracy. She was proceeding on blind instinct.

"Sure," said Del. "Pull out the drawer. There are a few things in there."

"I'll be careful," said the chief, knowing the dangers that might accompany touching unfamiliar firearms. Knowing how to unload them and handle them safely was job one, as he learned at his grandfather's knee. He picked up the classic 1902 Bisley, opened the loading gate, and made sure the weapon was unloaded. He dropped the magazine of the .45 1911 automatic Colt Pistol and racked the slide back, clearing the chamber. It was unloaded, too. He picked up the classic Walther. It was identical to Dasha's PPK in .380, but this was the PPK/S variant in .32, an ounce and a half heavier, with an eight-, not seven-, round capacity. The chief dropped the magazine and saw that it was loaded. He pulled the slide back. There was a round in the chamber, ready to fire.

Odd.

"All the handguns are unloaded except this one," he stated flatly to Del. "Any idea why that may be?"

"No clue," said Del.

The chief slid the one loose round from the chamber into the magazine and released the slide on an empty chamber. The gun was safe now. He kept the magazine separate, restored the handgun to the drawer, and closed it.

"We understand your husband liked to spend a lot of time in his workshop," said the chief. He was winging it. "Do you mind if we have a look?"

"Be my guest," said Del. "It's in the basement. I have no idea what he did down there." Tracy was amazed by the disinterest some women showed toward their husbands' lives.

The chief led the way into the basement, and they were struck by all the "stuff" they encountered. The upstairs, Del's domain, was pin sharp. Michael Aubrey inhabited a netherworld where he could investigate the principles and ideas that would later show up as ink on the page.

"Fascinating mind," said Tracy, running her hand over the books on his shelf. "A lot of how-to." Wood, simple electronics, listening devices, firearms . . . any fact Aubrey needed for his work could be summoned on demand.

"Look at this one on locksmithing," said the chief. "He seems to have had an interest in metalwork."

"Key making," said Tracy. "First make an impression out of clay, it says here."

"Wonder if you could make a knife that way," said DeFranco.

"Wouldn't that take hot metal, a forge, and some blacksmith tools?" asked Tracy.

"Why does it need to be metal?" asked the chief. "It just needs to be the same shape. Why not use something ceramic? Seems like it would be easier to work with."

"I had an artist boyfriend, a sculptor," said Tracy. "He used something he called investment casting. But he said ceramic casts take too much work. Once, he made a knife out of the melted-down alloy of a sports-car wheel."

"Hey, no old boyfriends," said DeFranco. "Especially clever ones."

"Down, mister. It's ancient history," said Tracy. "But I'm just thinking out loud. How could Aubrey's killer mimic Dasha's secret knife? Get an impression. Make a form."

"I think they do that with plastic foam now," said the chief. "It's easier to shape. Angelica took an art class one summer, and they fooled around with it."

"After that, pour in molten metal," said Tracy. "Grind, sand, buff, polish. A lot of work. How do you get the metal hot enough to melt?"

"Angelica's class used an electric forge," said the chief, "about the size of a hot water heater. Aren't these mental gymnastics fun?"

Tracy said, "Just trying to figure out how a knife shaped like Dasha's knife—"

"But not Dasha's knife," said the chief.

" —could wind up causing Aubrey's wounds," Tracy completed the thought.

"Lots of planning, time, significant work," said the chief.

"What about attention to detail?" said Tracy. "The same brain that produced Jayne's double-tap head wounds. And Aubrey's fatal injuries. Plus, the elegant ploy of framing an innocent party."

The chief and Tracy Taggart left the Aubrey residence and drove to the Westport Public Safety building on Jesup Street. They swung by Stanley Ferguson's cubicle, and the detective had his feet on his desk, reading the *New York Post*. The page 1 headline screamed GOLD COAST VIPER STRIKES TWICE, then, in a subhead, "Ex-CIA assassin eyed in second kill-for-money scheme."

"Don't tell me," said DeFranco, "Hawkes found out about the change to Aubrey's will."

"We were just with Mrs. Aubrey, and even *she* didn't know about it," said Tracy. "Or so she claims."

"Makita is the only one who had access," said Ferguson. "In any event, the gun, the knife, the boots. We've got to bring Dasha in, chief. For the sake of the department."

"She gets out of the hospital today," said the chief. "I'm going to ask you to interview her at her home. You can handle it with Jameson. Tracy and I are too close. We've got too many conflicts."

"I think that's wise," said Ferguson. "And that's why you're the chief."

DeFranco and Tracy walked to the chief's glass-walled office. Tracy sat down, and the chief closed the door.

"I think that was pretty gallant giving Stanley that assignment," said Tracy.

"Well, I think he's part of a faction that, along with Hawkes, doesn't think it looks too good for Mrs. Petrov," said the chief. "The physical evidence is piling up. But you know—and I know—Dasha's heart, mind, and character. We've gone into battle with her. We believe her. While Stanley is doing his diligence, you and I can dig in on the wives. What did you say Tammy's maiden name was?"

"Garcetti," said Tracy. "As in Paul Garcetti. Leader of one wing of the Gambino crime family. Rubbed out in December 1985 at Sparks Steak House on East Forty-Sixth Street. It was an unsanctioned hit ordered by John Scarpella."

"You've already started doing your homework," said the chief.

"Quick call to an intern to get some basics," said Tracy. "I'm spending the rest of the morning with the microfiche reader at the library. I have to figure out if Tammy is a part of the 'outfit,' as they like to say."

"What about Del?" asked the chief.

"A Garcetti? That would be way too weird," said Tracy. "I'll be chained to a desk in the library if you need me."

"And I've got a department to run," said the chief. "There's a stack of maintenance requisitions on my desk."

He watched her go and noticed she was carrying her purse with the special compartment for her Kimber. Technically she was on assignment, but he was glad she decided to "carry," the sanitized term for concealing a deadly weapon. Her research had suddenly shifted to organized crime.

Broken cruisers, faulty radios, leaky pipes—they all seemed to land on the chief's desk. He organized his plan of attack based on rough priorities. A leaky pipe might have to wait, but a bad radio could get one of his officers hurt. And he had some pull with the local Ford dealership to get his vehicles to the front of the line in the service department. His personnel challenges were under control, and he thought that might have something to do with what he'd learned commanding Swift boats in the Mekong delta. If the skipper spent time with the young people, everyone noticed and seemed to pull harder on the oar. Remaining aloof and out of circulation seemed to breed discontent. Giving young Jameson a chance to work with "Stan the Man" Ferguson would yield a deeper pool of departmental experience. He wondered how he could anoint his son Patrolman Sam DeFranco without showing favoritism.

There was a quick meeting with the first selectman, who wanted to know just what the hell was happening on Beachside Avenue. That was followed by a showdown with his school resource officer, who seemed to have had his back turned during a particularly virulent graffiti attack at Staples High School. Soon, the chief was shaking off this steady drumbeat of responsibility and joining Tracy Taggart in front of the old microfiche contraption at the Westport Public Library.

"I suppose this thing called the internet will do all this work for us in the future," said the chief as he got comfortable on the hard-backed seats.

"That's the word," said Tracy. "But for now, we've got to deal with that card index over there and these spools of plastic over here. You load the full ones on the spindle to the left, run through to your selected issue and page, then load up the reel on the right.

It makes a photocopy you can take with you. After that, rewind. Some fun."

"What have you learned?" asked DeFranco.

"Paul Garcetti was a highly respected figure, as made members of the Mafia go," said Tracy. "He was given the responsibility of running the Gambino family when Carlo Gambino died. Garcetti was no saint, but he concentrated on the white-collar side of the business, cornering the market in concrete. You couldn't build anything in Manhattan without paying Garcetti, and he had deals with all the unions. He was a clever, hardworking businessman."

"And the heroin pushers like Scarpella hated him," said the chief.

"But let's not get ahead of ourselves," said Tracy. "Here's where it gets interesting. Paul had a younger brother named Mario, who had a daughter named Tamara."

"That's our Tammy?" asked the chief.

"I found a wedding picture from the *Staten Island Advance*. Here's a photocopy. That's Tammy with her first husband, Lucas. I have to figure out what happened to Lucas, but I fear for the man's longevity in this family. That's Mario, her dad. That's the big guy, Uncle Paul. And that's Paul and Mario's sister Louisa."

"Happy as clams at high tide," said DeFranco.

"Louisa married a guy named DiCarlo, and they had a son named Donny, and Donny's first wife was a young woman from Queens named Adele," said Tracy.

"And her nickname is Del?" asked the chief. "She's come into the family from the outside. Don't tell me things didn't go too well for Donny and Del."

"Del was a bit of a nonconformist from what I can tell," said Tracy. "In this family, you were supposed to stay at home and make babies. But Del wanted a career, and she got into interior design. She kept her maiden name, DeLormée. After eight years and no babies, she managed to extricate herself. There are all kinds of references to Del DeLormée in the society pages. She married three times—her star, and her bank account, rising with each vow. Then she hit the Aubrey jackpot."

"It appears Del and Tammy kept in touch," said the chief.

"Close touch," said Tracy.

"Anything unnatural befall Del DeLormée's lineup of husbands?" asked DeFranco.

"Accidents," said Tracy. "An auto wreck. A hunting accident. A snapped carabiner in a climbing mishap."

"Jesus," said the chief. "The black widow. So, when Dasha saw Tammy and Del in a huddle, she wasn't imagining things."

"But they needed help, Tony," said Tracy, "if Dasha is right. If Barnaby was meeting Del on the seawall and someone came up behind him, it would take one big guy to lift Barnaby up and plop him in his chair."

"Let's assume two, then," said the chief. "But how did the trigger man get Dasha's gun?"

"It's staring us in the face, Tony," said Tracy, slapping herself in the forehead. "Del or Tammy switched Aubrey's Walther for Dasha's Walther. Dasha was walking around for a few days with a .32 caliber PPK/S in the pocket of her Barbour coat. They took a big risk she wouldn't notice. They used Dasha's gun to shoot Jayne, then managed to get Dasha's gun back into her coat."

"And get the PPK/S back into Aubrey's collection," said the chief. "When we get Dasha in a quiet moment, we'll query her about any occasions she might have been alone with Del or Tammy."

"Or when her coat was available," said Tracy. "But why not the stick, too? Dasha becomes separated from her knife for a minute or two. They make a clay impression. The knife goes back into the stick."

"Boots, Tracy," said the chief. "Dasha's Wellingtons."

"Same plan," said Tracy. "I've seen Dasha leave them in the little vestibule by the back door leading to the kitchen. Del comes down one night and swaps Dasha's boot with that nicked tread-line for another pair. Dasha's wearing a new pair, and Del uses Dasha's boots for her rendezvous with Barnaby. Del gives Tammy the boots for Aubrey's own rendezvous with destiny."

"Well," said the chief, "as theories go, it's a beauty. But it still means we've got one, possibly two, killers on the loose."

20

Pointing Fingers

As the chief predicted, the interview between Dasha Petrov and Stanley Ferguson didn't go well. She'd returned from Norwalk Hospital the next day, and she was anxious to feed her swans, but the detective and his young acolyte, Jameson, were taking up space in her living room and questioning her veracity.

"Let's talk about your pistol, Mrs. Petrov," said Ferguson. "Do you have a license to carry?"

"I'm sure it's around here somewhere, detective," she said. "You do know I carried a gun for a living."

"I'm aware of your history, Mrs. Petrov," said Ferguson, "but you still need a permit in Connecticut. And I am trying to deal with what's in front of us. It's been shown beyond a reasonable doubt that your firearm was used in the commission of a homicide."

"Explain," said Dasha imperiously, which only annoyed Ferguson more.

"Patrolman DeFranco picked up your Walther PPK at the Aubrey residence when you went into the hospital," said Ferguson. "We test fired it and captured the round in a bullet trap. We compared the marks on the test bullet with the bullet fragments from the Jayne murder. Your Walther PPK is most definitely the murder weapon. And that's why Officer Jameson and I are here," he said. "Did your gun leave your possession?"

"Absolutely not," said Dasha. "I take great care with my firearm, which I have owned since 1942, when I served in the Czech underground. You were probably in diapers. As you know, I have been accosted on this property, and on this avenue, and I have taken to carrying my pistol in my Barbour coat. It has not left my side."

"You fired it at the Aubrey residence," said Ferguson.

"I certainly did," said Dasha. "Twice. First time was target shooting with Michael. Two rounds. Two direct hits. Second time, there was man in the process of attacking me. I believe he's the man who killed Michael. I fired another two rounds—one struck my attacker in the chest, another went into a doorframe. It's in your police report."

"The gun was empty when Patrolman DeFranco secured it," said Ferguson. "What is the capacity of that model?"

"Seven rounds plus one in the chamber," said Dasha. "But I never carry it that way. I normally keep seven rounds in the magazine and keep the chamber clear. I rack the slide if I want to chamber a round. It's safer to carry. I am telling you, I fired the pistol twice when I was with Michael the first time."

"That leaves five bullets," said Ferguson.

"And I fired twice at the intruder," said Dasha. "One round hit him in the chest. But I suspect he was wearing body armor. He twisted out of the way, and my second shot missed."

"That leaves three," said Ferguson. "Why was your gun empty when Patrolman DeFranco found it in your possession?"

"I have no idea, detective," said Dasha. "It's what we're all trying to learn."

"Three rounds went into the body of Barnaby Jayne," said Ferguson. "Three rounds from your pistol. It's been proven. Mrs. Petrov, do you want to save us all a lot of time and explain why you might have wanted Barnaby Jayne dead? Was it for the money?"

"Your allegation is preposterous," said Dasha, fuming. "Barnaby was my dear friend and colleague."

"But you stood to gain a lot of money with Barnaby dead," said Ferguson. "The same thing with Aubrey. The medical examiner has shown that a knife identical to yours, if not actually yours, was used to kill him. And for the same reason, Mrs. Petrov. You somehow worked your way into their wills."

Dasha started to feel lightheaded, and sweat broke out on her forehead and upper lip. Jameson saw it.

"Mrs. Petrov, can I get you a glass of water?" the young officer asked.

"The doctor gave me some pills when he released me from the hospital," said Dasha. "I need to find them. Young man, can you bring me my bag? I think it's in the kitchen."

Jameson complied, and Dasha found her pills for her angina.

"Mrs. Petrov," said Ferguson, "I'm sorry to upset you, but we will have to have these questions answered."

"I'll tell you anything you want to know," said Dasha. "As long as it's the truth.

"That will be a good start," said Ferguson. "Why don't you get some rest, and I'll make another appointment tomorrow?"

"Thank you, officer," said Dasha. "This whole experience has been rather trying." When the police left the guesthouse, Dasha put the pill back in its plastic container and took a sip of water. Pills made her woozy and took away her edge.

She had a mystery to solve.

21

Send in the FBI

DeFranco looked across the table at Tre Scalini in New Haven and beheld his love and partner, who was cradling a glass of Chianti and trying to ignore the patrons who recognized her from TV. It seemed like the farther away from New York she traveled, the more buzz she seemed to generate. She was roundly ignored in celebrity-saturated Manhattan, piqued only mild interest on the chief's arm in chic Westport, but caused a stir in the hometown of Yale University. She signed a young lady's menu and turned her attention to the chief, the love of her life.

They were debriefing each other after a trip to the New Haven office of the FBI, where DeFranco's grumpy old friend Reynolds ran the records division. They knew each other through local law enforcement circles, and had even played on opposing softball teams. The chief was delighted to introduce Reynolds to Tracy Taggert. They ran through the normal catch up.

"You still eyeing retirement?" asked the chief.

"Too many kids to put through school," said Reynolds.

"You can always moonlight working security at the mall," said the chief, who spoke from experience.

"I hope we don't keep you too long," said Tracy, capturing the man's attention with her bright green eyes. "We need a crash course in the current tri-state mafia."

"Jesus wept," said Reynolds. "How far back?"

"The Gambinos," said the chief. "But a more recent generation."

"That narrows it down a little," said Reynolds.

"Garcetti in particular," said Tracy.

"Poor Paul," said Reynolds. "Got caught up in the civil war. There has always been tension between the old conservatives who want to steal money the old-fashioned way, through graft and kickbacks, and the young Turks who sell drugs."

"Nothing says it better than the way Scarpella's outfit whacked Garcetti and his bodyguards," said DeFranco.

"Bad one," said Reynolds. "Lucky no civilians got hurt. Scarpella watched it go down from his car across the street."

"We want to find out about any muscle Paul Garcetti might have been using back about twelve years ago," said Tracy.

"Paul had a reputation as a gentleman," said Reynolds, "but he knew how to remove obstacles that got in his way. Usually, the small-time guys who wanted to get in on his act. It didn't turn out so well for a lot of them. You didn't cross Paul."

"Any ideas on who he might have used?" asked DeFranco.

"Let me whistle up this new thing called a database," said Reynolds. "It's hooked up to a big-ass computer called the internet, courtesy of the federal government."

Reynolds stroked a few keys, and the Garcetti file was soon up on the screen, a long list of confidential reports, audio transcripts, and surreptitious photographs. "These are all capos, or captains, the guys who radiate outward from the center of the Garcetti organization and actually pull the levers. They got to these positions because they put in time busting heads when they were younger and in the ranks," said Reynolds.

"Removing obstacles," corrected Tracy. "Gotta start somewhere."

"Exactly," said Reynolds.

"Did Garcetti have any favorites?" asked DeFranco.

"Let's see," said Reynolds. "This is interesting. I forgot this. Scarpella started out as a punk ass-kicker for Garcetti. Very skilled. And then he splintered off a faction, and they went into narcotics, where they still ply their trade. Only now they're getting into opioids and other pain pills, sometimes with dirty doctors."

"I thought Scarpella was behind bars," said Tracy.

"Turnstile court system and a very good lawyer," said Reynolds. "Here's another one, Jimmy 'the Hammer' Lucchese. Mean bastard. Likes axes and machetes. Known for making a mess. He's definitely in jail. Attica. Here's another one . . . a real Garcetti favorite, almost part of the family."

Tracy looked at DeFranco and he returned the glance.

"What's his name?" asked DeFranco.

"Nicky 'the Artist' Addonizio," said Reynolds. "Mother worked in the Garcetti kitchen. Nicky played piano for the Garcetti dinner parties. Genius. Paul sent him to school."

"Where did he go?" asked Tracy.

"Rhode Island School of Design," said Reynolds. "Learned woodworking, metalworking, sculpture . . . very precise handling of tools and materials. Great illustrator. Kept up with his piano."

"How did he get involved in Garcetti's outfit?" asked Tracy. "Seems to me like he'd be destined for other things."

"He loved Paul," said Reynolds. "He'd do anything for him. Paul resisted, but Nicky wanted in, so he gave him a few low-key assignments, and it turns out Nicky had an aptitude. He also made good money, and he could support his mother."

"Did Nicky ever get busted?" asked DeFranco.

Reynolds stroked a few keys and brought up Addonizio's arrest record.

"He went to Sing Sing for five years on some kind of bullshit racketeering charge," said Reynolds. "Best the US attorney could come up with, just to take him off the streets. It's part of the RICO Act. It's not a single criminal charge but a blend of activities that combined are called the rackets."

"From what I hear, Sing Sing is like grad school for guys in the outfit," said DeFranco. "You haven't made it until you've done real time, and you learn a lot of the ins and outs when you're inside."

"You got that right," said Reynolds.

"So, do we know if Nicky the Artist has 'whacked' anybody, as they like to say?" asked Tracy. Reynolds stroked more keys, and Nicky's résumé spilled forth.

"He's suspected but not charged in twenty-three assassinations," said Reynolds. "Not a bad number for a youngster. And he's never gotten caught."

"What's the MO?" asked DeFranco.

"None of this Umberto's Clam House Sunday dinner with the family stuff. The way they got Joey Gallo. Right out in the open," said Reynolds. "No. Nicky takes his time, gets his guys alone, doesn't leave much of a trace and certainly no witnesses. One of the reasons they call him 'the Artist.'"

"Clever enough to get other people to take the blame?" asked Tracy.

"Nicky? Sure. There's a note here. He's got a pattern. Double tap to the back of the head. Then one through the mouth for good measure. Use somebody else's gun. Thoughtful. Very detail oriented. Maybe that's why Paul liked him," said Reynolds.

Tracy and DeFranco looked at each other. Dots were connecting.

"Do you have a physical description?" asked DeFranco.

"Do you think you're onto something he might be involved in?" asked Reynolds.

"Too early to tell," said DeFranco, wondering why he decided to be coy. Just being cautious. Involvement by the Artist was nothing more than a theory at this point.

"Okay, but be careful," said Reynolds. "Nicky is not a nice guy."

"Photo? Anything?" asked DeFranco.

"Printing it out," said Reynolds. "Mug shot and some clandestine surveillance stuff. But Nicky likes to change his appearance."

"Has he ever used a mask?" asked Tracy.

"All the time," said Reynolds. "And he's a master of disguise. Here's a description: *Suspect is five feet, seven inches tall. Slender build, but works out. Nice dresser.*"

"Good-looking," said Tracy.

"Movie-star quality," said DeFranco. "But he sounds a little small for the kind of job we had in Fairfield County where he might be considered a suspect. Does he work with anybody?"

"Yeah," said Reynolds. "Guy named Donny. Last name DiCarlo. They did time together."

"Big guy?" asked Tracy.

"Six three, two thirty. Good size," said Reynolds. "Kind of a meathead, according to a note here."

"He doesn't have to be brilliant," said DeFranco. "Nicky's the brains. Do you have a photo of DiCarlo?"

"It's printing," said Reynolds. "So, you're going to tell me what this is all about, right? It doesn't have anything to do with that Russian lady, does it? What was her name?"

"Mrs. Petrov?" said DeFranco.

"She was involved in stopping that serial killer," said Reynolds.

Tracy saw that the chief wanted to change the subject. "That had a happy ending," she said.

"Hey, I'm taking this young lady to Tre Scalini tonight. What's your favorite entrée?" asked DeFranco.

"I always go with the veal," said Reynolds, and Tracy and DeFranco withdrew after handshakes and a slap on the back and "Let's get together one of these days real soon." As they were walking through the lobby, Reynolds turned to Tracy and said, "I swear I've seen you on television."

"I get that a lot," she said, and they escaped into the night.

Tracy was picking at her lasagna, and the chief was mildly mesmerized by the veal, thanks to Reynolds.

"I swear we could do this at home," he said.

"Flash your badge in the kitchen, and I'm sure they'll give you the recipe," said Tracy.

"You're always the one with the good ideas," said the chief. "What did you think of our FBI friend?"

"Useful," said Tracy. "Nicky's MO fairly screams a connection."

"It's his trademark," said the chief. "But you said something about Del's first husband, Donny?"

"You heard it right," said Tracy. "Donny is Louisa's son, Paul and Mario's nephew. And yes, Louisa's married name was DiCarlo."

"So, Del still has a thing for Donny," said DeFranco.

"My take?" said Tracy. "Donny is crazy about her, but she's moved on. Reynolds called him a meathead. But Del finds him useful. And Tammy is still Mario's little girl. She'll always be a Garcetti. Nicky Addonizio probably pushed her on the swings at Uncle Paul's. Nicky and Donny are happy to help Del and Tammy build their nest eggs."

"Plausible," said the chief.

"Let's share this with Dasha and see what she thinks," said Tracy.

"On deep background," said DeFranco. "By rights I should bring Stanley in on the Garcetti angle."

"How is he going to handle that?" asked Tracy.

"Not well," said the chief. "Stanley is all black-and-white. He doesn't do well with amorphous tangents and convoluted conspiracies."

"Do we even discuss Nicky and Donny with him at this point?" asked Tracy.

"I think it needs to gel," said DeFranco.

22

Domestic Duties

A safe house was just a necessary evil in Nicky Addonizio's line of work. He'd inhabited dilapidated tenements, drafty warehouses, an abandoned car, a cargo container—all in the name of getting close to the subject without putting his name on a hotel register. As safe houses went, the double-wide trailer in the little park behind the car dealership on the Post Road in Westport afforded the basics of heat, light, a kitchen, modest furnishings, a television, and two bedrooms. That last feature was a must, because he would not under any circumstances share a bedroom with Donny DiCarlo, who became fragrant after a day or two in the field. Donny explained that during big jobs he became lost in the mission and just let himself go. Nicky suspected it didn't take a job for Donny to stop bathing. No wonder Del wanted to ditch Donny and begin her polyamorous journey those many years ago. But Donny would still do anything for Del, and Nicky would do anything for Tammy, who was like a sister, including the familial baggage. And that's how Nicky and Donny found themselves together on a quiet Friday night, Donny contentedly slicing garlic for a pasta sauce and Nicky slowly sanding a sandalwood box he was making for his little niece Lucy. Of course, they weren't blood relations, but when the Garcettis took you in, you were in.

The plan was proceeding brilliantly, except for that round Donny caught in the chest, blocked as expected by his body armor. He said it was like a bad bee sting, but the raised welt and the vivid blues, purples, and mustard yellow of the bruise suggested it was more than an insect bite. Nicky determined Donny's ribs were intact and told him to walk it off. He was happy their operation had been aided and abetted by that fool Adrian Hawkes at the *Post*, who was annealing the old Russian lady's reputation as a stone-cold CIA-trained killer. Lucy helped get that rolling with her call to the Hawkes Talks tip line, and she also helped plant the addenda to the Aubrey and Jayne wills. Del and Tammy were never in any danger of losing ten mil each. It would be easy to show the addenda were nothing more than Mrs. Petrov's tawdry money-grubbing. Lucy did a nice job of devising a way Jayne and Aubrey could sign blank sheets to lend an air of authenticity. Lucy even copied the relevant passage from the Connecticut family law code and typed it into place.

The knife. He was proud of that.

He'd needed to take the clay impression to his studio in the city, make a plug out of Styrofoam, build "gates" or pipes to pour in molten alloy, and make perfect copies of the old woman's blade. He'd looked it up. Standard-issue German paratrooper's two-edged dagger. Real piece of work. Collector's item. He gave it a wooden handle, sharpened it, and they were off to the races.

So, everything was working out.

Except now that they had Mrs. Petrov nicely teed up as their perpetrator, it was time to finish her, too. She was the patsy, highly expendable. And how convenient the old crone wound up in the hospital after the encounter at the Aubrey place? Now she could die of a heart condition and no one would ever know. This is where some serious research was needed. This is where he'd earned his keep.

Surgeons stop a human heart during vascular repair using a flood of potassium. The heart-lung machine takes over, and surgery can commence. Slick. Afterward, surgeons deliver an electric shock to the heart muscle, and the patient's heart is back in business. But doctors in Australia had just found a combination of two drugs that stopped the heart without the potassium: an injection of adenosine and lidocaine. They're undetectable. Poor old girl was going to have cardiac arrest.

She'd had a good run.

23

Paint by Numbers

It was Monday, May 2, and Barnaby Jayne had been dead seven days, Michael Aubrey five. Tracy Taggart, Anthony DeFranco, and Dasha Petrov felt like they were in the eye of a hurricane. They sat in the living room in the guesthouse and sensed the great pitch and moment of events hurtling toward a crescendo just outside Dasha's door. The chief wanted to lower the temperature and dial back the pressure mounting on his old friend. It was just like Tracy to sense this, too, and she gently guided Dasha toward memories of a different time, a time that offered more clarity, perhaps.

"When did you know you wanted to enter the field of intelligence, Dasha?" she asked.

"In the beginning, G-2, the intelligence wing of the US army, was a meal ticket and shelter for me and my family. My sponsor, Marcus Willoughby, lavished us with kindness, and I wanted to please and outperform. I was just a refugee thrown into the translator pool. My languages opened the doors. But then I learned about all the blessings of America, and I wanted to protect my adopted country with all my strength," she said softly.

"What's your assessment at this stage of your life?" asked the chief. "Is it still 'my country, right or wrong'?"

"America has made mistakes," she said. "There's no doubt about that. We've misjudged and overreacted and abandoned any sense of finesse in too many spheres. But we have also protected what Churchill called 'the last best hope.' The Kennedy murders showed both sides of the coin. Kennedy wasn't frightened by extending a hand to our Soviet competitors to lower the temperature after the Cuban Missile Crisis, to end our dependence on nuclear weapons. But his CIA—my CIA—believed in fomenting the East-West hysteria and had an interest in seeing it continue. That's what gave us Vietnam and more than fifty thousand American men and women killed, plus countless Vietnamese."

"But still, you kept up the fight," said Tracy.

"We still needed to understand the intensions of people who would do us harm," said Dasha. "There will always be spies and spying. And I was cursed by being good at it."

"Tell me about your interview with Detective Ferguson," said the chief. He enjoyed listening to Dasha, too, but Tracy knew the man had a murder to investigate.

"He's just doing his job," said Dasha, "and I know why you had to send him to me, chief. You need an honest broker, somebody with a second opinion. But he's sadly lacking in imagination. He's all paint by numbers. Sometimes you have to remove the blinkers and look around corners."

"What did he present you with?" asked Tracy.

"My gun. My knife. My boots," said Dasha. "They were at both crime scenes. Therefore X."

"We believe you, Dasha," said Tracy. She told her old friend her theories about the switch with Aubrey's Walther, the possibility of a clay mold as the first step in cloning her knife, the chance her boots might have been purloined from her back vestibule.

Dasha was impressed.

"You've done a lovely job advancing a plausible theory," said Dasha, "but it's still just a theory. It remains to be proven. I shudder to think how I might have been manipulated. I knew Del and Tammy were up to something, and I now can see where they might have had outside help. That's where the threats will come."

"But now we have to protect you," said Tracy.

"The process needs to play out," said Dasha. She turned to DeFranco. "We need to draw the killers into the open, chief. We need a clear field of fire."

"Without anyone getting hurt," said DeFranco. "Nicky Addonizio and Donny DiCarlo are bad dudes. And Nicky seems to be smarter than your average hit man. He's got a talent for deception."

"So Dasha," said Tracy, "you know what it's like to be the target, sad to say. Do we just wait until they knock on the door here at Seabreeze?"

"It's a little too obvious," said Dasha, "and I don't think they would get close enough. If Nicky is as smart as you say he is, he'll see the wrong car in the driveway, sense some kind of movement behind the curtains, and bide his time."

"What's the alternative, Dasha?" asked the chief.

"Let's let the atoms form into molecules," she said. "Now that I know I'm their patsy, served up to shield Del and Tammy, I think I know how to smoke these two out. Don't forget, I've been targeted by the best."

24

Body of Evidence

The chief and Stanley Ferguson were locked in a profound disagreement, and the chief knew he had to let Stanley win.

"We have to bring her in, Tony," said Ferguson, reverting to the familiar behind closed doors. "We've got probable cause right now on the physical evidence. And we might turn up more when we search her premises."

"I don't know," said the chief. "She's a frail old woman, and I smell a setup. The evidence looks planted." He was giving Ferguson some pushback, and he hated being less than frank. He knew it was necessary to arrest Dasha, but he also wanted to make it look like it was Stanley's idea. "She just doesn't fit the profile," said DeFranco, injecting the right note of exasperation.

"Beg to differ," said Ferguson. "Mrs. Petrov is a trained killer, courtesy of the US government. You were at the scene when she stopped Altman. She knows how to use that knife of hers, and she doesn't hesitate. And she no doubt popped a few bad guys during her time with the CIA in Berlin and French Indochina. She doesn't shy away from a fight. "

"She just turned eighty-one, Stanley," said the chief, "and Jayne and Aubrey were her friends. I'm just not seeing it."

"I dug into her finances, chief," said Ferguson. "She's overspent her bank accounts, her modest brokerage accounts, and her CIA pension, just trying to keep her place going. The property taxes on that street are insane."

The chief was privy to Mrs. Petrov's reserves, but he didn't feel it was the time or place to bring that up. She'd spent a lot of money on Seabreeze in the past three years—from a secret treasury she'd fallen into, courtesy of the serial killer central to the sea glass murders. Still, the chief would concede, that nest egg would not last forever.

"I want to subpoena her bank accounts," said Ferguson, "and tie her heavy outflows to the need to tap into the Aubrey and Jayne estates. That's her motive. I think the state's attorney will agree."

"Be careful going down a rabbit hole, Stanley," said the chief. "The wives had just as much motive to bump off their husbands."

"Let me bring in Mrs. Petrov," said Ferguson. "The wives will have to come in at some point, too. But let's start the process with Dasha. The physical evidence is massive. The town won't understand our failure to act if we don't bring her in. And she needs to explain the financial part."

"Okay," said the chief, "but I'll pick her up with Sam, and you can handle the interview. I don't want to upset her. I worry about her heart condition."

"I appreciate that, Tony," said Ferguson, "but this town needs closure."

"I get it," said the chief, a sentiment he recalled when he looked at a sad, depleted Dasha Petrov in the sterile interview room at the Westport Public Safety building on Wednesday, May 4. Stanley had opened with the timeline and wanted to know Mrs. Petrov's whereabouts on the night of the Jayne murder.

"The twenty-fifth of April, Mrs. Petrov. It was only a week or so ago," said Ferguson.

"Horrible night," said Dasha, a tear forming and slowly sliding down her wrinkled cheek.

"Can you tell us where you were that night?" asked Ferguson gently.

"I was with my sister at home. We had soup for supper and watched the news," said Dasha.

"Did you go outside?" asked the detective.

"Oh yes," said Dasha. "There was a full moon. The night was clear, and I could hear the geese calling to each other out on the water."

"So, you went to the beach?" said Ferguson.

"Of course I went to the beach," said Dasha. "The beach is my home."

"Did you go down to the Jayne estate?" he asked.

"I don't remember." She looked down and away.

"The evidence indicates your Wellington boots were in the sand in front of Barnaby Jayne's steps leading to the top of his seawall."

"How do you know they were my boots?" asked Dasha. The chief was wondering if she was trying to be evasive, and her putative attorney, Kelly, so far didn't sense anything that put his reluctant client in jeopardy.

"This is a photo and a footprint taken of your boots at the medical examiner's office. Your boots are distinguished by this nick here," said Ferguson, pointing a pencil at the third tread line. "This is the casting we took at the murder scene on the morning of April 26. You see this nick here?" He pointed to the casting. "This matches the nick there." He pointed to the photograph. "Any jury would place you at the crime scene."

The youngster Kelly woke up. "Chief, I have to object to this speculation. Mrs. Petrov has indicated she's been up and down that beach on a daily basis. There's plenty of reasonable doubt."

DeFranco turned to Dasha.

"Do you want to continue this, Dasha?" he said. "You don't have to. You have the right to remain silent," he said.

"Yes, let's continue. We need to put this nonsense to rest," said Dasha. "I didn't kill my friends, Detective Ferguson. And while you're harassing me, you're not pursuing the real killers."

"This is not harassment," said Stanley. "We're all just trying to get to the bottom of things."

Kelly spoke up. "Mrs. Petrov, you don't have to say anything," he said.

"I was interrogated by the Gestapo, young man," said Dasha. "I think I can handle Detective Ferguson."

"If you take the boot prints and marry them to the fact that your gun fired the fatal shots . . . ," said Ferguson.

Kelly felt moved to intervene and addressed DeFranco. "Chief, she doesn't have to respond."

"Chief, who is this man?" asked Dasha. "I told you I didn't need a lawyer."

"He's trying to protect you, Dasha," said DeFranco.

"It's clear my gun fired the fatal shots," she said.

Kelly began to sputter at what appeared to be an admission. Ferguson turned to the lawyer.

"I have enough to charge her right now on the Jayne murder," he said. "The case is coming together on the Aubrey killing. A knife very much like hers caused Michael Aubrey's fatal wounds. Hers boots were at that scene, too."

"Detective, this is not a courtroom, and this is not a trial," said Kelly.

"No, it's not," said Ferguson. "But I've got more than enough to book her."

Even the chief had to yield the point.

Kelly spoke. "If it leads to a charge tonight, she needs to be released on her own recognizance," he said. "She's hardly a flight risk, and she's not a danger to anyone."

"Tell that to Mrs. Jayne and Mrs. Aubrey," said Ferguson. "Chief, can I have a moment?" Ferguson nodded toward the door, and DeFranco got to his feet. He glanced at Dasha, and he detected a slight smile.

"Dasha, I'll just be a minute," he told her as he followed Ferguson out of the room. To Kelly, who remained seated, Dasha seemed to doze in her chair. Ferguson and the chief reconvened in the hallway.

"I am recommending an arrest. Tonight. And the people of this town need to see she's put in jail. She'll make bail and be back at home tomorrow," said Ferguson.

"Stan, she's an old woman," said the chief.

"She's a danger to society," said Ferguson. "She's pulled off two homicides inside a week. In the town we both care about. I talked to the first selectman. He wants to see some action."

"Stanley, the representative town meeting is my responsibility," said DeFranco. "You've overstepped."

"The first selectman doesn't think you can be objective on this," said Ferguson. "We need to arrest her, put her in jail for at least a night, let her make bail, and let the state's attorney handle the evidence when he marches this thing toward a trial. It's in everyone's interest. Especially yours."

"Why are you suddenly so interested in my hide?" asked DeFranco.

"I just see us heading for a big cockup," said Ferguson. "We can book her. Keep her comfortable. And we can arraign her tomorrow morning. She'll be home by noon."

"If she can make bail," said the chief. "It's double homicide, Stanley."

"I'm sure the judge will take her age into consideration," said Ferguson. "But understand, chief, we'll need to perp walk her to get fingerprinted."

It was an old police tradition. March the suspects before a salivating press corps so the community could see some action—and get the arresting officers' names up in lights.

"She can handle it," said DeFranco, resigned, floating along with the swiftly moving currents. "I've got to get her to sign on with Cohen and Wolf. She can't represent herself. She's already stoked too much speculation."

"That's where we disagree, chief," said Ferguson. "Personally, I'm convinced she did it. Nothing speculative about it."

DeFranco went back into the interview room and explained to Dasha what was about to happen. She smiled sweetly.

"You said the press will be in the room?" she asked.

"Unavoidable," said the chief.

"Delightful," she said. Kelly asked to accompany her through the process, and she agreed. "But I'll want Ken if things go further, young man."

For Dasha, entering the legal system was just as aggravating as she expected—handcuffs chafing her old wrists, the hot lights from the television cameras, the shouted questions. Detective

Ferguson effected a prolonged and painstaking effort to get her fingerprinted in front of the cameras. She saw Tracy at the front of the swarm, which offered a brief moment of comfort. But she also saw that cretin Adrian Hawkes—plus a young man who held a notebook and distinguished himself by his look of complete composure. He didn't seem like he was on deadline. Five seven, slight, muscular build, dark Italian good looks, and long hands that appeared capable of playing the piano. He had a penetrating gaze, and he gave Dasha every impression he was attending the affair neither as a member of the press nor as a disinterested party.

She started the evening in a holding cell and was joined by an inebriated young man who curled himself into a corner. At midnight, she was moved to a jail cell, and she was glad to see it had a single bunk, an acceptable mattress, a scratchy wool blanket, and a pillow with a clean pillowcase. She'd been in far worse jails. In the corner, there was a stainless steel toilet with no seat and enough paper to attend to her hygiene, should the need arise. As the door was being closed, she saw a large man in a coverall with the silhouettes of a mouse and a termite stitched on the back under the letters *RISD*. Dark, decent looking, and big, he kept to himself and went about his duties setting plastic rodent traps. But he looked up from time to time to inspect the old Russian lady they said killed those two guys on Beachside Avenue.

Dasha was pleased.

They were coming to get her.

And they weren't wasting any time.

25

The Smell of Trouble

DeFranco called the lockup and learned Dasha had been moved from the holding cell to a jail cell, with the standard-issue pillow and blanket. She insisted on no special treatment, so he resisted the idea of doubling the watch and arranging greater privacy. A check kiter and a DUI were in adjacent cells tonight, but for all intents and purposes, it was a quiet night at the Jesup Street station.

DeFranco and Tracy went back to their abode on High Gate, and Tracy fiddled with a personal computer while the chief engineered a big salad with anchovies, hard-boiled eggs, and fingerling potatoes. Preparing dinner let him take his mind off things. Tracy, meanwhile, inserted the disk the chief had taken from Barnaby Jayne's study with the "Family" folder clearly labeled. In the press of work, with a second homicide now dominating their thoughts, they hadn't had a chance to peer into the contents. Tracy clicked the mouse, and a dozen or so subfolders spilled across the screen. They were marked "Cars," "Miguel," "Felicity," "Property Improvements," and with other titles that spoke to mundane facets of modern living. One folder was marked "Tammy," and she opened it to find more folders for "Jim" and "Lucy," along with her rather impressive expenses. Her 1991 calendar, beginning January 1, was clearly labeled. Tammy had blocked out April 24 through April 30 for her vacation in Turks and Caicos and had met with a company called RISD Pest Control every Wednesday in March and April.

The chief opened a bottle of Sancerre, and they ate their salad and consumed their wine, and the conversation covered dinner-party plans, an eagerly anticipated walk in the woods, and getting their Grand Banks trawler, *Paisano Too*, ready for spring commissioning. It was these little intimacies that created the edifice of their life together. Tracy did the dishes, and the chief called the station house to check on their prisoner. He learned she was sleeping soundly, and all was well.

Tracy and DeFranco toddled off to bed, and they were soon spooning into position for their well-earned slumber—when Tracy sat up in bed and turned on her bedside light. As usual her red hair was tousled, and her flannel nightie was slightly open, giving DeFranco a moment's pause. But he collected himself— and read Tracy's mind. Something was wrong.

"We shouldn't have left her alone," said Tracy.

"It's what she wanted," said the chief.

"What did Reynolds say about Nicky's alma mater?" asked Tracy.

"Rhode Island School of Design," said the chief. "Nicky's got a knack."

"RISD?" said Tracy.

"Those are the school's initials," said the chief.

"Tony, Tammy had RISD Pest Control in her calendar every week in March and April," said Tracy.

"Why do I know that name?" said DeFranco, pausing. "We found some mouse droppings in the lockup. The RISD name popped up on an ad flyer, and they made a follow-up call. I gave them a quick assignment to see what they could do."

"Were they there today?" asked Tracy.

"Not sure," said DeFranco. "Let me call the desk sergeant." He picked up the phone, dialed, muttered a few sentences, and looked at Tracy. He turned white.

"They're at the station now," said DeFranco. "Some kind of special nighttime inspection service."

"I have a bad feeling," said Tracy.

"I've learned to trust those bad feelings," said the chief.

"Something else has been bothering me . . . I've been around the press in Fairfield County enough to know most of the players, usually by name if not by sight. There was one guy at Dasha's booking tonight I didn't recognize. Medium height and build, dark Italian—almost as good-looking as you."

"Don't make me laugh," said DeFranco. "I didn't see him, but I was busy with other things."

"You don't suppose that was Nicky, do you?" asked Tracy.

DeFranco looked at her—hard.

"Basement. Strong room," said DeFranco in that urgent yet understated way Tracy adored.

He was out of bed putting on his pants, and Tracy was shifting into slacks, a blouse, and a sweater. A minute later they were out the door and down the stairs. They got to the cellar, and DeFranco used his keys to open a double steel door. Ever since the case of the sea glass murders, they'd paid extra attention to matters of personal security. DeFranco had installed the secure locker to contain certain high-value tools. The chief had transitioned to a full-frame Glock 17, consigning his little snub-nosed .38 to an ankle holster for backup. Tracy, the Hoosier Marine Corps veteran, preferred her Kimber in .45 ACP. And they both went in for a matching pair of Remington .12-gauge riot guns loaded with 00 buckshot. In the world of international journalists, there was a small coterie of fellow correspondents who would understand Tracy's professional interest in Kevlar body armor. But few could match Tracy Taggart's quiet appreciation for self-reliance when it came to defending herself, or her love, the chief of police, who was donning his tactical carry vest over his body armor and loading it with extra magazines of nine-millimeter Parabellum. They made their way upstairs toward the kitchen door leading to the driveway. They were in the chief's unmarked Crown Vic, rolling, in less than seven minutes from the moment their feet had hit the bedroom floor. The chief radioed the desk sergeant to stop and hold the technician from RISD Pest Control, and to approach with caution. "He's considered armed and dangerous. Call for backup."

However, as with many police activities, there was always the danger of arriving at the scene of the crime a half step too late.

26

Any Weapon Will Do

When she entered her cell in the small lockup under the Jesup Street station, Dasha knew her first order of business was to find or fashion some kind of weapon. She'd experienced the same challenge back in the Gestapo dungeon in the basement of the Petschek Palace, down the street from Prague's imposing Národní Museum. Back then, pieces of cloth pulled from the lining of her skirt might have served as a makeshift garrote, and a length of wood pried from a bunk could be fashioned into a club or a shiv. She cursed the modern conveniences in the average American jail. There was no glass in the windows, because there were no windows. And her metal cot was riveted together in such a way it would be difficult to pull apart. A shoe might work as a club, the pillowcase could offer a quick blindfold, and the blanket wrapped tightly around the neck might render any attacker unconscious until help arrived. And, as always, Dasha Petrov, the elderly pensioner, enjoyed the element of surprise.

She laid awake, contemplating these possibilities, when she heard the sharp metal-on-metal clank of a key in a lock and then a squeaky hinge as the door to the cell next to hers was opened.

"Pest control," said the officer, only to be greeted by the sleepy surliness of Dasha's next-door occupant.

She had removed the pillowcase and it was under her blanket, which was untucked and ready. She heard the key inside the lock of her cell door, and she contemplated a rough outline of what might come next. The night officer opened the door and stepped aside. He immediately went down to the ground, bleeding and unconscious, after a blunt object wielded by the heavyset man from RISD Pest Control connected with the back of the officer's head. The heavyset man entered her cell. He knelt over her bed, and she could see a hypodermic needle in the half-light washing down the hall. It was in his right hand as he bent at the waist and lowered himself, arm extended. He held the hypodermic in his fist like a knife. He was ready to stab her in the chest, and he had his thumb on the plunger. When he was low enough, with the needle hovering, she whipped the pillowcase over his head, and he stood. She got out of bed and worked her way behind him with the blanket, throwing it over his head, then hit him in the face repeatedly with the heavy heel of her shoe. Stunned, he struggled to get the blanket and the pillowcase off his head, and he let go of the hypodermic needle, which landed intact on the mattress. Dasha picked it up and jabbed it through the man's sleeve into the fleshy part of his tricep. It didn't take long for Donny DiCarlo to crumble in a heap at her feet, just as Chief DeFranco and Tracy Taggart arrived on her cell block, shotguns shouldered and safeties off.

Next, the chief was on the radio requesting backup and an ambulance. Tracy checked on Dasha, then went back to the injured officer. She applied direct pressure using the pillowcase to sop up the blood, then advised DeFranco how to perform chest compressions on the assailant, who was out cold on the floor. Her training as a corpsman was kicking in.

"Dasha, there's an automated external defibrillator in the office, hanging on the wall," said Tracy. "Go grab it, and we'll see what we can do for this guy."

Dasha complied and came back with a small valise marked *AED*. Tracy took the box out while the chief continued compressions. She opened the man's coveralls and stuck two probes to his skin, one on the center of his sternum, over his heart, and one on the side of his chest. She shouted, "Clear," the chief withdrew, and she pushed a green button. Dasha's attacker bounced once, and the color returned to his cheeks. Tracy put her ear to his chest and sensed he could breathe on his own. The chief rolled him on his side and handcuffed him.

Donny DiCarlo was alive.

27

Bad News

The next day, Adrian Hawkes awoke fully clothed face down on his Murphy bed at his Murray Hill studio. The night before, he'd been the toast of the Blarney Stone, where the gin martinis flowed freely. He'd walked in at nine p.m. with the bulldog edition of the next day's *Post*. His page 1 headline had been an inspiration: Angel of Death, Ex-CIA KILLER CHARGED IN GOLD COAST MURDERS.

His Hawkes Talks article opposite Page Six was another "luminous gem of lucidity," as he described it to his fans, who made sure Adrian never lacked a drink.

THE LADY KILLED TWICE

Retired CIA agent Dasha Petrov was booked on charges of double homicide yesterday in Westport, Connecticut, facing allegations in the brutal slayings of two of America's most beloved mystery writers.

The elderly grand dame of Westport's tony Beachside Avenue was motivated by greed, according to sources close to the investigation. She'd inveigled both Barnaby Jayne and Michael Aubrey into naming her in their last wills. She then callously murdered them, according to the charges filed. Jayne was discovered with three well-placed gunshot wounds to the head on the morning of April 26. The Fairfield County medical examiner's office linked Jayne's fatal wounds to Mrs. Petrov's classic Walther PPK.

His neighbor and rival Michael Aubrey was found stabbed to death two days later, his throat mercilessly cut by a knife bearing the same shape and size as the knife Mrs. Petrov keeps hidden in her walking stick.

The murders of Aubrey and Jayne have sickened the well-heeled bedroom community, and indeed they've sent the entire Gold Coast reeling in their unseemly aftermath.

Mrs. Petrov retired as an intelligence officer in the Central Intelligence Agency after more than forty years of service. She was born in czarist St. Petersburg, later Leningrad, and earned a reputation in postwar Europe as one of America's most efficient, if not prolific, operatives.

"She was fearless," said one former colleague, who preferred to remain anonymous. "She could work her way into and out of any situation and come away with secrets the opposition didn't know it had. She could also remove any obstacle—and that often meant proficiency in all kinds of weapons."

Westport police chief Anthony DeFranco declined to comment after the Petrov arrest, but Detective Stanley Ferguson told Hawkes Talks that Mrs. Petrov's footwear had been connected to both crime scenes following a detailed forensic examination.

Barnaby Jayne's funeral is scheduled for tomorrow. Michael Aubrey's funeral arrangements have not been announced.

Watch this space as the Connecticut state's attorney builds his case.

~

Hawkes's reporting that day, which culminated in this breathless dispatch, included interviews with Dasha's former colleagues in McLean, Virginia; revelations from a Soviet-era competitor who had run afoul of Mrs. Petrov in Moscow; plus a backgrounder from an old CIA hand who offered a catalog of verifiable violence she'd committed for God and country. Hawkes had had chats with her Beachside Avenue neighbors, who expressed surprise and sadness at the events' ugly turn.

As he was regaining consciousness, Hawkes was wondering if Lucy and Jim, or even Makita, might furnish more nuggets from the Jayne and Aubrey files—and he reminded himself he'd need to visit the accounting department soon to collect more bribe money.

He got to his feet, stripped off his stinking clothes, and stood in the shower for a few sobering minutes. Wrapped in a towel, he walked to his galley kitchen and made coffee. Desperate for a drink, he twisted the cap off an airplane bottle of Stolichnaya, downed it in two gulps, and felt somewhat restored. He got into his last pair of clean underwear, found a shirt from the previous week, and put the same suit back on. He needed to make the 12:05 out of Grand Central. Keys, wallet, pen, notebook, cash, flask of Bombay. He checked his personal effects and got himself out the door, down the street, and into the station. He found his platform and boarded the last car before the doors closed. So far his bowels were cooperating, his headache the same familiar throb, and he managed to sleep all the way to Stamford. When he got to Westport, he rented a small Toyota at the Hertz office near the train station and drove to the Jesup Street police headquarters to soak up some flavor. That's when disaster struck.

He asked Madge, the chief's media maven and all-around fixer, when Mrs. Petrov would be moved to a more secure facility.

"Oh, she's been released, and charges have been dropped," said Madge. "Isn't that great news?"

Hawkes sputtered. "What? When?" He saw his investment of time and money turning to ash.

"Is there a new suspect?" asked Adrian.

Madge deflected. "The chief will have an announcement soon," she said.

"Where is Mrs. Petrov?" he asked.

"The chief drove her home early this morning," said Madge. "I can't say any more."

Hawkes saw Stanley Ferguson walking across the lobby and through the double-swinging doors leading to the warren of cubicles where the officers performed their deskwork.

"Detective?" Adrian asked, chasing him across the floor. "A word?" Ferguson stopped and looked at the disheveled reporter, seeming to recoil from the man's olfactory essence.

"Yes?" asked Ferguson.

"You booked and fingerprinted Mrs. Petrov last night. Now Madge tells me she's been released and charges have been dropped. Do you have a new suspect?" asked Hawkes.

"The investigation is continuing," said Ferguson.

"What happened to the charges against Mrs. Petrov?" asked Hawkes. "Her gun shot Jayne. Her knife stabbed Aubrey."

"Dropped," said Ferguson. "We've got new information."

And the detective disappeared behind closed doors. Hawkes was panicked. The chief was protecting her. They'd had a prior, collaborative relationship. It was the obvious answer. He went upstairs and approached the secretary outside the chief's office.

"I wish to speak to Chief DeFranco," said Hawkes.

"Media inquiries go through Madge downstairs," said Angela, the chief's secretary.

"Madge is not telling me why Mrs. Petrov was released," said Hawkes, showing his exasperation.

"It's embargoed," said Angela.

"Where is the chief?" asked Hawkes.

"He's on official business," said Angela. "Everything goes through Madge. Sorry."

Angela went back to her typing, and Hawkes stalked off, fuming. He recovered his rental car for the quick drive over to Assumption Cemetery off Green's Farms Road, guided by a Hertz map. He arrived to find the Jayne family seated under a tent before a polished wooden coffin. Tammy was dressed in black, flanked by a grieving Lucy and Jim. Del Aubrey was in the clutch of mourners closest to the family, signifying her propinquity to the family of the dearly departed. Hawkes saw what appeared to be Jayne's older progeny, with spouses and young children of their own. There might have been an ex-wife or two. Hawkes couldn't be sure. A sobbing Miguel was seated in the front row, a nice egalitarian touch, thought Hawkes. On the outer periphery, he thought he detected some attendees who might have been on Jayne's retainer—a lawyer or two, a banker, a broker, certainly his accountant. Casting his eyes around the group, as the hired preacher offered solace from the Book of Thessalonians—"For we believe that Jesus died and rose again . . . "—Hawkes's gaze fell on an old woman in black, her face obscured by a broad-brimmed chapeau and an elaborate veil. She was seated next to the chief of police and that tiresome Goody-Two-shoes Tracy Taggart, who always seemed to have the best access. No wonder. Sources said she was sleeping with the chief. He'd have to find a way to insert that little parenthesis in his next piece of copy.

The preacher transitioned to John 3:16, and soon the coffin was lowered into the earth, to great wails from the children. Barnaby Jayne was at last laid to rest. At the conclusion of the service, the attendees made a point of greeting Tammy and the Jayne offspring, and then started to stroll toward their automobiles lining the roadway. He watched the old woman pay her respects to the widow Jayne, noting Tammy's neutral reaction when confronted by the woman, who, up until that morning, had been charged with killing Barnaby Jayne. Where was the slap on the face? The clenched teeth? The swell of anger? What happened to his open-and-shut case and all those beautiful, damning headlines?

Hawkes approached the old woman in black, confirming, as he drew closer, it was Dasha Petrov. The chief, spotting Hawkes's approach, stood before Dasha with his arm out.

"No interviews," he said, cutting Hawkes off. Tracy shot her fellow journalist a menacing look and followed the chief and Dasha as they made their way toward the chief's unmarked Crown Victoria. Hawkes walked back to his car and made a decision that would change the course of his gin-soaked life. He got behind the wheel of his rental and followed the chief, three cars back, then two, then one. The Crown Vic mounted I-95 at Exit 17 southbound and drove in the middle lane at precisely sixty-five miles per hour. The chief's car left the interstate at Exit 15 and worked its way toward Norwalk Hospital. The chief co-opted a favorable parking place near the front door, and Hawkes's luck held as he found a nearby metered spot and plugged in quarters. He got to the lobby to see the chief, Tracy Taggart, and Dasha Petrov enter an elevator. He watched the semaphore indicate a stop on six and inquired at the information desk as to the specialties performed on that floor.

"That's our heart center," said the helpful matron in the pink striped dress. She wore two badges, one that said, *Hi, I'm Carolyn*, the other *Ask me about TWIG*. Hawkes idled by the desk and overheard Carolyn on the phone.

"What do you mean he can't come in today?" she said into the handpiece, mildly agitated. "I've got his uniform, his name badge, and his transport chair. Now I have to find someone else."

Carolyn paused.

"All right, tell Lionel to get well soon." She rang off and scratched a pencil behind an ear. Hawkes watched her peruse a schedule and a roster. It was clear Carolyn was in a bit of a jam.

"How can I volunteer?" asked Hawkes.

"Well, I could use you right now. We just had a transporter call in sick," said Carolyn. "But you need an orientation and a background check."

"Maybe I could start those today," said Hawkes.

"Sure. Go see Ruth in Room 119 near the cafeteria. She can get you set up. And do me a favor? Push that wheelchair over to Ruth's office please," said Carolyn. Hawkes saw Lionel's uniform with the man's name badge draped across the back of the chair.

"Happy to help," he said and moved toward a sign indicating the dining hall. He slipped into a men's room on the way, found an empty stall, and took a sip of Bombay from his dented flask. He removed his suit coat and shirt, folded them, and placed them in a small basket under the chair. He donned Lionel's attire and pushed the wheelchair to the elevator bank. Carolyn's back was turned. He boarded an elevator, rode to the heart center on the sixth floor, and stepped off. He cruised without interruption past the nursing station and finally found what he was looking for. There were two uniformed police officers standing outside the closed door to Room 611.

Guard duty.

He went back to the nursing station and inquired of the young nurse behind the desk: "I'm supposed to take the patient in 611 to imaging." The nurse looked at his name badge.

"Well . . . Lionel, I don't know who told you that, but the patient in 611 is not scheduled for imaging," she said.

"Oh bother, I'm so sorry," he said. "What is the patient's name? I'll go back to four and straighten this out."

"Mr. DiCarlo," said the nurse. "Donald DiCarlo."

"His condition?" asked Lionel.

"Recovering from cardiac arrest," said the nurse.

"Why the police guard?" asked the wheelchair volunteer. "Some kind of VIP?"

"He was handcuffed to his gurney when they brought him in," said the nurse. "So, he's being charged with some kind of offense. They're interviewing him now."

He paused. The story was getting away from him. There were elements beyond his ken, and he had deadlines. His original plan had been to cover the Jayne funeral and craft a second-day follow-up of the Petrov arrest. Cut. Dried. Simple. His friends in circulation would agree. But now Mrs. Petrov had been released, and the mystery of Donald DiCarlo suddenly loomed. He looked at his watch. He needed to phone in a rewrite. He'd kick it down the road one more day. He took out his notepad and used his Bic pen to draft the first take of a piece he'd phone in that would run the next day under the banner headline: WHAT'S THE CHIEF HIDING?: DEFRANCO ESCORTS ACCUSED MURDERESS TO JAYNE FUNERAL. He thought the page 5 headline particularly enterprising:

The Lady Wore Black

Booked for his murder the night before, accused Barnaby Jayne killer Dasha Petrov was observed at Jayne's graveside service yesterday at Westport's Assumption Cemetery. She was being escorted by Westport police chief Anthony DeFranco, with whom Mrs. Petrov enjoys a well-documented friendship.

A tight lid on this developing Gold Coast mystery has been clamped down, and this is what we've learned so far: Yesterday Mrs. Petrov was charged with the slaying of Barnaby Jayne, and charges are pending in the stabbing death of author Michael Aubrey. Police investigators have told Hawkes Talks that Mrs. Petrov's gun fired the fatal shots that killed Jayne, and her knife was likely used in the Aubrey killing. Additional evidence has placed Mrs. Petrov at the scene, and, we've learned by analyzing information exclusive to Hawkes Talks, points to her possible unlawful access to the victims' finances as her possible motive.

But now, Hawkes Talks has learned Mrs. Petrov has been released from police custody, and charges have been suspiciously and unceremoniously dropped. Westport police chief Anthony DeFranco and the ex-CIA suspect are known to have a long-standing personal relationship, begging the question, is the chief somehow protecting his Beachside Avenue intimate? Add to this puzzle the unwavering presence of *NBC Nightly News* reporter Tracy Taggart, who, we're told, also enjoys a particularly close relationship with DeFranco.

Concurrent with the dropped charges comes a new player on the stage, who is being kept under police guard at Norwalk Hospital. His name is Don DiCarlo, and he could prove central to the murders of Barnaby

Jayne and Michael Aubrey. There's more, much more, to this ongoing Gold Coast mystery.

~

It would have to do. He was happily anticipating spending the next year covering the trial of the century, Mrs. Petrov clapped in irons. Now his plans were in a muddle, and he'd have to rebuild the story from scratch. He'd start with DiCarlo. Who was he? Where did he fit? Why were the chief, Dasha Petrov, and Tracy Taggart with him behind a closed door under police guard?

Adrian Hawkes finished with his rewrite and hung up the pay phone in the hospital lobby. He didn't see the slender dark-haired Italian gentleman walk through the front door of the building. The man was wearing scrubs, and he made his way to the elevators to push the "up" button.

28

Like a Canary

Dasha Petrov knew she didn't have much time to interrogate the prisoner before he'd be released into the legal system. DiCarlo had the right to remain silent and to be represented by counsel, so time was of the essence. It was the like the old days at the black sites along the East German border. You'd work to hide the arrestees—hospitals always did nicely—and get them to spill before the opposition stepped in to silence them, often permanently. Now she was working against American jurisprudence, which she'd taken an oath to defend. Of course, the man had rights, but she and the chief had urgent challenges of their own. She just wanted a few minutes with him. It wasn't much to ask.

Dasha reflected on what had brought them here. It had been quite a harrowing sequence of events—from the time DiCarlo had tried to kill her in her jail cell, to their surreptitious arrival at the hospital, where DiCarlo's heart attack could be treated. The syringe with the remnants of the drug he'd wanted to push into Dasha's chest was now in a lab inside the building. A report was due.

After Tracy brought DiCarlo back to life with the AED, she'd found a stethoscope among the station's first-aid supplies and pronounced DiCarlo's heart functioning normally. The EMTs soon took over, and the chief secured the syringe. The chief, Dasha, and Tracy drove behind the ambulance and assured themselves DiCarlo was tucked in for the night. The chief and Tracy went back to Seabreeze to drop Dasha off.

"If this is Paul Garcetti's nephew, and Del's former husband, how long will it take for his buddies to come and spring him loose?" asked Tracy ominously as they pulled into the Seabreeze driveway.

"I'll double the guards," said the chief. "I'll also let hospital security know we've got a career criminal enjoying their hospitality on six."

Now it was the next day, and they'd attended the graveside services for her friend Barnaby. She didn't know how she'd be received by the family, given that they'd probably succumbed to some bad information regarding her arrest. She had whispered the particulars to Tammy after Barnaby was lowered into the ground, and Tammy expressed surprise. Or was that dismay? Dasha couldn't quite tell, and that's what you got when you went up against a seasoned liar. The chief and Tracy took Dasha to the hospital, and now the problem was extracting information from this DiCarlo fellow. As always, wasn't it a pleasure to converse with the person who'd just tried to kill you? When her two novelists had perished, she thought she wanted to recede into her own private oblivion, but now she sensed the exhilaration that came with being back in the game. Dasha Petrov was on the hunt.

"Chief, can you give me a few minutes alone with Mr. DiCarlo?" asked Dasha.

"Tracy and I were just headed down to the cafeteria to get a sandwich," he said with a wink. "Can we bring you back anything?"

"Some soup," said Dasha, "if they have it. And if not, a small green salad." The chief and Tracy left the room, but not before the chief handcuffed DiCarlo's free wrist.

Dasha pulled up a chair and sat next to the bed. DiCarlo looked a bit dazed due to the sedative the doctors had ordered, but he was still compos mentis.

"You're in a tough situation, Mr. DiCarlo," Dasha opened. "It's always helpful to start with the facts. Do you know who I am?"

"You're that old Russian bitch," said Donny.

"Let me clarify that," said Dasha. "I'm the old Russian bitch you tried to kill last night. What's in the syringe?"

"I have no idea," he said.

He would turn to her as she helped him find the bright center at his core.

"You loved your Uncle Paul, didn't you?" asked Dasha.

Donny was stricken by memories of how Paul died that night. Dasha could see it on his face.

"Must have been wonderful times when you were growing up," she said. "Paul's big house on Todt Hill, one of the biggest places on Staten Island. Nicky's mom baking muffins in the kitchen. The smell wafting through the rooms. Tell me, Donny. What did she like to bake?"

"Banana nut muffins," said Donny, with a smile.

"Banana nut muffins," said Dasha. "I love them, too. And Nicky. Was he playing the piano? Was your cousin Tammy there, too?"

"We called Nicky 'the Maestro,'" smiled Donny. "He can play anything. Bach. Gershwin. Duke Ellington. Amazing guy."

"Was Del there, too?" asked Dasha, finding Donny's reward center.

"Later on," said Donny. "When we were a little older."

"Who introduced you?" asked Dasha.

"Tammy brought her over," said Donny. "She'd met her at the Barbizon. Del liked the family. She didn't come from much."

"Sounds like she just liked being included," said Dasha. "Or was it the banana nut muffins?"

Donny laughed, and Dasha thrilled at the return of the man's humanity. She was helping him rediscover himself.

"I like to think she came over because of me," said Donny.

Dasha wanted to press the point. "Of course she did, Donny," she cooed. "She recognized your worth. But you probably realize being married means marrying the whole family. She probably felt a bit stressed. Did you have kids?" Dasha surmised the answer.

"Del couldn't," said Donny. "Messed-up uterus."

"Pity," said Dasha. "You two would have made wonderful parents. But here we are. Del is out there under suspicion. You're handcuffed to a bed. The police will charge you with my attempted murder—no hard feelings—and certainly as an accessory in the Jayne killing. And they'll throw the book at you for Michael Aubrey. But it doesn't have to be this way, Donny." Her voice was like milk and honey. "You can win this. You don't have to go to jail. You can cut a great deal." She had no power to offer clemency, but she offered it anyway.

"They must think I'm stupid," he said at last.

The moment!

"But we both know how smart you are," said Dasha. "You can finally show them. All you need to do is come over to me. I can protect you. Here is my number. If we get separated. I want you to call me." She put a piece of paper in the breast pocket of his hospital gown. "Day or night, Donny," she said. "Just call me."

He nodded.

"What were we discussing?" Dasha continued. "I know. Confirmation. Del and Tammy agreed to kill each other's husband. But they needed help. Del called you, and Tammy called Nicky. It was convenient. You two had worked together before. Did time together, too, as I recall. How am I doing so far?"

DiCarlo, mute, only nodded.

"Good, so Del switched Michael's Walther for my Walther the day I visited the Jayne household for tea," she said. "And Tammy made an impression of my knife so Nicky could copy it."

Again, DiCarlo could only nod in agreement.

"It was a great plan," she said, "but they couldn't pull it off without you, Donny. You were the critical link. Sure, Nicky could shoot Jayne in the back of the head plus one in the mouth, but he needed you to get Jayne off the seawall and into the chair by the pool, isn't that right? And why was that? Why not just leave him?"

"Nicky wanted to stage it," said Donny. "That's why he's the Artist."

"He likes to think things through, doesn't he?" said Dasha. "Very precise. Very methodical. But he'd be nowhere without you."

"We work together," said Donny. "I do the heavy lifting."

"And he really needed you at the Aubrey gazebo, isn't that right?" she asked.

Donny nodded, and Dasha continued.

"But I'm curious about a few things," she said. "Help me here. You slit Michael's throat. Came up behind him? Was Tammy in there with him? Del was down in Mustique, as we know. But it must have been your cousin Tammy in there . . . to keep Michael distracted. And we both know how Michael liked pretty ladies."

Donny nodded.

"The stage was set. You were waiting in the wings. Tammy was playing her part. And just so I get this straight," said Dasha, "Tammy had my boots on, isn't that so?"

"Del stole them off your back doorstep," said Donny. "Switched them with another pair."

"So, Del wore them to see Barnaby, and Tammy wore them when you slit Michael's throat? Came up behind him while he was chatting up Tammy," stated Dasha. "I'm curious. Did Tammy leave right away, after Michael was killed?"

"He wasn't dead yet," said Donny. "Tammy stabbed him in the chest. Then she left, down the beach. Later she cleaned your boots off and replaced the new pair you'd been wearing with your old pair."

"Hmm," said Dasha. "Thought as much. Let me get back to Michael Aubrey's murder. A professional job of it, from what I'm told," said Dasha. "Stuck the blade right up under his ribs to hit the right blood vessels. And she literally broke Michael's heart. Why did she show up at the Aubreys' to begin with?" asked Dasha. "Was she seeing Michael?"

"She told Michael she wanted to get it on with him," said Donny.

"This is rich," said Dasha. "Del was having an affair with Barnaby, and Tammy was reeling in Michael."

"It was Nicky's plan," said Donny. "He said it would help us get closer."

"Beautiful. That Nicky . . . he's something. Shakespearean. Secret identities. Switched roles. Secret loves. And tell me, Donny." She moved closer to him. "Who was upstairs in the Aubrey house? When you accosted me with your mask on. After I shot you in the chest, I heard footsteps upstairs. Was that Nicky?"

"It was Lucy," said Donny. "She was trying to get more stuff for the newspaper guy. Hawkes."

"Ah, so Lucy is the person who's been spilling the beans to the *Post*," said Dasha. "That makes sense. And it was Lucy who fiddled with Barnaby's and Michael's last wills, is that right?"

"She got the signatures," said Donny.

"How?" asked Dasha.

"Jimmy helped. He told Barnaby he needed a lesson in cursive. Told him he was being punished at school because his handwriting was so bad. Jim asked Barnaby how to make a nice signature, and of course Barnaby fell for it," said Donny. "Del figured out how to get Michael's signature, slipped a blank in among some checks he was signing."

"I can see Barnaby supplying his signature to the child," said Dasha, "but Michael wasn't that sloppy."

"Del had him wrapped around her finger," said Donny. "And Lucy came up with the legal mumbo jumbo. Smart kid. I knew her dad. He got whacked, too . . . the night my Uncle Paul died."

"He was at Sparks?" asked Dasha.

"Held the car door open for Uncle Paul," said Donny. "Took the first round. Back of the head. Lucas didn't feel a thing."

"One big happy family," said Dasha. She felt the air move. The door was swinging open. The chief and Tracy had returned with her soup. She turned around to greet them.

But it was a healthcare worker in scrubs, a cap, and a face mask. He was pushing a wheelchair. He reached into a cloth shoulder bag and pulled out a small handgun fitted with a suppressor. He also had a small bolt cutter, and he moved toward Donny's bed while he trained his pistol at Dasha's forehead.

"I was expecting you," said Dasha, now hoping the chief and Tracy would somehow get delayed. Bad time to be walking in with soup. "You must be Nicky." She took a hard look at his firearm. Beretta in .22 long, favored tool of the assassin.

"And you're that old Russian bitch," he said. "You really messed up my plans."

"You can call me Dasha," she said, smiling.

He leveled the pistol and approached the bed, opening the jaws of his bolt cutter one-handed.

"We'll be going," said Nicky. "But you're coming with us."

"Happy to," said Dasha. *No better way to get to the bottom of things,* she thought.

"Use this bolt cutter to cut him loose," said Nicky.

"I'll try," she said. Dasha clamped the jaws of the tool around a link in the little chain that connected Donny's wrist to the handcuff attached to the bed. The handles offered the expected resistance, and she cursed the gods of time that had allowed her to grow so old. She felt Nicky's hand on the handle, and her abductor was now sharing the load. The link in the chain snapped. He directed her around the foot of the bed to attack the next one. She struggled with the cutter, and Nicky again pushed his weight against it before it, too, yielded.

"Get that shit off you, Donny," said Nicky, and Donny started removing wires and pulling out needles. The EKG machine was making a racket, and Nicky went around the head of the bed to unplug it. Dasha was watching the door, expecting the guards or a nurse. She knew Nicky wouldn't hesitate to shoot anyone who came in. The safest way out was to comply.

Nicky had Donny out of bed. "You push him," he told Dasha. "I have this gun aimed at your back. You fuck this up, you'll be dead before you hit the floor. Donny, hang on and we'll get you out of here."

Nicky put his mask back on, left his bolt cutter for the enjoyment of the police, and put his bag back over his shoulder. Dasha watched him put his gun hand into the bag. He'd have his finger on the trigger for every second they made their escape.

"Wait," he said. There was a pole for mounting a plastic bag filled with intravenous drugs. He hung a bag on the pole and put the tube up Donny's sleeve to make it look like they were on official business. He used a blanket to cover up the broken hand-cuffs on Donny's wrists.

More staging, thought Dasha.

"Move . . . slowly," said Nicky. "I'll talk to the guards. Keep walking toward the elevator. If you screw this up, Mrs. Russian Bitch, those guards won't get to go home to their little kids and their little wives. It's up to you."

That's putting an exclamation point on things, thought Dasha, and she lost some of that fearlessness that had gotten her through decades of dangerous intelligence work. Make a mistake, someone dies—stark in its simplicity. Above all, she needed to get into that elevator with these two before the chief and Tracy came back. She couldn't let her friends stumble into her abduction.

Nicky was opening the door.

Dasha pushed Donny into the doorway, and the two guards stood.

"We've got to take him downstairs for his nuclear stress test," said Nicky.

Dasha silently begged the police officers to stay away.

"We'll go with you," said a nice young man with the last name of Jameson, and she wondered if she'd met him at Barnaby's crime scene.

"Great," said Nicky. "Officer, can you go ahead and push the button for the basement?"

"Basement?" said Jameson. "*This* is the heart center."

"They put the radioactive stuff on the lowest level," said Nicky, orchestrating another of what Dasha thought was an impressive string of saves.

Dasha did a double take. The other nice officer was Sam DeFranco, the chief's stalwart son.

"Hi, Dasha," he said. "I just came on shift. Let me do that." Sam pushed the elevator button, and they all boarded. She had that strange, wet heat between her eyes, the signal she first experienced as a little girl with the Bolsheviks banging on the door. It had always been her early warning sign: when the Prague Gestapo threw her into a rat-infested cell, when the Stasi chased her through the streets of a shattered Berlin, when the Viet Minh were setting up their booby traps. That sweat between her eyes told her trouble was near.

The chess game playing in her head now came down to a single move.

What happens when we get to the basement?

29

Nicky to the Rescue

Chief DeFranco looked across the cafeteria table at the ravishing Tracy Taggart and said through all the clatter and din of the busy hospital lunchroom: "I love you."

"Oh, Tony," she returned, smiling, "I love you, too." She reached across and took him by the hand, and he felt a surge of energy from this simple touch. Yes, he loved his kids, and he'd always love his long-deceased wife, Julie, but there was something about the way Tracy gave herself to him, and to their small-town life, that filled him with gratitude. She could be anywhere with anyone, yet this beautiful Hoosier Marine—who'd be jetting off to Seoul in three days, and after that, Beijing—chose to be with him.

"I just hope we can wrap this thing up before I leave," she said.

That was another thing that grappled Tracy to every beat of his heart: She was a partner, and she knew how to use a gun.

"I'll let Stanley interrogate the wives," said the chief. "They'll lawyer up and throw a few roadblocks in the way. But Donny's testimony will shut that down fast. And Donny can point us toward Nicky."

"Nicky sounds like a mean one," said Tracy.

"Mafia killers usually are," said the chief. "We definitely need some help. I placed a call to Reynolds, and he's got a team from the New Haven FBI coming."

"Can't happen fast enough," said Tracy. They rose to leave. "Don't forget Dasha's soup."

"Damn it," said DeFranco. "I have to go back into that line. Why don't you go upstairs? This won't take long." He kissed her on the cheek, and they separated.

Tracy Taggart grabbed her purse, thankful she wasn't technically on assignment and could therefore carry her Kimber with a clear conscience. She went out to the main lobby and pushed the elevator button. She got to the sixth floor, hackles raised as she walked closer to Room 611. Donny DiCarlo's two-man police guard was gone, and there was no in-house hospital security. She pushed open the door to the hospital room. Dasha and DiCarlo were gone, too, replaced by an empty, unmade bed and a pair of compact bolt cutters.

"Shit," she said, all she could manage as she ran back to the nursing station in the center of the wing near the elevator bank.

"The patient in Room 611 is gone, and so is his police guard," she announced to the first nurse she encountered, who sat behind a counter typing at a computer. "Where did they go?"

"I didn't see anyone," said the nurse, turning to a compatriot. "Ruthie, did you see the patient in 611 go by?"

"Ten minutes ago. Patient in a wheelchair. Two cops. A male nurse in scrubs. And the old woman," said Ruthie.

"Do you know where they went?" asked Tracy.

"It seemed a little funny," said Ruthie. "I watched where they stopped. The elevator went straight to the basement."

"Okay, that's extremely helpful, Ruthie," said Tracy. "I need you to dial security."

Ruthie complied and handed the phone to Tracy, who stated the prisoner in 611 was missing and presumed to be in the basement with Westport PD guards but also persons considered armed and dangerous. "We might have a hostage situation," she added, to a yawning silence, signifying disbelief, coming from the other end of the line.

She opened her BlackBerry and dialed the chief, who answered on the first ring.

"I'm at the cashier. What's up?" he asked.

"Dasha, DiCarlo, and two Westport PD guards are gone," said Tracy, working hard to remain calm. "Tony, they were escorted into an elevator and went to the basement with a male nurse in scrubs."

"Did that nurse have a mask on?" asked Tony. Tracy restated the question to Ruthie, who reported that yes, the nurse wore a mask.

"Affirmative on the mask, Tony," said Tracy. There was a pause.

"Stay on six, Tracy," said the chief. "In case they come back. You can keep me advised. I am going to roll the backup and get Reynolds to move his ass a little more aggressively."

"Tony, I want to be with you," she pleaded.

"Please, Tracy. Help me by staying right there. I'll call you when I know more." He hung up, and Tracy walked back to 611. She circled the room, then stood outside in the hallway. She reached into the secret compartment of her generous purse and felt the mute power of her Kimber .45. She racked the slide, chambered a round, and flicked up the safety. She was now cocked and locked, as she went to the end of the hall, found the stairs, and started down, taking the steps two at a time.

30

Going Down

Dasha Petrov watched the annunciator in the elevator flash the floors they were passing through. They continued nonstop down to the basement. Nicky was behind them, and she wanted to catch Sam's attention. She stared at Donny's arms concealed under the blanket, hoping Sam would follow her gaze and understand that DiCarlo's handcuffs had been cut. She sensed Sam shifting on his feet, and he was clenching and unclenching his fists around the handles of the wheelchair. Jameson was at the front of the elevator car, waiting patiently. But Dasha thought Sam might be developing an understanding of the predicament they were in.

"Great day, huh, Mrs. Petrov?" Sam said. Was he trying to buoy her? Was he trying to enlist her in the gunfight that was about to happen? Or warn her? She'd never wanted her Walther or her stick so much in all her life.

"So far," said Dasha, "but I'm afraid it might get stormy very soon." Would Sam understand her veiled warning? Would Nicky pick up on the chatter and pull the trigger on his lethal, silenced Beretta?

They reached the basement, and the doors opened. Sam stopped.

"What's wrong?" asked Nicky from behind his surgical mask.

"Wheels are stuck," said Sam. "I think the wheel is pushing against the blanket."

He knelt down to get the blanket out from under the wheel. And when he came back up, he went straight for Nicky's shoulder bag, lifting it toward the ceiling of the elevator car while simultaneously kneeing Nicky in the crotch. They all heard the *pfssst* sound of a round passing through the suppressor, and Dasha saw the jagged hole open up in the ceiling. Another round went off, this time high in the wall above the elevator buttons. Dasha grabbed one of Nicky's arms and bit down hard, only satisfied when she heard the man scream. A third round exited the bag, hitting Jameson high in the left arm as he stood outside the elevator holding the door.

Jameson was able to get to the mic on his epaulet and announce, "Shots fired."

Sam was turning to see his friend bleeding badly when Donny DiCarlo got out of his chair and pulled it out of the way. Jameson didn't have his gun out, which was a good thing, they later reflected, because it was kept in place thanks to a snatch-proof holster. Donny was trying to grab it as he reached back into the elevator car. He finally let go of Jameson's holstered gun and grabbed Dasha. He pulled her into the basement, with its gray floor-to-ceiling paint and overhead pipes and wires. Another round from Nicky's Beretta split the air and landed somewhere near a sprinkler pipe. Donny, the recent heart patient, had enough strength to grab Sam DeFranco by the scruff of his neck and pull him out of the car. Nicky Addonizio was now free to do his worst, but Donny stood in front of him.

"Let's go, Nicky," he said.

"I want to finish these fuckers," said Nicky.

"No time. There's an exit sign. It points north. Closest to the parking lot. Let's go."

Nicky had his gun out, walking backward as he moved with Donny toward the exit.

That's when Tracy Taggart arrived, out of breath, from the opposite stairwell.

"Get down!" she shouted.

Jameson was already down, his left arm bleeding handsomely. Dasha knelt on the floor. Sam covered her with his arms, and Tracy fired two quick rounds at their retreating attackers. The bullets penetrated the steel door leading outside just as Nicky and Donny made it through. Tracy ran to Jameson to fashion some kind of tourniquet, while Sam ran toward the exit door with his Glock service piece out, yelling into his mic and running into three hospital security guards plus the chief as they lunged into the hallway from the west stairwell.

"This way," he yelled, out of breath. "Nicky and Donny are getting away."

The group followed the young patrolman outdoors into the sunlight. They all ran through the parking lot, looking car by car. But after an hour of searching and a floor-by-floor lockdown, it was clear that Nicky Addonizio and Donny DiCarlo were gone.

31

Live to Fight

"Here's to being alive," said Dasha Petrov, raising a glass of wine around the table at the chief's and Tracy's abode on High Gate Road. Young Sam, man of the hour, was sipping a bourbon, and Jameson, his arm in a sling, was certainly a danger to himself and others, considering the tall vodka tonic he was consuming on top of a Percocet.

"Careful there, partner," said Tracy to the wounded patrolman. "Mixing that stuff will play havoc with your liver."

"Bring it on," he said, lightening the mood.

Even the chief was enjoying the moment. He had two escaped killers on the loose, but aside from Jameson's flesh wound, his team was intact and would live to fight another day. The ER docs were pleased Nicky's .22 round hadn't broken Jameson's humerus, and aside from grazing a vein, his vasculature was in one piece. Dasha had been extolling Sam's selfless step into the breach, and the young patrolman seemed glad to be able to put more goat cheese on his cracker as he reached for the Jim Beam.

The chief had a surprise. He'd sent a patrol car over to the medical examiner to pick up Dasha's chestnut stick. After all, it hadn't been used in the commission of a crime, and it needed to be returned to its rightful owner.

"That's very nice, chief," said Dasha, "but where's my pistol?"

"Unfortunately, Dasha, it's in an evidence locker at the ME's office," said DeFranco. "There's no doubt it was used to kill Barnaby. You can petition to get it back when the perpetrator is sentenced."

"You'll have to catch him first," said Dasha. "I hope I'm still alive when that happens."

"I have no doubt of that. Here's the second surprise," said DeFranco. "I tasked our department armorer to find you a replacement. This is a Walther PPK in .380, but I'm afraid it's postwar."

"Well, chief, it doesn't have the same patina, but I am happy to keep it safe until my original is restored. You are a real gentleman."

The chief watched her drop the magazine, clear the chamber, and put the extracted round back in the magazine—all the muscle memory standing at attention. She put the magazine back in the pistol and kept the chamber clear.

"And I've got a surprise, too," said Tracy. "This is a Motorola flip phone. We got an early version at NBC. I've set up an account for you on Sprint. Keep it charged, and keep it in your pocket when you're out and about."

"I'm not old-school enough to reject technology," said Dasha. "I had to use illicit listening devices in my day . . . so I accept this sweet gesture, dear."

Dasha grew reflective.

"Let's turn our attention to the matter at hand. There was a moment just before Tracy arrived, guns blazing, when Donny DiCarlo had a choice to make," she said. "He stepped in front of Nicky's pistol and persuaded his compatriot to make for the exits."

"He was trying to take my gun," said Jameson.

"And do what with it?" asked Dasha. "Is it possible he was going to stop Nicky?" Dasha explained the course and tenor of her conversation with Donny while the chief and Tracy were getting lunch.

"I spent a lot of time trying to get some facts, but I also tried to build him up," said Dasha. "That's what you do with your spies. Make them feel safe, even appreciated, so they turn in your direction. I put my phone number in the pocket of his pajamas. Let's see if my asset checks in."

The chief was once again amazed at the powerful Mrs. Petrov. She might have succeeded in saving his son's life.

"Donny's no angel, Dasha," said the chief. "Lab results came back with the contents of that syringe he wanted to stick you with. Adenosine and lidocaine. The combination literally stops your heart. It's attempted murder."

"Well," said Dasha. "The tables turned, thanks to you and Tracy."

"We'll see what he has to say about that," said the chief.

"You're expressing confidence you can bring them in, chief," said Tracy.

"We've broken their momentum," he said. "They're on the run. But that only means they'll have to surface soon."

"And chief," said Dasha, "we can interfere with their plans even more if you bring in the wives, certainly Tammy. Donny told me she was in the gazebo with him when he slashed Michael's throat. And Tammy put Nicky's fake knife under Michael's ribs and finished him."

The weight of it made the little gathering grow silent.

"First thing in the morning, we'll bring in Tammy and see what she has to say for herself," said the chief. "I'll let Stanley request an interview. Sam, I'd like you to go over to Mrs. Jayne's with him to pick her up."

"I serve at the pleasure of the chief," said Sam.

"What are my ground rules, Tony?" asked Tracy. "I'd like to report that Tammy is a person of interest. And the Westport PD hasn't announced Dasha's release or DiCarlo's escape."

"Yes," said Dasha, "the announcements might flush Nicky and Donny into the open."

"I've tasked Stanley with looking at closed-circuit camera footage from Norwalk Hospital security," said DeFranco. "We think we have a shot of Nicky in nursing scrubs entering the lobby a little after one p.m. today."

"Do you have a shot of Nicky getting out of a car?" asked Dasha. "It would be nice to have a make and model."

"Stanley is digging into that," said the chief. "We think we've got him entering the stairwell leading up to the lobby. He's in civilian clothes, carrying a paper bag. Then, a few minutes later, we have a male nurse exiting the stairwell to the garage and heading for the lobby entrance. Height matches."

"License plate?" asked Tracy.

"No joy," said DeFranco.

"Another angle," said Dasha. "Costume stores. Don't forget Donny's *Scream* mask. Where did he buy it? Can they show us a credit card receipt? Can we query the credit card company to get Donny's street address?"

"Chief, let me make some calls," said Jameson, eager to get in on the investigation.

"Sure," said DeFranco. "It might take your mind off your painkillers."

"Tony, I can get my camera crew over here ASAP," said Tracy. "I can get the news on the air about Dasha and Tammy."

"Should I powder my nose?" DeFranco asked with a smile. "Where should we set up?"

"How about our front yard?" Tracy said. "And Dasha," she said turning to her old friend, "I would like to interview you, too."

"Lovely," said Dasha. "I might be able to get a message to my spy." Tracy and the chief weren't quite sure what she meant by that.

They finished supper, and soon Tracy's camera crew was knocking on the door. They set up lights in the chief's front yard as the sun was setting to the west. Tracy could anticipate her anchor tossing her the interview with her opening sentence.

"Thanks, David," she said. "This is Tracy Taggart reporting from Westport, Connecticut. It's been a whirlwind twenty-four hours as the Westport Police Department grapples with the double homicide of two of America's favorite mystery writers— Barnaby Jayne and Michael Aubrey.

"Their bodies were discovered at their respective Beachside Avenue estates last week. Evidence developed since then points to the possibility that one of their neighbors, Mrs. Dasha Petrov, may have been involved. Mrs. Petrov was arrested, but charges were dropped when new information came to light."

Tracy's editors would splice in B-roll footage of the coming interview with Dasha.

"Police now believe the Jayne-Aubrey murders may have been carried out by members of the Garcetti crime family. Paul Garcetti had sprawling interests in the construction trades in the tri-state area in the sixties, seventies, and eighties. Garcetti was killed at Sparks Steak House on East Forty-Sixth Street in December of 1985. Garcetti's niece is Tammy Jayne, Barnaby Jayne's widow. Garcetti's nephew is Donny DiCarlo. DiCarlo was in police custody last night, implicated in the Aubrey-Jayne affair, but he escaped with the help of a Garcetti hit man named Nicky Addonizio, who is also wanted in connection with the double homicide. We spoke to Westport police chief Anthony DeFranco about these fast-moving developments. Chief DeFranco, what do we know tonight?"

"Thanks, Tracy," said DeFranco, "and thank you for giving me a chance to let my friends and neighbors in Westport know the state of the investigation. We released Mrs. Petrov early this morning when new information came in. We are concentrating now on searching for Donny DiCarlo, Tammy Jayne's cousin, who may have information regarding both authors' murders. Mr. DiCarlo is also the ex-husband of Del Aubrey, Michael Aubrey's widow. And yes, DiCarlo managed to break away from our custody at Norwalk Hospital. But we have a lot of confidence we'll be able to track him down. "

"Chief, that's quite a twisted tale," said Tracy. "How did DiCarlo escape, and what evidence leads you to the conclusion that DiCarlo is a person of interest?"

"DiCarlo escaped custody at gunpoint, assisted by Addonizio. One of my officers, Hank Jameson, was injured. But thanks to Mrs. Petrov, we were able to get some information from Mr. DiCarlo that helps shed light on what really took place on the Jayne and Aubrey properties on April 25 and April 27."

"What are you concluding?" asked Tracy, knowing she had to ask the question, and knowing DeFranco had to refuse to answer it.

"It's of an evidentiary nature at this point," said the chief, "but we'll have more in the coming hours and days as the investigation continues. I would like to thank Detective Stanley Ferguson and Patrolmen Hank Jameson and Samuel DeFranco for their work in helping solve these crimes."

"Chief," said Tracy, "should people be concerned DiCarlo and this person named Addonizio are at large tonight?"

"I'm not going to sugarcoat it," said DeFranco. "Addonizio and DiCarlo are considered armed and very dangerous, but we are getting excellent help from the New Haven office of the FBI, and Connecticut State CID has also been notified. People should lock their windows and doors, and they can call the Westport PD tip line if they see anything out of the ordinary. As we like to say, if you see something, say something."

"Good advice tonight as the Gold Coast grapples with two murders and a manhunt. From Westport, Connecticut, for *NBC Nightly News*, I'm Tracy Taggart."

Once she'd signed off, Tracy turned to DeFranco. "Good job, Tony."

"I hate to say we've got those two galoots out loose," said DeFranco, "but people have a right to know what's going on."

"Expect to be hassled by the first selectman," said Tracy.

"I would like to answer the first selectman with an arrest," said the chief.

Tracy turned to Dasha. "Ready for your interview?"

"Ready as I'll ever be," said Dasha.

Tracy's cameraman announced, "We're rolling and recording," and Tracy turned toward her dear old friend.

"Mrs. Petrov, you were charged in the Aubrey-Jayne murders last night, and today you are out of jail and the charges have been dropped. How do you feel?"

"I feel fine, dear. I was never worried. Barnaby Jayne and Michael Aubrey were wonderful friends. And I am just as appalled as anyone that they are now gone."

"Did the police explain why you were being charged?" asked Tracy.

"The police were just doing their job and doing it well," said Dasha. "Evidence was manipulated to make it look like I had something to do with these murders. We now believe two individuals, Nicky Addonizio and Donny DiCarlo, are the real persons of interest. Chief DeFranco saw the merit of this conclusion and released me. Mr. DiCarlo was in custody, and unfortunately he got away."

"Is there a connection between Addonizio and DiCarlo, and a connection between Barnaby Jayne's and Michael Aubrey's widows?" asked Tracy. She had to ask it, but she was pretty sure Dasha would follow the chief's lead and deflect.

"That awaits confirmation," said Dasha. "I'm just happy I can go home to feed the birds and bake some nice banana nut muffins. I want nothing more than to invite my friends over for some baking and tea, get warm in front of the fire, and put this business behind us."

"There you have it," said Tracy. "Big developments tonight in the Gold Coast murders of Barnaby Jayne and Michael Aubrey." She paused a minute or two and shouted, "Wrap" to her team. Dasha was walking back into their little house on High Gate Road, and Tracy Taggart was left to wonder, *What was that about banana nut muffins?*

32

Lawyering Up

Chief DeFranco and Detective Ferguson watched Tammy Jayne from behind a one-way mirror at the Jesup Street station. She sat staring straight ahead with her hands folded in front of her, obviously coached by her attorney, Derek Sanders, who remained stern and immovable at her side. Sanders had a decades-long career defending the Gambinos, root and branch, including the offshoots like the Garcettis. Sanders was old-school and white shoe, and he enjoyed skewering anyone who criticized his choice in clients. "Everyone is entitled to a defense," he liked to shout. And Sanders knew Tammy from the time she was a little girl, having played golf with Paul and Mario, and having dined on numerous occasions with the DiCarlos while Donny was still in knee pants.

The chief was struck by Sanders's stone-cold, straight-ahead look, and it occurred to DeFranco that the man got paid for coaching his clients to remain silent, each void in the interview earning more dollars. The first part of the exchange went badly, from the chief's point of view, and went downhill from there. Stanley Ferguson had opened.

"Mrs. Jayne, thanks for coming in, and please accept our sympathies for your loss," he said. DeFranco thought a casual pleasantry might break some ice. Not with Sanders in the room.

"My client has just lost her husband in a brutal murder, and she is here against her will," said Sanders. "We are making this accommodation just once, and then we will countersue for harassment. The town of Westport better have insurance, because this is going to be very expensive."

DeFranco ignored Sanders and added a light frosting on the cake.

"Rest assured we are doing our utmost to track down your husband's killers," said the chief, directly to Tammy, avoiding eye contact with her legal shark.

"You *do* know Mrs. Jayne was out of the country when Barnaby was killed," said Sanders.

DeFranco thought his next pronouncement might be able to get a rise out of Tammy and Derek.

"I am quite aware of that," said the chief. "I was in contact with the constabulary in Turks and Caicos the morning Mr. Jayne was found. There is no doubt Mrs. Jayne was enjoying her stay at the Paradise Lodge with her children. This morning we wanted to talk to Mrs. Jayne about the murder of Michael Aubrey. We believe we have at least two witnesses who will place her at the scene of that crime."

"Preposterous," shouted Sanders. "And I will sue for defamation if this blasphemy gets into the press, where I know, chief, you have unique connections."

"Let's back up," said the chief. "Mrs. Jayne, your maiden name is Garcetti, and your father is Mario Garcetti, brother of the late Paul Garcetti."

Tammy looked at Sanders and Sanders nodded his consent for her to answer.

"Yes," she said with studied coolness.

"Mario and Paul have a sister, Louisa," said the chief. "And Louisa is your aunt?"

"Yes," said Tammy.

"And Louisa's married name is DiCarlo, and she has a son named Donald, also known as Donny? Donny DiCarlo is your first cousin?" DeFranco waited while Tammy went through the ritual of asking her attorney if she should speak. All these elements were in the public record, so DeFranco didn't think Sanders would object. The attorney nodded, and Tammy responded.

"Yes," she said.

"And Donny DiCarlo was married to Adele DeLormée, also known as Del. The former Miss DeLormée is Michael Aubrey's widow, with whom you enjoyed a long-standing prior relationship."

"I don't see the point of this," fumed Sanders, who intended to throw down challenges, as DeFranco expected.

"Mrs. Jayne and Mrs. Aubrey were acquaintances. Mrs. Aubrey was married to Mrs. Jayne's cousin Donny," said Ferguson, happy to get a word in. "We have information that Donny was involved in the Aubrey murder— "

"Why don't you talk to this Donny person, then?" said Sanders.

"And Mrs. Jayne helped Donny either distract or subdue Mr. Aubrey in the gazebo," finished DeFranco. He watched Tammy for the barest flicker of recognition or remorse, but she was a porcelain statue—her Turks and Caicos tan leaving faint, even traces on her perfect, professionally maintained skin. Her blush and makeup were understated, mascara applied with the delicate whisk of a brush, lips lightly glossed. DeFranco was impressed at Tammy's ability to keep her emotions in check. Dasha had said she lacked in intellectual gifts, but maybe this was her God-given talent—to become the ideal, unmoving client to the sputtering Mr. Sanders.

"What it comes down to is this," said Detective Ferguson. "Donny DiCarlo told us while he was in our custody that you and he, jointly, murdered Michael Aubrey in the gazebo at his home on April 27."

"Tammy, don't respond in any way," said Sanders. "Chief, you are way out of line. I don't know where you came up with that piece of unmitigated bullshit, but it amounts to hearsay. It's inadmissible, not to mention unmentionable. You are out to destroy my client, and I won't let you."

"Just trying to get some information," said Stanley. "I was pretty sure Mrs. Jayne would like to help us. But this appears to be hostile."

"Do not take Mrs. Jayne's right to remain silent as a failure to cooperate or an admission of any kind," said Sanders.

"Let's look at it from another angle," said DeFranco. "When is the last time you saw your cousin Donny?"

"You don't have to answer that, Tammy," said Sanders.

"Innocent question, counselor," said the chief. "Mrs. Jayne, do you and Donny stay in touch? We would like to get ahold of him."

"You had a chance to interrogate Mr. DiCarlo yourself," said Sanders. "He was in your custody, but you let him go."

"Escaped," said the chief, "but not before he told us about Mrs. Jayne's involvement in Michael Aubrey's murder," said the chief without emotion. "He told us Mrs. Jayne delivered fatal stab wounds to Mr. Aubrey's chest. Her fingerprints will be on that murder weapon when we find it."

"The murder weapon belonged to Mrs. Petrov," said Sanders, "and you let her go."

"The murder weapon did not belong to Mrs. Petrov, as it turns out. Charges against Mrs. Petrov were dropped when Mr. DiCarlo tried to kill her. It was a case of attempted murder. She was being set up as a patsy. To be silenced. To make the whole affair go away. But Mrs. Petrov turned the tables, and we managed to take DiCarlo into custody. That's when he told us all about what really happened in the gazebo." DeFranco looked straight at Tammy. "Mrs. Jayne, where is your cousin Donny?"

"No more questions," said Sanders. "Are we free to leave?"

"My colleague and I would like to take a break," said DeFranco. "Can we get you some coffee? Some water?"

"We don't need anything," said Sanders. "How long will this break take?'"

"Give us five minutes," said DeFranco. The chief and Ferguson left the room and reconvened in the anteroom with the one-way mirror.

"Brick wall," said Stanley. "Sanders is a ballbuster."

"He gets paid top dollar to bust balls," said DeFranco. "Ideas?"

"Without hard evidence, we can't keep her," said Ferguson.

"We need Donny, and even then it's not clear whether or not a jury will believe him," said the chief.

"FBI have anything to report?" asked Ferguson.

"Nicky and Donny have gone to earth," said DeFranco. "But Reynolds has a theory they didn't go too far. Otherwise, we'd see CCTV footage at bridges, tunnels, and tolls, and credit card usage would be showing up."

"I have a buddy who works records at NYPD," said Ferguson. "Addonizio sometimes uses the name Arnold Simms, and Donny has been known to go by DeLormée."

"Wait, that's Del's maiden name," said the chief. "It came up in Tracy's research. That man fell hard for Del and never recovered."

"Let me see if that name is getting any traction, even at grocery stores," said Ferguson.

"Credit card companies, but real estate brokers, too," said the chief. "Maybe they're holed up locally. I'll let these two birds go." DeFranco went back into the interview room. He wanted to inject a bit of displeasure into the cool, unflappable veneer of Tammy Jayne.

"Mr. Sanders, your client can leave," said the chief, "but I will be asking a judge to revoke her passport this afternoon. I will be sending around a patrolman to pick it up."

Sanders flew into the anticipated rage, and Tammy appeared aghast at this latest insult as they stalked out of the room, bristling with contempt.

33

The Trouble with Assets

How many times had Dasha Petrov waited in the dark for an asset to check in? She trolled the dim corners of her recollection. Wasn't it always late at night? Wasn't there always rain lashing against the windows? Tree branches brushing against the shingles? Embers in the fireplace losing their last glow? Didn't all her assets leave her waiting and alone? She sensed that familiar panic—for the potential loss of vital intelligence, for her sneak thief's mortality, for the sudden unmasking that would leave her people maimed or dead. It had been ten years since she'd run agents in the field, and they still kept her up at night.

Her spies may have been faceless underlings, but to Dasha Petrov they were priceless stalwarts, knights of the resistance, even those of dubious morality and checkered background. They stood against their various tyrannies—and yes, of course, they had their hands out. Bills to pay, like all of us. A signals clerk, an adjutant, a rising bureaucrat, all manner of résumés and occupations. There had been hundreds. Some had suffered abuse and slander and demotion. They wanted their revenge. They'd betray their country, revealing all they knew. But her best spies were the ones who would do it all for free.

So where did Donny DiCarlo, née DeLormée, fit in this parade? What would motivate the man to give up his associate, Nicky Addonizio? Donny had always played second fiddle. He didn't have the temperament, the drive, or the skills to be the leader. He was good at cracking heads. The cook's son, Nicky, had the looks, a knack for playing the ivories, Uncle Paul's respect. Nicky was good-looking, but Dasha wondered why the fabulous Del, the ingenue from the Barbizon, hadn't gone for the Artist.

Dasha decided, in the end, Nicky was still the cook's son, a contractor, a tool to be used in the furtherance of Garcetti family business. Maybe Nicky was gay. Del's clearest pathway into the rich, vibrant world of the Garcettis was through Louisa's hapless boy Donny. And all right, that didn't work out too well, especially when it came to the challenge of contributing to the Garcettis' familial increase. Poor Del was barren, and that meant she had to go. Or was she pushed? Or did she leave Donny of her own volition, and thence move on to some new vapid plaything—a race-car driver, a mountain climber, a yachtsman, what have you. She'd have them lining up, our Del. And poor Donny would be utterly destroyed when he saw her go. Had they kept in touch through each one of her doomed romances? No doubt. He'd want to remain on the periphery, catch her if she fell. But where would he turn if Del cast him aside one more time?

Dasha was pondering these permutations when the phone rang. There was danger in relying on the telephone, she knew. Normal tradecraft would find her schooling her spies in dead drops, brush passes, burst transmissions, coded classifieds in the *PennySaver*. But she didn't have time. She would have to trust the fact that Donny could get himself to a phone and dial the number she'd left in his pocket. She answered on the fifth ring, and all she heard was breathing.

"I'm not as talented in the kitchen as Nicky's mom, but I have a great recipe for banana nut muffins," she said. It was their passkey, impromptu and informal, employed by expediency.

"Those were the days," mumbled Donny DiCarlo into the handset on the other end.

"Let's talk about your safety," said Dasha. "I presume you can talk? You're out of the house or the apartment. No one listening on the extension?"

"I'm down the street in a phone booth," said Donny. "I needed some fresh air."

"It's raining," said Dasha. "Do you have a coat?"

"And an umbrella," said Donny. Dasha felt a thrill. He was nearby, in the same rainstorm.

"We don't want you catching cold," said Dasha.

"You're not my mother," said Donny, and Dasha gave herself a stern rebuke. Mothers. You either loved them or you despised them.

"No, I'm not," she said, "and I'm not going to tell you to turn yourself in."

"You're not?" he asked.

"You can make up your own mind when it comes to that," said Dasha, empowering the man. "I should think you'd want to be with Del, now that she's free."

"I'm afraid she'll reject me again," said Donny.

"Isn't Del the reason you got into this affair?" Dasha asked. "Isn't she the reason you joined Nicky in getting Barnaby and Michael out of the way? You want her back. You've always wanted her back, Donny. And now she's free as a bird."

"I guess I made sure of that," he said.

"I won't judge you," said Dasha. "You had a choice to make, and you made it. Michael has left the stage. And now Del may really see you for who you are. Strong. Decisive. Those are your true qualities, Donny. And now Del has had a chance to see you up close. She didn't know the real you when you were younger. Now she sees a man of daring and accomplishment."

"How will I know if she really wants to be with me?" asked Donny.

"You have to go to her," said Dasha. "It's dark, but it's not too late. You have to tell her how you feel. It could mean a new life together. Tomorrow the police might close in. You can't let this chance go, Donny."

"Do you really think so?" he asked.

"Donny, I'm an old woman," said Dasha. "I've seen lost causes and missed opportunities, and it's always because of a lack of imagination and impulse. You can do this, Donny. And Del will welcome it. Can you get a taxi?"

"I can walk," he said. "I know the way. It's not far. Maybe twenty minutes."

"Don't let her get away, Donny," said Dasha, and her asset rang off.

Dasha's mission had been twofold: Set Donny up for rejection, turning him against Nicky and the wives. Her second goal was to find the knife he'd used to kill Michael Aubrey, the one with Tammy Jayne's fingerprints. Donny knew where it was, and he was only a twenty-minute walk to Beachside Avenue. She arrived at a point of inflection. Call the chief, and send in the posse? They might be able to apprehend Donny, but what about Nicky's knife? And might Donny's apprehension warn Nicky? *A lovely layer cake of imponderables,* she thought. And then she finally arrived at her plan, just as a thunderclap filled the guesthouse with a furious light.

As she had so many times before, she would take the battlefield alone.

34

Quite a Couple

Donny DiCarlo trudged through the wet, wrapped in an old London Fog coat he'd picked up at a secondhand store when he'd arrived in Westport incognito. He was carrying a black umbrella, and he was glad something was going right. It wasn't one of those cheap damn things you could buy on any street corner in Manhattan, the ones that usually disintegrated in the mildest zephyr. This umbrella was full-size and able to stand up to the gusty winds that shook the trees on his walk that night toward Beachside Avenue . . . and his destiny. He'd given his life to Del, suffered the indignities of her prolific betrayals, and stuck with her through marriage after marriage, hoping she'd choose him yet again, and forever more.

This time he'd killed for her, erased her latest husband in a perfect plan that envisioned Donny taking his place at Del's side. The fucking Russian bitch was supposed to take the fall, then collapse and die from cardiac arrest, case closed. But she'd refused to die, and now, strangely, the old woman was on his side, nurturing his decision to pursue Del, come what may. Of course, the old woman had shot him in the chest, and he'd tried to snuff out her life with Nicky's syringe. But couldn't they let bygones be bygones? Now Dasha Petrov wanted to protect him on his journey toward a reunion with his one true love.

The rain was letting up. He pushed the intercom at the stone-and-iron gate leading to the Aubrey residence. Del answered, and she sounded worried.

"Donny, the place is probably being watched," she said anxiously.

"I walked over here from the Post Road," he said. "There isn't a soul out on a night like this, except your old friend." He detected a sigh, and a buzzer. The lock to the gate was thrown electronically. He walked up the winding driveway to the huge wooden double doors. He lifted the knocker, but the door opened anyway.

Del had been waiting for him, and his heart took flight.

"Come in," she said. "I don't want anyone to see you." She made him stand on the mat while he removed his outer garment and propped his wet umbrella in a corner. He took her all in. She was even more gorgeous now that she had arrived in her middle years. She had her crisply laundered blouse and a gold necklace that bedecked her décolletage and matched her gold earrings. Her twill slacks fell to a clean break at her stiletto heels. Her makeup was understated and applied with care. Did she always look this good? Or was she waiting for someone? Would he always have these trust issues?

"Come sit in the study, Donny," she said, and he noticed she refrained from offering him a drink.

He followed her into Michael Aubrey's masculine domain, the true home of the legendary Max Gunn.

"I've been going through Michael's papers," said Del. "He's got at least four more manuscripts in the works. I want to keep those alive. I am soliciting a ghostwriter."

"Why do you want to keep Michael going?" asked Donny, wondering if she'd moved on.

"No use in letting these projects go to waste," she said. "Max Gunn is too valuable. His agent called. It's money."

"He's left you with plenty," said Donny. "Why not just let him go, so we . . . so you can get on with your life." He wanted to add "with me," but some sense of self-preservation, of wanting to keep the conversation going, held him back. He didn't want her to shut him down. He didn't want to push her away. He fought against the urge to hold her.

"It's all in the discussion stage at this point," said Del. "We'll see what happens." Donny could tell she wanted to get off the subject. And he needed to find out where her heart was leaning.

Toward him? Toward the life together that he'd dreamed about? Del gave him an opening. "Donny, why did you come here?"

"I want to get back together," he said. There was a hopefulness shining through his big, sad eyes.

"You always want to get back together," said Del. "We split years ago. And every time I change husbands, you come around."

"This time is different," said Donny. "I removed Michael. For you. That's what you wanted. I thought it was because you wanted us to reconnect. Make a new start. With money." He looked around the room.

"The plan changed, Donny," said Del. "The old woman was going to take the blame. Now she's alive and kicking. I'm scared."

"I can protect you," said Donny. "I've always protected you, even when we were apart. I always made sure you were okay." He moved close enough to smell Del's lavender bathwater. He craved her right then, but the look on Del's beautiful face darkened.

"I've always looked after myself, Donny," she said. "It was you and Tammy who put Michael away. And you helped Nicky kill Barnaby. Your fingerprints are all over this."

"You and Tammy planned it," said Donny. "You helped get Barnaby into position. I don't know what they call it. Conspiracy? An accessory? You'll do time."

"Donny, stop talking like this," said Del. She edged closer to the drawer where Michael Aubrey kept his prized pistols. Barnaby had destroyed only the long guns. The pistols were still in the drawer. She needed to get to the Walther. It was loaded. She was already formulating what she'd tell the police. Donny DiCarlo had come back to the Aubrey estate to kill her. She'd had to shoot him.

It would be self-defense.

35

Bearing Witness

Dasha Petrov stood on the uppermost step of the stairs leading to the top of the Aubrey seawall. She was wearing her Barbour coat and an old sou'wester rain hat that had belonged to Constantine. She had her Leupold field glasses around her neck, her replacement Walther in her pocket, along with the chief's Motorola flip phone and a mini Maglite "torch," as they called it in England. The rain was less torrential, but it was still coming down, and her binoculars were fogging up. She could see Del and Donny talking in Michael's study, and she didn't envy the job Donny had cut out for himself. It would take some doing to convince Del to take the man back into her embrace. Dasha didn't want to remind Donny, but how many times had Del turned him away? For most men, once would be enough, but Donny had kept at it, and here he was, ready to take the leap again. He'd get points for trying.

Dasha could tell the conversation wasn't going well. Her objective was to drive a wedge between Donny DiCarlo and his accomplices, and it looked like that plan was proceeding grandly. They were screaming at each other. Dasha saw Donny edging closer to her with his arms outstretched, pleading. Del was backed against the gun case. She turned to open the drawer filled with Michael's pistols.

"Oh dear," said Dasha. And then she thought, in a spasm of self-reproach: *Dasha, you should have seen this coming.*

36

Between the Eyes

Del was panicked.

She had the pistol in her hand, but where was the magazine? Michael had shown her how to use it. Push it into the grip, then pull the slide back, putting a bullet in the chamber, and flick down the safety. Could she do all that with Donny standing there screaming at her? She got the first part accomplished. The magazine went into the well in the grip. She turned around and pointed it at Donny.

"Don't come any closer," she said. She pulled the slide, chambered a round, and worked the safety. She knew the pistol was ready to fire.

"Del," he said, "it's Donny. We go back. We're perfect together. Don't do this."

"I want you out of my house. And out of my life." She spat the words. She was angry. Donny hated it when she got angry.

"Don't push me away again, Del," he said. But he'd crossed this bridge. When he saw Del's flashing eyes and bared teeth and heard her shrieking tone, he knew he would never get her back. He had only one card to play.

The evidence.

"The knife, Del," he said slowly. "The one I used to kill Michael. The clothes I wore that day. They still have his blood and Tammy's fingerprints. I'm taking her down, and when she goes, you'll go with her. I'm giving you one last chance."

"Go to hell, Donny," she fumed. But she couldn't pull the trigger. Not inside the house. Too much of a mess.

"I'll make sure you go with me," he said. He left the room and went to the front of the house, which faced the sound. He walked out into the rain, and Dasha Petrov watched him march across the wet grass heading for the east end of the seawall, away from her and toward another little stairway leading down to the beach. She went back to that awful day when Michael was killed, when she'd chased Donny in the black duster down the lawn. He had been angling off toward the east end of the seawall then, too, like he knew where he was going. Now Donny was walking in the same direction—toward Michael's little clay target house hidden in the shrubbery, where Aubrey's mechanical target launcher was stored.

Donny got closer to the bushes, and Del came running out of the house into the rain, ruining her hair. Dasha watched as Del Aubrey kicked off her shoes and ran up to Donny, leveling a pistol at his back.

"Stop," she yelled, but Donny kept walking away from Del toward the other end of the seawall. He wanted to recover something. Dasha was sure of it. She had to intervene. She had to protect her asset. Dasha had placed Donny directly in this impending line of fire. He was a thug and a murderer, but he was still her responsibility.

Dasha had her hand in her pocket, gripping the Walther the chief had given her. She was desperate not to use it. She walked up to Donny as Del ran down the lawn, three people with very different missions converging on the rain-soaked grass. Dasha tried to read the situation. Donny was trying to recover something, something compromising. Del was trying to stop him, resorting to deadly force. Donny had his hands up—hardly a threat.

"I give up, Del," he said holding out his arms with his palms up. Dasha thought for a fleeting second she might have to shoot Del to stop her from killing Donny. She resisted the impulse. She was torn. Would Del really do it?

Del Aubrey looked at Dasha, and Dasha tried to read her mind. Dasha expected rage and worry, but Del seemed utterly composed. Del's state of calm gave Dasha the impression she wanted to scare Donny, not shoot him. That's why Dasha hesitated.

Then Del looked at Dasha and stated with a cool reserve: "He came here to kill me." She raised the gun and pointed it at Donny.

His arms flew up and out in a defensive reflex: "No, Del. It doesn't have to be this way."

Del took one more step, then shot Donny DiCarlo in the face. Donny collapsed in a heap on the wet lawn, and she threw the pistol down on his lifeless body. She looked at Dasha and said, "He killed Michael and threatened me tonight." She turned on her stocking feet to walk back into the house.

Dasha Petrov looked down on Donny DiCarlo, having met his inevitable end. She hadn't put the gun in Del's hand, but she certainly put Donny in front of the muzzle. Yes, he was a thug and a killer. But God help her, he was still an asset—and she felt a crashing wave of grief.

She pulled out her new flip phone and dialed the chief. After she finished calling out the cavalry, she was even more resolved.

"The Artist," she said aloud to a rising wind. "Let's see how artful you really are."

37

Not Another One

DeFranco and Tracy were trying to have a quiet dinner at home on their beautiful dead end when the phone rang. Dasha Petrov stated the facts plainly, and the chief let out a deep sigh. Another unnatural death had visited the Aubrey residence, and he took one more sip of his Cabernet before telling Tracy what had transpired. He rose to don the shoulder holster for his Glock, and Tracy cleared the dishes and got her Kimber out of the locker in the closet. She wasn't going to leave his side. The chief notified the ME's office, and he called Stanley Ferguson at home—hoping all hands could break free of their domestic respite to meet him on Beachside Avenue.

The chief and Tracy Taggart rode in silence over to the Aubreys', and he parked the Crown Vic under the porte cochere. Tracy banged the knocker, and soon Del Aubrey answered with a terry cloth towel in her hand, drying her rain-soaked hair. She'd removed her makeup, slipped on a pair of flat moccasins, and changed into a pair of blue jeans and one of Michael's Notre Dame sweatshirts.

"He's in the front yard," said Del. "He tried to kill me."

The chief and Tracy went outside to find Dasha Petrov standing over the lifeless corpse of the love-besotted Donny DiCarlo, who had a bullet-entry wound in the middle of his forehead. There was a Walther pistol thrown down on his body.

"You witnessed this?" the chief asked Dasha, who seemed to be expecting the chief's raised eye. "How did you know he was coming over here?"

"He called me," said Dasha. She hated to lie, but couldn't reveal sources and methods. "I'm in the book." Technically true.

"Did he threaten Mrs. Aubrey?" asked Tracy.

"Do you want my opinion? Or the facts?" said Dasha.

"Let's start with the facts," said the chief.

"They were in Michael's study. They were arguing. He did not appear to have a weapon. Del pulled Michael's gun out of a drawer and followed Donny as he walked out of the house. He walked toward that corner of the seawall, angling off to the east side, the same direction he ran the day Michael died—after I shot him in the chest. I think he was looking for something."

"So, she comes up to him and he turns around to face her?" said the chief.

"With his hands up," said Dasha. "He said, 'I give up, Del.' They were six feet apart. She raised that pistol there and shot him in the face. She then turned to me and said, 'He came here to kill me.'"

"Self-defense, Tony?" asked Tracy.

"Not really," said DeFranco. "He was out of the house, moving away, and she came after him. You said his hands were up in the air?"

"Yes," said Dasha, "and she was pursuing him across the lawn with her shoes kicked off."

"In Connecticut, the shooter pleading self-defense has to be cornered, no way out except over her attacker's dead body," said the chief. "To enter a plea of self-defense, she first has a duty to retreat. The lawyers will have fun with this one. Where do you think Donny was headed?"

Oliver Snell had arrived, and he began inspecting the corpse. Stanley Ferguson was ensconced in the Aubrey living room with the lady of the house.

"The little structure in the shrubs where Michael kept his electronic target thrower," said Dasha. She had put away her pistol and had her beloved stick in one hand and her flashlight in the other. "Let's go look."

They walked behind a small hedge in the corner of the yard. The small square building was hidden therein, with an opening on one side to allow the thrown targets to escape. There was a door on the other side large enough for one person to stoop through. Dasha went in, preceded by her torch's oval of light. The target thrower had stacks of orange clay discs loaded into a dozen magazines, and there was an arm in alignment with the opening on the side of the building facing the sound. There were cardboard boxes of White Flyer brand targets. She looked in one of the open boxes on top of the pile and saw a collection of round clay "birds." Everything else in the small room was neat and orderly. Overhead there were three sheets of plywood resting on crossbeams. She poked them with her stick, and they were loose. She could lift a board up and slide it over its neighbor, then stand up in the opening with her flashlight. She swept the light over the space, and it fell on a pile—black cloth, a black hat, a *Scream* mask, and the glint of an alloy knife. She came back down out of the little attic and went outside to report her findings to the chief.

"You'll want to send Mr. Snell down here to process more evidence," she said. "The black duster Donny wore the day he murdered Michael. Plus, Nicky's handcrafted knife."

The chief took his own flashlight out of a breast pocket and had a look, and Tracy couldn't resist witnessing this link in the chain of evidence. They walked back up to Oliver's team, which had erected a small four-pole tent over Donny, along with some powerful lights. They were rolling Donny over to see the ragged exit wound made by Del's .32-caliber bullet from Aubrey's PPK/S.

"Tony, I want to get a film crew over here," said Tracy. "Do I need Del's permission?"

"It's my crime scene, so go ahead," said the chief. He was growing weary of the merry wives of Beachside. Tracy stood off to one side under her own umbrella to call her night assignment editor. The chief turned to Dasha.

"So now it's all about Nicky," he said. "Donny really called you?"

"He said he was coming to get Del back into his good graces," said Dasha. "He said he was only a twenty-minute walk away . . . through the rain."

"But why would he call you?" asked DeFranco, still puzzled.

"Maybe Del knows," said Dasha, despising herself for leading the chief astray.

"We'll come back to it," said DeFranco. "He walked here from somewhere that's twenty minutes away. Narrows it down. I'll get Sam and Jameson to start checking real estate listings and the Westport Inn."

Tracy came back to the little tent on the lawn.

"We're using a pool team from News 12 Connecticut," she said. "This will be like old times."

Her resulting news bulletin filmed on the Aubreys' front yard described the shooting death of Donny DiCarlo, an offspring of the Garcetti crime family. It threw suspicion onto DiCarlo as the murderer of Michael Aubrey and introduced a cryptic reference to a homemade knife found on the Aubrey property that may be implicated in Aubrey's death. Her piece described eyewitness accounts of Del Aubrey shooting her husband's killer dead after he'd threatened her. And at the close of the piece, Tracy mentioned the crucial role of a reported Mafia assassin named Nicky Addonizio, now considered a person of interest in the killing of Barnaby Jayne.

~

Fifty-five miles away, Hawkes watched the news bulletin from his Murray Hill studio. The circulation department had expressed dismay that he couldn't give the double homicide of Jayne and Aubrey more ink. He watched the bulletin and phoned in a perfunctory recap of Del Aubrey's sterling initiative in ending the life of Danny DiCarlo. He hated cadging another outlet's scoop, but he had no choice. If the *Post* didn't cover DiCarlo's death, there'd be bigger hell to pay. He sipped one of his shorties of Stolichnaya and contemplated his next move. In order to get back in the good graces of the higher-ups—especially after the false and defamatory headlines implicating Dasha Petrov—he would have to pull a very special rabbit out of a very big hat.

He'd have to land an interview with a Mafia killer named Nicky Addonizio.

38

Triangulation

Chief DeFranco knew it was going to be a very long night, and he was cheered by Dasha and Tracy's willingness to stand at his side in the Jesup Street station as they went over Sam and Jameson's research.

"We drove due north from the Aubreys' house up Maple Avenue at about five miles an hour. Jameson drove, and I walked," said Sam. "That pace takes you a little north of the Post Road, so if you get out your protractor and draw an arc, you can get an idea of where DiCarlo may have started his evening."

"Stellar work, my boy," said Dasha, patting Sam on the arm.

"So, let's assume Donny and Nicky were holed up at the farthest point on the arc," said the chief. "East and west, you've got some of the nicer neighborhoods in Green's Farms. I can't see our trained killers hanging out in suburbia. They'd draw attention to themselves."

"Did you check any real estate listings?" asked Tracy.

"We went back three months to see availabilities along our arc," said Jameson.

"Three potentials," said Sam. "A room for rent above the barbershop at the corner of Maple Avenue and the Post Road. One bedroom, small sitting room, galley kitchen, a bathroom."

"Too small," said the chief.

"There was an in-law place over a garage behind the video rental store," said Sam. "One bedroom."

"Getting warmer," said Dasha. "What else?"

"The one we like is in the trailer park just east of Oakview Circle," said Jameson. "There was a double-wide for rent in there three months ago. Living, dining, big kitchen, two bedrooms, two baths. Short-term, month to month. The owner is out of the country."

"I like it," said the chief. "Jameson, you're done for the night. We need you to rest. Sam, I'm going to ask you and Stanley to take up surveillance of that place while I work up a search warrant and get state CID to whistle up a SWAT team."

"You'll be the clearinghouse, chief?" asked Ferguson.

"Yes. All comms go through me," said DeFranco. "Plain clothes, binoculars, watch and wait. If anything moves in or out, call me. Use your flip phones. Stay off the radio for now."

Stanley and Sam left the room, and DeFranco rousted a judge to get his search warrant. He also called the state police barracks and advised the night sergeant of the matter at hand. The nice thing about the SWAT services was that you didn't have to beg and plead for a dozen very rough, well-armed police officers to blast into position. They lived for breaking down doors. DeFranco wanted to make sure it was the right door.

"Sergeant, I am going to have eyes on this address in about twenty minutes," he said. "I want to make sure your guys don't scare the crap out of some nice family watching TV."

"Understood," said the SWAT leader. "We'll stage in the Stop and Shop parking lot."

They exchanged contact information, and DeFranco rang off.

"The funny thing is, this address is less than two hundred yards from our house on High Gate," mused Tracy.

"Excellent tradecraft," said Dasha. "They may have been right under our noses. Reduces all the exposure associated with moving around."

"Our people are getting into position," said DeFranco. "Dasha, why don't you tell me how it came to pass that Donny DiCarlo called you tonight and wound up dead on Del Aubrey's front lawn?"

"We're old friends, chief. But I need to keep some things classified," said Dasha. "I need to protect my sources and methods."

"Not when it comes to my murder investigation," said the chief. Dasha knew when the chief was irritated. "I wanted Donny

DiCarlo alive. Nicky, too. They're the key to nailing down what the wives may have been up to."

"All right, chief," said Dasha. "You and Tracy have always kept my secrets. I recruited Donny when he was in the hospital. I gave him my number. I wanted to drive a wedge between Donny and Nicky *and* the wives. And I wanted Donny to give us the knife he used on Michael. With Tammy's fingerprints."

"We have partial success, chief," said Tracy. "The ME can process the knife. Things don't look so good for Tammy." It was easy for Tracy to rise to Dasha's defense.

"And we may have triangulated the location of their safe house," said the chief, resigned, "but you've shortchanged the legal system, Dasha. Donny won't kill again, but I sure would have liked knowing what he knew."

"Sorry, chief," said Dasha. "Now we just have to bring in Nicky."

"Let's see if your work tonight getting Donny out of the house results in finding Nicky," said DeFranco. "Then all will be forgiven."

"How about we move to High Gate Road?" said Tracy. "The chief can lead the orchestra from there, and it's closer to the action."

"Agreed," said DeFranco, as the cell phone in his pocket rang. It was Sam, reporting he and Stanley were in position.

39

Home Invasion

Nicky Addonizio was sitting in the living room of their rented double-wide, trying to figure out where his best-laid plans had turned to utter shit. Donny's mysterious departure in the rain to get some fresh air had caused a mild, momentary stir. But Donny's failure to return after what? Three hours? It did not bode well. Nicky suspected Del had somehow contaminated the man's already addled brain. He had crossed over to the other side. Continuing his tour of the coming disaster, Nicky quickly fell on their failure to assassinate the old Russian woman. They'd teed her up brilliantly. It hadn't been easy making that knife. But she engineered a reversal, and Donny wound up in the hospital, where they very nearly got caught. Now Nicky's bags were packed, and it was time to get out of Dodge. Donny could figure out things for himself. Nicky wanted to leave before something else could go wrong. He had two duffel bags for clothes and supplies, plus his little Beretta with the suppressor. He also had a big Colt .45, cocked and locked in a holster on his belt. He had wiped down the surfaces in the kitchen and bathrooms with a rag and a spray bottle of Fabuloso he'd found under the kitchen sink. He turned out the lights and walked out to the carport, to the used Ford F-150 pickup truck he'd purchased for just this mission. It would be in a crusher in the morning. He put his bags in the back of the truck and hopped behind the driver's seat.

He turned the key to the single click of the starter solenoid and the glaring, gaping absence of a functioning engine. He emitted his customary cloud of curse words, then performed a quick analysis. The switch for the dome light was in the "on" position. It had drained the battery. He would never have done that.

"Donny, you fucking asshole," said Nicky Addonizio. He got out of the truck and stood with his hands on his hips, looking up and down the tidy row of mobile homes on this well-positioned back street. He left his bags in the back of the truck and went inside. He left the lights out and observed the street. A car drove slowly by with a man at the wheel. The man took a good, long look at Nicky's "unit." And directly across the street, between two more mobile homes, he thought he saw someone standing next to an outdoor metal shed. There was a glint from a pair of binoculars.

The police were closing in.

40

Battering Ram

Sam DeFranco called his father on a cell phone and reported movement at the subject residence. He also reported he'd run the plates on the pickup truck. It was recently registered to RISD Pest Control, Fifty-Fourth Avenue and Vernon Boulevard, Long Island City. The chief was delighted with this news, which made him confident the SWAT team would take the right house. He called the SWAT commander and asked him to move with all deliberate speed. He called Sam back and told him to wait in the road with his badge out for the SWAT crew. Sam would point out the target. DeFranco called Ferguson and told him to take up a position behind the house to make sure Nicky didn't get out through any backyards.

The chief, Tracy, and Dasha got into the Crown Vic and moved slowly toward the objective. They pulled up behind the SWAT team's panel van and had a good view of the assault. A two-man crew led the way with a battering ram, followed by a four-man entry team. There was a dog handler with a German shepherd on a leash, plus the sergeant in command standing off to direct the coming show. The chief noted the team didn't waste any time getting into the home. Soon the lights were on, and the team was coming back into the street to pack their gear and load it into their transport.

The SWAT sergeant came over to the chief's vehicle.

"You can come inside," he said. "Nobody's home. Place looks clean."

"Damn it," said the chief. "We needed to take that suspect tonight."

"Happens," said the sergeant. "At least my guys got in a little practice."

DeFranco, Tracy, and Dasha walked up the street and found Sam and Stanley huddled in conversation.

"A screwup," said Stanley, mortified. "Nicky got in the truck, tried to start it, then went back inside. Battery's dead. Then he bolted before I could get into position."

"We have to assume Nicky's walking around out there with no ride," said the chief. He got on the phone to the night desk sergeant back at Jesup Street. "I need every available unit to flood the area at Maple Avenue and the Post Road," he said. "We're looking for a Caucasian male, slender build, dark hair, dark complexion. Wanted for murder. Considered armed and dangerous. Subject's name is Nicholas 'Nicky' Addonizio. Last known address Fifty-Fourth Avenue and Vernon Boulevard, Long Island City, Queens." He knew the dispatcher's call would go out over the police band radio, to be picked up by radio scanners at media outlets. Couldn't be helped.

The chief's entourage walked over to Nicky's safe house, and DeFranco noticed two duffel bags in the bed of the pickup.

"He was on his way," said Tracy.

"Stanley, put those bags on the tailgate and inspect the contents," said the chief. Ferguson turned to the task while DeFranco went inside. When the sergeant said "clean," he really meant it. DeFranco sensed the bleachy chemical aroma of a cleaning solution. Tracy and Dasha went into the bedrooms. The beds were made, the closets were empty, and the bathrooms were immaculate.

"Fastidious," said Dasha.

"Remember, this is the guy who delivered the neat double tap to the back of Mr. Jayne's head," said Tracy. "There's nothing sloppy about Nicky the Artist."

"That's why the dead battery is such a puzzle," said Dasha. "Nicky would never do that."

Stanley came into the living room of the mobile home. "Just some clothes," he said. "And this . . . " He handed the chief a Beretta .22 with a suppressor. "It's unloaded."

"He left his favorite tool behind," said the chief. "It only means he panicked, and he's running . . . hard."

Actually, at that moment, Nicky Addonizio was in the center lane of I-95, just passing Exit 14. He was traveling at the speed limit behind the wheel of a late-model Chevrolet Malibu he'd hotwired after he'd made his hasty retreat. He was fresh out of vitriol for Donny DiCarlo and instead gave himself entirely to the mission: driving to his studio in Long Island City. He had to recover a carefully prepared go-bag filled with money, another pistol, his Arnold Simms passport, and essential hot-weather clothing. Destination: Bogotá and his offshore account at Banco Popular. But he had one last errand. He needed to settle his affairs with Tammy and Del. They had agreed to give him two million each. He had wiring instructions, and he wanted to personally impress upon the wives the importance he placed on getting paid.

So, he was in for some driving tonight. He'd get his backup Mitsubishi, and he'd be back out to Connecticut. It was two a.m. He was passing Port Chester, and traffic was light. He was getting a handle on things. Later on, after he'd cruised the Malibu over the Whitestone Bridge and worked his way over to Long Island City, he didn't bank on a knock at his studio door—nor did he expect to see Adrian Hawkes of the *New York Post* standing on the front steps, greeting him in that misplaced London accent.

"Mr. Addonizio. May I have a word?"

41

Story Time

The street-by-street search for the escaped killer Nicky Addonizio wasn't going well, and the chief knew he was looking at an all-nighter. Stanley Ferguson was out cruising in an unmarked Ford, and he reached him on the cell phone. "We need to liaise with NYPD tonight. I'm going down with Sam. You want to come?"

"Do I have an option?" said Ferguson.

"You've had a long day," said the chief. "Why don't you call it a night?"

"Thanks, chief," said Ferguson. "We'll get the little bastard. My phone will be on if you need anything."

So, the forces were converging: The chief, wanting closure, with Sam, Tracy, and Dasha buckled in. The NYPD special services unit, already alerted, tasked with taking down dangerous criminals. The Artist himself, comfortable in his secret lair, if not for the unexpected arrival of the unrivaled Hawkes, whose thirst for a scoop exceeded his thirst for dry Bombay gin martinis, straight up.

To Nicky Addonizio, the sight of Adrian Hawkes banging on his studio door was one more surreal experience in a string of endless missteps in this star-crossed operation.

"Who are you looking for?" he said.

"You are Nicky Addonizio, aren't you?" said Hawkes.

"Never heard of him," said Nicky. "Get the fuck out of here."

"I've seen your mug shot," said Adrian, pressing. "You're Nicky the Artist. I want to interview you. I want to tell your story."

"I'm busy," said Nicky.

"It won't take long," said Adrian. "And I can be discreet. We can embargo the release of the interview until after you've made your escape. I can only assume you're leaving the country?"

That's it, thought Nicky. *There's no way I can let this little asshole live.*

Nicky paused.

"Why don't you come inside?" he said, with his hand on the grip of his .45. "This is my studio. It's where I do my best work."

"I was hoping to see your work," said Adrian. "It will give the story an important dimension. What's your favorite medium?"

Nicky couldn't comprehend why the idiot from the *Post* wanted to engage in conversation at three in the morning. Were all journalists this stupid?

"Come inside," said Nicky. "It's not much, but it's home."

To Adrian, the transition from junkyard to palace was striking. There was a living room with a polished wood floor, lush drapes, overstuffed seating, a massive kitchen with hanging pots, a Steinway grand piano, and a Viking gas stove.

"My mother likes to come over to bake," said Nicky, "and I like to cook Italian."

There was an alcove with a double bed, a bookshelf, and a small desk with a personal computer.

"Where does the art take place?" asked Adrian.

Nicky threw a switch to illuminate his workshop: lathes, cutting machines, a forge, woodworking tools, paintings completed and in progress. Adrian noticed reds and blacks and dark macabre themes. Also Manhattan cityscapes.

"I like to go down to the point to paint the skyline," said Nicky. "Helps me relax."

All good fodder for his forthcoming page 1 triumph, thought Hawkes. *Exclusive: Inside the Assassin's Den. The* Post *gains access to the inner sanctum of the Gold Coast killer.*

"I was wondering how you spend your downtime," said Adrian, "but can we talk about the Jayne-Aubrey murders?"

The guy is clearly out of his fucking mind, thought Nicky.

"What do you want to know?" he said, convinced now more than ever the intrepid *Post* reporter wasn't going to make it out alive.

"It was an impressive piece of engineering," said Hawkes. Flattery was always useful in oiling the waters. After all, the killer was an artist and no doubt carried himself with a bit of pride. "The ladies offering to kill each other's husband, the ironclad alibis, Mrs. Petrov the patsy. It's brilliant. Was it all your idea?"

"Of course," said Nicky.

"Not your usual mob rubout," said Adrian. "There's real finesse here. Who inspires you?"

"I always strive for perfection," said Nicky. "I learned it from my mother." Nicky was thinking about where he was going to leave this guy's body. Trunk of the car, maybe. A dumpster. The Bronx. Of course. He knew a good spot off Pelham Parkway.

"Do you prefer working alone?" asked Adrian, who wondered if Nicky knew about the police activity at the Aubrey residence that night. "Where is your collaborator?"

"Not sure," said Nicky, suddenly growing tired of the charade.

"I have to ask you, what's next?" Hawkes was fawning now. "Do you think the wives are in the clear?"

"Remains to be seen," said Nicky. "We still have some business."

"Back to Connecticut?" asked Hawkes. "Let me ride with you. We can talk in the car."

There was nothing Nicky Addonizio would like less. The interview was over.

"Let me show you something over here," he said. He walked deeper into the studio, where he picked up a piece of rebar and a burlap sack. He turned around and grabbed Hawkes by the throat and put the bag over his head. Then he hit Hawkes once in the head and was satisfied when he heard a disagreeable *oomph* coming from under the sack and saw an expanding bloodstain. Nicky could smell the gin and cigarettes on Hawkes's clothing. Maybe that was the answer. The man was drunk.

"You need me," was all Adrian, still conscious, could muster. Nicky frog-marched him to a wooden chair. He sat him down and grabbed a roll of duct tape. He started taping Hawkes to the chair. But Adrian, undeterred, kept sputtering out questions.

"I want to tell your story, but I would like some historical context," he said. "When did you first start your career as a hit man?"

Nicky found himself compelled to answer. He wasn't sure why. Maybe he liked the attention.

"I was still in college. Providence. A friend of Mr. Garcetti, my mom's employer, needed a favor. Simple job. The enemy of the friend wound up in pieces, then I stuffed him into a big coal-fired kiln at RISD."

"Fascinating," said Adrian. "Do you mind if I use that in my article? The readership loves a good anecdote."

"Suit yourself," said Nicky. He heard sirens in the distance, not unusual in New York City. But these were coming closer. "How did you get my address?"

"Police scanner," said Adrian. "I have a dial-in number, so I can always get Westport PD. I can only assume they ran the license plates on your truck. Shame about the dead battery."

"That asshole Donny," said Nicky with contempt. "Fucking meathead."

The sirens were getting louder. It would be so easy to put a bullet in this guy's brain. But maybe Nicky appreciated a little show of enterprise. He grabbed his go-bag, walked into the junk-yard, and found his downtrodden Mitsubishi. He put his bag in the back, started the car, and froze. He opened the door and went back into his studio. He approached Hawkes with his gun out and leveled it at the man's head, which was inside the burlap bag. Hawkes was still asking questions about the young Nicky and early signs of talent. Was it true he played the piano?

Killing the reporter would be so easy.

But Nicky Addonizio whipped off the sack, holstered his firearm, and started cutting the duct tape with a box knife. He handed Hawkes a dish towel for his head, grabbed the scribe by the neck, and marched him outside. Nicky threw Hawkes into the passenger side of the Mitsubishi. The sirens were getting louder as Nicky Addonizio pulled away from the junkyard.

"You want a story?" he asked the author of Hawkes Talks. "I'll give you a fucking story."

42

Return to the Scene

The NYPD had secured the building, and the chief walked in, followed by his entourage. The special service officers with their body armor, helmets, and assault weapons looked out of place in the homey if not lush environment. Tracy and Dasha walked around the kitchen, marveling at Nicky's taste in pots and crockery, and they both fell for the six-burner Viking with the special spigot for pasta water.

"Lovely setup," said Tracy. "And if you're into making things, the shop is splendid. Did you see the woodworking equipment?"

"I'm impressed with the works in progress," said Dasha. "Tremendous output, but I guess it's hard to access the market if you're a Mafia hit man."

The chief was seated at Nicky's desk. "But if you're Arnold Simms, maybe you have a gallery on the Upper East Side that buys your stuff." He was nosing through statements, business cards, notes from satisfied clients, a burgeoning to-do list.

"I have to hand it to Nicky," said Tracy. "Industrious. Any press clippings?"

"Some reviews with photos of his artwork," said Dasha, "but none of the man himself. Review here says Simms is 'reclusive.'"

"He was noodling on a scratch pad recently," said the chief. "Tammy, two million; Del two million. And then a bank in Colombia, with a routing number, an account number, and a correspondent bank for handling the details. This was Nicky's take."

"Do you think he collected?" asked Tracy.

"He's been off stride and out of step," said the chief. "Things started to go wrong for Nicky's plan when Dasha knocked out Donny with the syringe. It all went downhill from there."

"He was in the safe house in Westport waiting for the right moment to present his bill to the wives," said Dasha. "Then we ruined his plans."

"But he still wants to get paid," said Tracy. "Tony. He's heading back to Beachside Avenue."

43

Personal History

Nicky Addonizio had a lot he needed to get off his chest, as he and Adrian gamboled through the night in Nicky's rattletrap Mitsubishi. He and Adrian had endured a rocky start, but they both seemed energized by the ensuing conversation. In the back of his mind, Nicky felt he might have to eliminate the reporter at some point, a feeling that became less urgent with each passing mile. Adrian kept coming back to a single question each time Nicky described a critical moment in the arc of his life: "How did that make you feel?"

No one—well, maybe his mother—had ever asked him that question.

Adrian learned Nicky Addonizio was the bastard child of the Garcettis' cook, Nicola. He and his mother lived over the garage on the Garcettis' Staten Island estate, and he spent his early years observing the Garcettis enjoying their sumptuous lifestyle. Men in smart suits came to discuss important matters with Paul Garcetti, the don, and were dispatched to do this bidding at the far reaches of the Garcetti empire. There were beautiful women and boisterous children, elaborate parties, and endless music. When he was older, he put on a white jacket and served drinks and hors d'oeuvres. Always, he wondered how he might become a part of this closed world.

At one point, his mother expressed some concern that young Nicky might not have enough stimulation. She bought him an upright piano and dragooned a few Garcetti soldiers into hefting the monster into their small apartment. Mrs. Addonizio could manage "Chopsticks" and "Mary Had a Little Lamb." But she bought Nicky lessons, and it soon became apparent that Nicky was destined for bigger things. He taught himself Chopin, interlaced with a bit of Gershwin and even a flavoring of Rachmaninoff. As with everything Nicky pursued, he leaned into the task and discovered talents that could open doors.

He liked to draw, play with clay, build things with stone, learn how to use tools. And when his mother's employer invited him into the great man's study, he absorbed the lessons that spilled freely from Paul Garcetti's busy mind. To succeed in life, you needed to corner a market, remove the competition (sometimes with brute force), smooth things over with the stakeholders like police and judges, and form lasting alliances. "Respect, Nicky," said the elder Garcetti. "Respect is everything. If they don't respect you, you're nothing. And sometimes you have to earn that respect by breaking a few legs."

Hawkes was taking notes and snuck key questions into Nicky's monologue.

"When did you realize Garcetti's business was founded on a history of violence?" he asked.

"I think I was three when I saw my first dead body," said Nicky. "Some poor bastard stuffed into the trunk of a car. Hands tied. Head bashed in. To me, this was normal."

Adrian wrote furiously in his pad.

"How did that make you feel?" he asked.

"I don't know," said Nicky. "Special, I think. How many kids got to see that?"

"When did you start playing with Mario's daughter Tammy and Louisa's son Donny . . . the cousins?" asked Adrian.

"I think we were in the cradle together," said Nicky. "Paul's wife, Dorothy, didn't like me, though."

"You were a cute little child," said Adrian. "How come she didn't like you?"

"That's something I didn't mention," said Nicky. "Something big. Paul Garcetti was really my father."

Adrian Hawkes blew out a whistle and saw the complete, freshly painted fresco on the ceiling of the cathedral. It was a revelation. Nicky was the illicit issue from a forbidden liaison between the cook and the master of the house. Tammy and Donny were Nicky's actual cousins, Garcettis all. But Nicky's lineage could never be mentioned. He was "the other," so he needed to work that much harder to rise and shine on his own.

"Nicky, that's massive," said Adrian, who, for once, refrained from asking Nicky how he felt. "When did you find out?"

"I think I knew in the back of my mind from a young age. But they confirmed it on the car ride up to RISD to start my freshman year," he said. "Paul and my mother took me in Paul's big Cadillac. I don't know what he told Mrs. Garcetti. Errand out of town or something. Best trip of my life."

"Why is that?" asked Hawkes.

"It was normal," said Nicky. "I've led a life of the abnormal, everywhere you turn, and that was one occasion that was completely straight. Mom and Dad schlepping up to Providence with their kid. Of course, Paul started to rely on me, and of course would do anything for that man. Kill for him, in fact. Many, many times. It's because he respected me. His respect was everything."

"Where were you the night Paul died?" asked Adrian.

"My mom and I were in my studio making sausage or something," said Nicky. "We heard it on WPIX 11. We saw pictures of him lying there, half in and half out of the Cadillac with a cigar still in his mouth. We curled into a ball and cried all night. But I vowed right then and there that rat scum bastard Scarpella would pay. I'll get the fucker. I'm just biding my time."

"And in the meantime, you excelled at your craft . . . or I should say all your crafts. Painting, sculpture, music, murder," said Adrian.

"It's been a living," said Nicky. "I should have known working with family would fuck things up. Cousin Donny is a dope, and Tammy just invites trouble. It's time to take a break."

"It's your valedictory," said Hawkes.

"Come again?" asked Nicky.

"Your farewell, a final triumph," said Adrian. "You'll get paid, take a breather, and figure out next steps. It's time to stop and reflect. Take stock. How are you going to get out of the country?"

"Alias. Second passport. Driving to Canada and flying to Colombia out of Montreal," said Nicky. "But now you know too much, Mr. Hawkes."

They both laughed, but Hawkes grew silent. Then he figured out a way to save his own life.

"You're a book, Nicky," said Adrian. "And after that, film rights and maybe even a serialization. I know how to put it together. Let me come with you. I'll take a month's leave from the paper just to set things up. I know this can work."

Adrian thought he might have captured Nicky's interest, expressed in the studied silence and the scratching of the chin. Nicky was thinking.

"Who gets to play me?" he asked.

"Always the first question," said Hawkes. "My thoughts tend toward Brad Pitt."

"I don't know," said Nicky. "I like Clooney."

"Clooney's another fine choice," said Adrian, thinking perhaps he might have avoided a bullet as the night transitioned to a slowly gathering dawn and the Mitsubishi drove through the stone gate at the estate of Barnaby Jayne.

It was going to be another beautiful day on the Gold Coast.

44

Slings and Arrows

Sam drove, and the chief worked the phone. The state police CID was again moving into position. On information and belief, the chief was trying to explain that Nicky Addonizio was going to be visiting either the Aubrey residence or the Jayne estate.

"My bet is the Jayne residence," said Dasha. "Tammy and Nicky go back. Del will always be on the periphery." The chief emphasized the Jayne estate with the SWAT sergeant, then he added, "We could be looking at a hostage situation. We might need a profiler and a negotiator."

"No can do," said the sergeant. "Our hostage negotiation apparatus is not working because our negotiator just retired. We might be asking you to take that on, chief."

"Understood," said DeFranco. He related the coming challenges to his team in the Crown Vic, as the vehicle mounted the ramp at Exit 18. Sam was piloting the big car toward Beachside Avenue.

"Can we surmise you'll want to talk to Nicky without weapons?" asked Dasha.

"Correct," said the chief, "but let me establish some ground rules first." He called the SWAT team leader back, and they agreed to keep the entry team out of sight behind the seawall.

Sam turned into the Jayne drive, and they saw a Mitsubishi up by the front door.

"I don't recognize that car," said Dasha. "New York plates?"

"Affirmative," said Sam.

"Let's assume he's here," said the chief. He called the Westport PD desk sergeant and got the Jayne number out of the phone book, then started dialing. He got Lucy on the first ring.

"This is Chief DeFranco," he said. "Is your mother there?"

"She's a little tied up," said Lucy, as she watched Adrian Hawkes duct tape her mother to a chair under the supervision of family friend Nicky Addonizio, who trained his .45 on the couple. Nicky was waving at Lucy. "Wait, Nicky wants to speak with you."

Nicky Addonizio came on the line.

"Hello?" said DeFranco.

"Didn't take you long to figure out where I would be this morning," he said.

"Just following the breadcrumbs, Nicky," said DeFranco.

"Where's your SWAT team?" Nicky asked. "I watched them break into my house last night."

"On standby," said the chief. "I thought you and I should talk first."

"Thoughtful," said Nicky.

"Who do you have with you?" asked the chief.

"Cousin Tammy, of course. Lucy. Jim. And Adrian Hawkes of the *New York Post*. He's my biographer," said Nicky.

"Hawkes?" asked the chief. "What's he doing there?"

"Showing some enterprise," said Nicky. "Guy's got balls."

"Okay, so how can I help you this morning, Nicky?" said the chief, wishing to lower the temperature. Separating Nicky from his hostages was the objective.

"No SWAT team," said Nicky. "Tell them to stand down."

"Agreed," said the chief, who would tell the SWAT leader to remain out of sight but within reach.

"And I'm not feeling comfortable," said Nicky. "I want you to come inside with anyone you came with."

"I'll come in," said the chief. "But I'll be alone."

"I'm looking out the window," said Nicky. "You've got the old Russian woman, the redhead from NBC, and a patrolman. Bring them all in, chief. No weapons of any kind."

He wants a human shield, thought the chief.

"It will have to be up to them, Nicky," said the chief. "I can't force my colleagues to do something that might be dangerous."

"The more, the merrier," said Nicky. "This should be fun. Come in with your team, and we'll talk about how to end this peaceably."

"I'll call you back," said the chief. He huddled with Tracy, Dasha, and Sam. He described the predicament, and they all agreed to go inside. The chief was squeamish. Somewhere in hostage negotiation 101 there must be a rule about exposing more people to harm, especially civilians. And he wasn't too keen on putting Sam in harm's way, either.

"The idea is to send Nicky on his way so he can be apprehended in a timely and efficient fashion," said Dasha. "That won't happen here. Too many people."

"Okay," said DeFranco. "But no weapons. Including your stick, Dasha. Leave everything in the car, and Sam, you can lock it."

They all complied and went to the front entrance. Adrian Hawkes, with a nasty welt on his forehead, standing bloody and proud, opened the door and showed them into the living room. Nicky was sitting at the piano, and Tammy was taped to a chair with a gag in her mouth.

"Don't mind her," said Nicky. "I couldn't get her to shut up. The only one missing is Del. But I'll get to her. She killed my cousin Donny, you know. He was a meathead. But he was family."

"Condolences," said Dasha.

"Thank you, Mrs. Petrov," said Nicky. "If my plan had gone forward, you wouldn't be here right now."

"Sorry to upset things," said Dasha. "And I've been held against my will before, so I don't take this personally. Tell me, Mr. Addonizio, how can we help you get what you want so you can be on your way?"

"I want $4 million," said Nicky. "Tammy and Del were supposed to split it. But Del isn't here, so it's all up to Tammy, and she and Del can sort it out later. Mr. Hawkes, could you remove Tammy's gag, please?"

Adrian complied.

"Cocksucker," said Tammy when she could talk again.

"There are children present," said Nicky. "You always had a foul mouth."

"Fuck you, Nicky," said Tammy. "You're being an asshole."

"Pick up the phone and ask Barnaby's broker Crawford to wire $4 million into this account," said Nicky, handing her a piece of paper. "Then we can part friends." He pulled out his .45 and aimed it at Lucy's head.

"You know I'll do it, Tammy. Then Jimmy, too. Get busy."

Tammy was stifling a cry.

"Nicky, if you please, I know where the Crawford file is in Barnaby's desk," said Dasha. "Do you mind if I go get that? It probably has all the contact and account information Tammy will need."

"Yes, Mrs. Petrov," said Nicky. "That would be very nice."

All the action in the living room seemed to freeze as Dasha Petrov left the little assembly and entered Barnaby's beloved space. The bookshelves. The huge desk. The window overlooking the sound. She could hear Barnaby clacking away on the computer keyboard, see him hunched over his reference works, his reading glasses slipping down his nose as he contemplated the murder and mayhem his fans had grown to love.

Dasha didn't hesitate.

She removed Barnaby's modern hunting crossbow from the wall, stepped on the stirrup, and used the lever, called a gaffe, to tension the string back to the trigger nut that held it in place. She found a steel bolt with a razor-sharp broadhead point and crisp fletching at the tail. She fitted the grooved nock at the back of the bolt into the string and laid the bolt in the groove on top of the weapon. She removed her hat and coat to give herself more freedom of movement and practiced sighting in the weapon on a bookshelf. She made sure the safety was in the "fire" position, checked and settled her beating heart, and banished that liquid heat that seared the skin between her eyes.

She had one bolt, and one chance, to stop Nicky Addonizio.

She walked closer to the door and heard the party talking. Tammy was scurrilous in her condemnation of her accomplice.

Lucy was starting to cry, and the chief was quietly suggesting Nicky put the gun down so they could settle this matter without anyone getting hurt. She noticed that Nicky was standing as he talked to the chief. He had his pistol in his right hand, away from Dasha, pointed at Lucy's head, and he was growing agitated at the child's whimpering. Adrian Hawkes sat mute, for once. Dasha thought he might be making a rare visit to a place called reality. He was a mere storyteller after all, forever arriving at the scene of the crime well after the crime had been committed.

Dasha knew the arrowhead was designed for a quick, humane kill of deer and other moderate-sized game. It was so sharp it could pass through tissue without the game realizing it, until the animal collapsed from massive blood loss. It was her only option. She took in a breath, expelled it from her lips, felt her heart settle, then stepped into the doorway. Nicky saw her and saw the weapon. He had to turn 180 degrees to take the gun away from Lucy's head and aim it at Dasha. In the span of time he spent twisting in Dasha's direction, she pulled the trigger, and the bolt split the air and struck Nicky Addonizio in the left pectoral, entering his chest. It sliced through both the pulmonary artery and the aorta and continued through his trachea and the upper lobe of his right lung. It exited his body through the lymph nodes just behind his right armpit, but not before cracking a rib. The bolt stuck in the wall over the fireplace, and Nicky's dark, crimson blood began to drip onto the hearthstone beneath.

After the bolt had left her crossbow, Dasha's real concern was whether or not Nicky would have enough life left in him to pull the trigger on his big pistol. But Chief DeFranco jumped out of his chair and went straight for the gun, forcing Nicky's arm up in the air. Nicky was coughing up a fountain of blood but managed to squeeze the trigger of his .45, sending a round into the ceiling. The massive report from the pistol could be heard by the SWAT team waiting on the beach below the seawall, who stormed the house as Nicky Addonizio toppled over and drew his last breath on the parquet floor.

Dasha thought of Lucy and Jim, and she crossed the room to hold them. The young ones would remember this dreadful day for the remainder of their lives. Dasha had witnessed violence in many forms, having been both the deliverer and the recipient. And now, in her twilight, she was grateful she had never gotten used to it.

Epilogue

Dasha was mortified she'd neglected Galina during those tumultuous days at the beginning of May. Now, she sat with her sister on the broad lawn in front of the manor house, wrapped in blankets to ward off a slight chill. They watched the sound and the birds and the mullet pushed up to the surface of the water by a boil of ravenous bluefish.

"The oyster beds are thriving again, Galina. Isn't it wonderful?" There were three dredgers going about their tasks offshore. Galina pushed her little wooden squares around her Scrabble board and stated, simply, "Heaven."

The chief and Tracy had come and gone with their after-action reports, always accompanied by a worthy selection of wine. Del Aubrey was arrested for first-degree murder in what the state's attorney determined was the contract killing of her husband, Michael. The prosecutor was also examining her singular role in the death of Donny DiCarlo. Had Donny been a threat when she pulled the trigger? Testimony from Mrs. Petrov suggested the man was in full retreat, which would adversely affect her defense. She was in the town lockup awaiting trial. Michael's children were lining up to handle his final affairs, and they'd already wired a million dollars into the account of Mrs. Petrov, who had been instrumental in bringing the whole sordid business to a proper conclusion.

Tammy Jayne's encounter with the law was different. Her fingerprints were found on the handcrafted knife that had killed Michael Aubrey. The authorities were warming a cell for her at the Corrigan-Radgowski Correctional Center in Uncasville, where it was quite likely she'd live out her days. Lucy and Jim were now in the custody of Jim's dad, who accepted the orphaned Lucy into his home. There was talk of a reformatory for each of them, but Mrs. Petrov had vouched for their character—"and they really are characters," she told the judge.

Adrian Hawkes would get his chance to write a string of stirring headlines in a series he was calling "Killer Wives of the Gold Coast." He led with the news: GOLD COAST HIT MAN DEAD, followed by PATH OF DESTRUCTION, ASSASSIN'S LAIR, NICKY'S LIFE OF CRIME, ALL IN THE FAMILY, and THE CROSSBOW KILLER, wherein he extolled the many talents of Dasha Petrov, who declined to be interviewed. She had better things to do: feed the swans, host Makita and Prince on their daily beach walks, contemplate the annuals she'd plant following Constantine's design—and look into a strange package she'd received from far-off Vietnam, something about missing gold bullion from the South Vietnamese treasury and nefarious characters. There were calls for help from former trusted colleagues.

Something to look into, perhaps.

But now, all she wanted to do was hold her sister's hand and admire the birds.

Acknowledgments

A novelist takes nourishment from early feedback, and I have a wonderful team of beta readers who have taken a liking to Dasha, Chief DeFranco, and the ravishing Tracy. I want to thank Allison Murdoch, Judy Hammer, and Lynne Neff for their early and enthusiastic critique of *Murder This Close*. My friend Bonnie Barney gave *Murder This Close* her usual keen eye, and I am grateful for her unflagging interest in Dasha's occupational development. My brother- and sister-in-law, Walter "Skip" Smedley III and Stephanie Scanga Smedley, devoured this one, even though they didn't have to, and have become ardent Dasha Petrov cheerleaders. My son, Andrew Cole; my brother, Robert H. Cole; and my sister, Dr. Susan Farmer, also offered nods of approval and always helpful comments. I am delighted to thank Peg North and Laura Woolpert, dear old friends from my early days as a marine journalist, for their support, and also Peter Kappel, Victor Tchelistcheff, and John Pfeifer for some down-range evaluations of Dasha Petrov novels currently in the works.

I would also like to extend my thanks to Westport's finest lawyer, Ken Bernhard, and to my friend of four decades, Anthony Giunta, lately retired from the Westport Police Department, where he served the people of Westport with distinction. People who know Tony will see the same can-do spirit that drives Dasha's friend Chief Anthony DeFranco and will understand where the inspiration for DeFranco originated.

No acknowledgment would be complete without the mention of my beautiful, hardworking, and constantly supportive wife, Sarah Smedley—crewmate, dance partner, cooking instructor, and consummate friend. You are my Polaris, the faithful star that helps guide the way.

Timothy Cole's thirty-year career as a journalist, editor, and author has taken him aboard America's nuclear Navy, to ozone depletion studies at the South Pole, and to particle physics cyclotrons in Siberia. He is an instrument-rated private pilot and holds a fifty-ton captain's license from the US Coast Guard. Currently, Tim serves as the editorial director of Belvoir Media Group, publishers of health information products from Harvard Medical School, the Cleveland Clinic, Massachusetts General Hospital, and other health centers. In prior roles, he served as an editor at leading marine magazines and was the science/technology/aerospace editor at *Popular Mechanics*. He is wrapping up *Moscow Five*, third book in the Dasha Petrov series, and is preparing to send Dasha on more exploits in *Last Reich* and *JFK: American Ambush*. Tim and his wife, Sarah Smedley, live in Greenwich, Connecticut. Learn more at TimothyColeBooks.com.

CPSIA information can be obtained
at www.ICGtesting.com
Printed in the USA
JSHW031957300422
25411JS00002B/3

9 781610 353854